Please return/renew this item by the
last date shown to avoid a charge.
Books may also be renewed by phone
and Internet. May not be renewed if
required by another reader.

www.libraries.barnet.gov.uk

BARNET
LONDON BOROUGH

The Last
Summer of the
Water Strider

The Last Summer of the Water Strider

TIM LOTT

SCRIBNER

LONDON NEW YORK TORONTO SYDNEY NEW DELHI

First published in Great Britain by Scribner, an imprint of Simon & Schuster UK Ltd, 2015
A CBS COMPANY

1 3 5 7 9 10 8 6 4 2

Simon & Schuster UK Ltd
1st Floor
222 Gray's Inn Road
London WC1X 8HB

www.simonandschuster.co.uk

Simon & Schuster Australia, Sydney
Simon & Schuster India, New Delhi

A CIP catalogue record for this book
is available from the British Library

Hardback ISBN: 978-1-84737-304-5
Ebook ISBN: 978-1-84983-584-8

Typeset by M Rules
Printed and bound by CPI Group (UK) Ltd, Croydon, CR0 4YY

Simon & Schuster UK Ltd are committed to sourcing paper
that is made from wood grown in sustainable forests and supports the Forest
Stewardship Council, the leading international forest certification organisation.
Our books displaying the FSC logo are printed on FSC certified paper.

In memory of Alan Watts, 1915–73

One

It was one of the distant, lost afternoons of the 1970s when I first met Crazy Uncle Henry. The week, the month, the year – they don't matter. Henry taught me that. The divisions of the calendar and of the clock are nothing more than ripples sketched on water.

I was seventeen years old. I had heard rumours of Uncle Henry, but I had never actually met him. Visits weren't encouraged by my father, and, so far as I knew, were never solicited by Henry either.

All I knew about Henry was what I could find out from my father when he dropped his guard – a rare event. It emerged then from time to time as a garbled bulletin. Henry was on the run from the police in Mexico. Henry had made a 'packet' smuggling 'pot', but had blown it all on a sports car that he crashed into a tree in Cap Ferrat. Henry had hooked up with the Maharishi Ji in Rishikesh and had converted to Vedantism. Neither my father nor I had much idea what a

Vedantist was, but my father was convinced that it was in some manner disreputable, or inauthentic – 'a con'. Most recently, the story was that Henry was living on a riverboat in the West Country with a waif – a ballet dancer by some accounts, a singer by others – who suffered from bouts of schizophrenia, or paranoia, or common-or-garden madness.

These dispatches were delivered to me by my father with a speck of reluctant amusement that was edged by a corona of disapproval. Ray worked hard and followed the rules. He smelled faintly of leather and other people's socks, and bore a slight stoop from undertaking too many fittings in the shoe shop he managed. He died at the age of sixty-three of a heart attack, selling a pair of Doc Marten boots disapprovingly to an impertinent Goth who had goaded him about his display of buckled patent-leather loafers. He did the right thing all his life and as a result he never really had a life. So the idea that his brother could profit from reckless and irresponsible behaviour offended his sense of natural justice.

Henry, two years older than my father – he had just turned fifty when I first met him – was, according to Ray, a 'weirdo'. He'd trod the Katmandu trail, he'd ridden the Marrakesh Express, he'd worked as a roadie for the Stones, he'd met Timothy Leary in San Francisco, he'd been on the Haight-Ashbury before it degenerated into a freak show. Lately, he was claiming to have cleaned himself up and to be working on a Book That Would Change the World.

From the photographs I'd seen, he was physically impressive, long and lean with chiselled cheekbones and heavy-lidded, mesmeric grey eyes. It would have been impossible to guess, at a glance, that he was my father's brother – Ray was four inches shorter, with a face that was somehow deeply generic; you could imagine that there were thousands of Rays, but only one

Henry. The roundness and redness of middle age, the lank brown hair that was losing its struggle for purchase, the eyes that held no distinguishable colour at all, the softening of the angles of a face that had never been very angular in the first place.

Henry, said Ray, never quite without bitterness, always had money. This good fortune, coupled with Henry's reckless-ness, was another source of grievance for my father. Ray was not quite sure where Henry obtained his alleged money – my father suspected it was from the rich, beautiful women Ray believed he consistently picked up and discarded like motes picked idly out of the air – but he had managed to get through most of his adult life without a straight job.

It was my father who christened him Crazy Henry. So far as I know, no one else ever called him that.

Although I feigned indifference – my personality being scarcely formed, indifference was all I had in the way of psy-chological stock – I was intrigued when Ray told me that Crazy Uncle Henry was coming to visit. I was looking for-ward to something – anything – that might interrupt the inertia of the passage of time in Buthelezi House, the very ordinary low-rise council block in which we lived.

The name of the block belied its absolutely quotidian nature. A far-left council, infiltrated by Trotskyists, named the block after the Zulu Chief Mangosuthu Buthelezi, founder of the Inkatha Freedom Party, who was in those days at least as well known a symbol of the South African strug-gle as his rival in the ANC, Nelson Mandela. Whether Chief Buthelezi was pleased with the honour bestowed on him, I could not say, but certainly all the residents I ever met had their doubts, envying those neighbours in the more conven-tional Chesterton House or The Pines. 'I mean, who wants to say they live in Buthelezi House? It's not exactly Hyde Park Gate, is it?' was Ray's view of the matter.

I didn't really think of living in Buthelezi House as living at all. It was a process, a situation, that fell well short of life. Worse, there was no sense of latency – merely the certainty of further stasis. It felt that it would be for ever. I sometimes wished it was violent, or crumbling, like some nearby council blocks – there was at least a certain grim drama to poverty and decay. But it was well kept and respectable, with carefully tended communal gardens and lifts that worked.

It wasn't only our location that oppressed me. The entire decade seemed to have got stuck somewhere, in the craw of something, choked off, the flow of air restricted. It was as if we were waiting for a new time to bloom while the old one was on life support, waiting for the plug to be finally pulled. The cheap brightness of the 1960s was exhausted, but there was no sign that its long vapour trail was ready to evanesce, leaving the sky clear for new beginnings. The stultification expressed itself in triviality: novelty records crowded the charts; adults dressed as children in violently coloured dungarees and stacked cartoon shoes. Terry and June had replaced JFK and Jackie O as icons of the age.

My father warned me what to expect of Henry, despite the rumours of reinvention and literary aspiration. Henry was liable to be dirty, dishevelled and barely articulate. He would be high on some psychotropic substance or other. He would inevitably ask for money, or a favour, since there was no other reason my father could imagine him coming to visit. Ray hadn't seen Henry for fifteen years – although he had received the occasional letter, and even more occasional phone call – but he had little doubt that his brother would be unchanged, that was to say, feckless, self-involved and entirely out of touch with what Ray liked to think of as reality.

He would not necessarily be unhinged – my father had spoken to him on the telephone in the shop several weeks before, at which time the visit was arranged (we did not yet have a telephone at home), and had reported him to be fundamentally coherent. But it was suggested that I would be unable to make much sense of anything he had to say. Ray's theory was that the drugs would have reduced his brain to residual tissue a long time ago.

When Uncle Henry actually arrived, one monochrome afternoon, on a late-winter day stillborn by a sterile, uncommitted sun, he was nothing like my father had described. As he stepped into our bland, overly kempt hallway, he was wearing a verdigris-coloured Harris tweed suit and polished chestnut leather brogues of the kind that I had seen the landed gentry wear in nostalgic films. It was clear that my father had expected tatty jeans, a scruffy beard and possibly a kaftan, and was taken aback by Henry's businesslike appearance – even though the business might have been that of a sturdy yeoman buying livestock at a village fair fifty years before.

He was clean-shaven and clear-eyed. He moved fluidly, as if the nine-tenths of his body that were water dominated the grosser, material parts. When he said hello to me he looked me directly in the eye for a long moment. I broke the gaze, then with a beckoning gesture of both hands, and a slight splaying of his arms, Henry tried to summon my father forward for a hug. Ray shrank before him, confused. Henry capitulated and offered his hand instead, which my father half-heartedly took, then swiftly let go, as if Henry might be carrying a dangerous communicable disease. I remember he called my father Raymond, rather than the accustomed Ray.

His hair was reasonably long, but well groomed and combed back from the brow, as if the wind had swept it and continued, somehow, to secure it there. There was a streak of grey like a badger's stripe running from crown to nape. If I tried hard enough, I could register faint traces of my father in his face – the slightly jutting ears, the nearly linked eyebrows – but on the whole he seemed to be from a different genetic pool altogether.

He had in his mouth, unlit, a burnished cherrywood pipe, somehow managing the performance without appearing pretentious. When he spoke, the vowels were clipped, the consonants precise, like a Third Programme announcer. He had been public school-educated until my grandparents' money ran out – another source of resentment from my father, who had attended a local Church school before leaving at the age of fifteen. Henry, on the other hand, had read Divinity at Cambridge, and been awarded a doctorate.

Henry gave a sense of being impressively cultured, punctuating his conversation with literary quotations and even repeating chunks of poetry from memory. During his visit he recited excerpts from Allen Ginsberg's 'Howl' and a few lines from Auden's '1939'. This made my parents suspicious, as if culture itself were another dangerous narcotic that would get you into trouble sooner or later.

Evie – Eve was her given name, but I never heard anyone call her anything but Evie – my mother, was a kind, lightly built, scared-looking woman with an ingrained defensive smile that remained, even at rest and without company, as an after-image on her lips. This smile was stitched on to her face as she ushered Ray and Henry into the sitting room. I followed at a safe distance — far away enough, I hoped, not to get dragged into any small-talk, which I found excruciating. Henry was offered a drink, a choice between a glass of Amontillado sherry or a dusty bottle of London Pale Ale. The sitting room was furnished with Ercol chairs and contained a spindly, 1950s-style circular coffee table decorated with a pattern that suggested space satellites and circulating planets.

Henry politely declined both the proffered drinks, even when pressed urgently by his nervous brother, and requested instead a glass of tap water, which Evie set off to fetch. Then he lowered himself into a worn but comfortable green plush wing-back armchair — normally reserved for my father — with an air of entitlement, like a visiting bank manager.

I noticed that although he sat perfectly still — uncannily so, like a mime artist — his eyes rarely stopped moving, albeit lazily, around the room, taking everything in, holding the images momentarily like a mirror then letting them go. Although his urbanity conjured in me a sense of shame in our surroundings — in the shape, quality and surfaces of our life — I could detect no judgement in those eyes, only a quiet, analytical curiosity.

I could see why he made my parents uncomfortable. Without his ever saying a word, the apparition of Henry seemed to question everything my father stood for; and under Henry's gaze I felt that my parents' life, as well as my own, reduced itself. Henry — I imagined — was viewing each of us through the wrong end of a telescope. It was obvious to me that Ray wanted him out of the flat as quickly as possible. In the state of perpetual, sullen resentment towards my parents that I sustained myself in, it made me warm to Henry somewhat, despite my determination to have nothing to do

with the adult world and what I saw as its ubiquitous, suffo-
cating hypocrisies.

I wasn't sure that I entirely liked him, however; neither
was I convinced that he liked me. He certainly made no
effort to reach out to me, or accommodate my discomfort,
which I signalled by refusing to sit down and by doodling
pointlessly with a blue ballpoint pen on the back of my hand.
He seemed to find my behaviour – and everything else for
that matter – faintly amusing.

There was certainly a gentle humour about Henry, but
with an undertow of gravitas, as if he commanded an
Olympian view of life. This aura of unforced amusement was
particularly disconcerting. He made you feel foolish, without ever really trying to be anything but affable and dry. I'd
never met anybody who occupied their skin so completely
and comfortably.

Surprisingly, during that brief meeting, we managed to
form the semblance of a bond. It was when my mother and
father both left the room briefly – one to use the toilet (I
noticed that Henry looked slightly pained at the word
'toilet'), the other to fetch a resupply of Royal Scot biscuits.
This left Henry and me briefly alone.

He looked me up and down in the manner of a biologist
studying a specimen. I was wearing a bottle-green grandad
vest – three buttons at the top, no collar – and a pair of
burgundy loon pants, low on the hips, vast at the ankles and
tight around the buttocks. I may have been wearing an absurd
pair of platform boots with a wooden heel. I had vaguely
imagined, before he arrived, that Henry might see me as
some kind of kindred spirit. But Henry looked very little like
the scion of the counterculture that Ray had led me to
expect.

He asked me, conventionally enough, how school was going. I told him I thought it was stupid. Then he asked me how I was getting on with Raymond and Evie. I told him I thought they were stupid. He calmly lit his pipe, taking what seemed a very long time, and eventually puffed out a cumulus of blue, fragrant smoke. Then he gave me a curious look, and asked me what I thought of him. Taken aback, I replied that I hadn't had time to form a proper impression. This was not strictly true, as I was unable, despite my best efforts, to find him anything other than intriguing.

A silence fell, within which Henry seemed entirely comfortable. I began to hope for the return of one or other of my parents. Just to make a dent in the noiseless space, I asked him what he thought of me. He inclined his head to one side, and answered, 'Pretty stupid.' But he said it in such a kind, wry way, it made me laugh. I tried to disguise it as a cough, but Henry wasn't fooled. In response, he laughed too. In contrast to my brief, high, anxious bark, his laugh came in thick, heavy waves, great booming reverberations, rich and purple-brown like old port. When Mum and Dad walked back into the room a few moments later, we were still laughing, him taking the baritone, me the falsetto. A fresh shadow of resentment worked its way across my father's face. The frown lines around his eyes contorted into question marks. Ray and I rarely laughed at the same time, or about the same things.

Henry stayed for an hour or so in all. The longer he was there, the more uncomfortable my mother and father became, and the more the silences made pit-holes in the conversation, until the talk almost entirely ran out of juice. The new supply of Royal Scot biscuits remained untouched, though Evie had pressed them on Henry twice. When at last he got up to leave, claiming, not inaccurately, that he had overstayed his welcome, my father didn't try to conceal his relief. His shoulders relaxed and for the first time he conjured what seemed to me a genuine smile.

It was never clear why Henry had come that day. When my father asked him, as Henry was making ready to leave, he said that it 'seemed like it was time'. It was my first intimation that Henry didn't think like my parents, or most of the people I knew. I later found out that he felt no particular need to invent reasons for the things he did. He just did them, without too much reflection and without regret. My father, I knew, found this irritating, since he, in contrast, overthought nearly everything. He was paralysed by fear of consequence. I simply found Henry's attitude bewildering. How could you 'just do' anything? Didn't everything have a reason?

Henry offered me his hand as he left. I can remember the smell of his pipe tobacco – the mysterious inscription on the tin read BORKUM RIFF – and the gentle, almost feminine clutch of his long fingers, with their buffed and rounded fingernails, as if very recently manicured. His palm felt dry and warm and I imagined it to possess the character of sweetness in some way. It made me think, oddly, of cake.

In those days people, outside of formal situations, didn't shake hands very often – it was considered rather 'continental'. Henry made it seem very natural. He smiled at me – as I remember it, after shaking my hand, he even ruffled my hair, thoughtfully pushing it back down into style afterwards. My father would never have dared do such a thing. Had he ventured it, I would have shrunk away and he would have wiped his hand on his shirt afterwards – but it seemed quite acceptable, even reassuring, coming from Henry.

He made his way out to his car, which was of a shape and style I had never seen before, both domestic and faintly sensual at the same time (it was a Volkswagen Karmann Ghia, a swan among ducks in the midst of the Morris Minors, Anglias and Cortinas that made up the inventory of vehicles in my street).

He waved through the open car window, still with his pipe poking from his mouth, inclining it slightly downwards in farewell. Then there was the blare of the exhaust pipe, a cough of backfire, and he took off at what seemed a dangerous rate of acceleration.

For all the impression he had made on me, his light and colour faded like an expiring firework. Buthelezi House had that muffling effect on all experience. Even memory was submerged in a grey-green tide of non-eventfulness which I believed would never withdraw.

But it did, and when it did, I looked back on that drowned banality as a blessing. It was all, really, I knew of innocence.

Two

Ten months after Henry's visit, my mother and I were having breakfast together. With her carefully bobbed hair, mail order-catalogue clothes and a perpetual pinafore that miraculously never showed a stain, she lived her life by principles of kindness and self-sacrifice towards my father and myself, qualities that both of us took entirely for granted. Evie always had a worried look on her face, because she was, in fact, perpetually worried – about nothing in particular and therefore everything.

I had one A-level paper left to sit – in History – and I was way behind in my revision. My thoughts that morning were all of the First World War and its causes. My studies seemed to ask of me why wars in general happened, a conundrum that I considered insoluble. As I ate, I was chewing over the assassination of Archduke Franz Ferdinand and weighing its effects on the future against those of the Triple Entente. I barely registered – as usual – my mother's presence. She was sitting in front of me with a copy of the *Daily Express*, eating lumps of old white bread spread with large chunks of peanut butter – peanut butter was possibly her only strong preference in food, always the crunchy variety – and she didn't look like she was enjoying herself. But she hated waste, so she would always eat anything in the larder or fridge, even if it was going off, rather than throw it away. I had seen her scrape mould off any variety of provisions, declaring its effects to be harmless, even beneficial.

I heard a small sound, rather like glottal stop without a word to make it manifest. It was enough to make me look up. On my mother's face, an expression had fixed itself that made her look even more worried than usual.

For once her anxiety had a cause. She seemed unable to breathe. She pointed frantically at her throat, then began clawing at it with her fingernails. She seemed like she was about to vomit, but didn't.

I was in the midst of taking the final bite of a Danish-bacon sandwich. Her fist, holding a butter knife, was suspended in mid-air, as if an invisible force was supporting her wrist while the rest of her was collapsing. Then the knife fell, and she followed it. I waited, numbly, stupidly, for her to get up, but she didn't move. I could not tell if her chest was still rising and falling under her pinafore. Her right arm had become jammed awkwardly under her torso.

Her eyes bulged like pale green grapes invaded by tendrils of red veins. Her face, in contrast, was draining of colour. She didn't move or speak. It all happened too quickly for me to be frightened. I rose, knocking my plate to the floor, where it shattered into two symmetrical fragments. Ketchup smeared the tiles and for a second I thought about fetching some paper towels to wipe it up. I even reached down to pick up the plate, before letting it drop again, understanding finally that there was a more urgent task to be undertaken.

Having no phone, I considered running to the kiosk on the corner, but it was unlikely to be operative. It was always being dismantled by vandals. I knew because I was one of them. Instead, I bent down and freed my mother's arm from under her. She grunted, but otherwise remained insensible. Her eyelids fluttered, revealing yellow-white underneath. If she had had a heart attack — which I for some reason assumed — I knew that if the brain was starved of oxygen for more than a few minutes, it would suffer irreparable damage.

I bent over Evie and put my lips to hers in order to give her mouth-to-mouth resuscitation. I had done a safety drill in swimming class as a child — that would have been about six or seven years previously — and I only slightly remembered the technique.

Her lips were warm, but bluish in tinge. I could taste saliva on them, and felt a shamed revulsion. I blew, feeling as ridiculous as I was panicked. I straddled my mother, there on the kitchen floor. I pressed down on her ribcage. But I wasn't sure at which point I should apply pressure. When I was breathing into her? Or when I stopped breathing into her? I didn't know what I was doing. But I kept on doing it — doing something, anything that might have an effect, that might restore the suddenly precious safety and predictability of my life. I could feel my mother, lumpen, beneath me. I felt certain that her respiration could be repaired, even though she had made no noise or movement since I had freed her arm.

I kept working at it. I thought as it went on I would get more proficient, but I fumbled it even more. Because of my indecision, I kept changing my technique. One moment I would be breathing into her as I pushed the torso down, the next when I let go. I improvised like this for several minutes. My mother remained stricken, falling further, deeper, it seemed, into immobility and unconsciousness. I decided I had no choice but to leave her and to go and ask someone for the use of their phone.

I didn't know anyone in our block who had a phone. But there were two neighbours, in the private houses over the road, who were connected to the telephones lines that were strung across our street like social boundaries. One was to the south of the block – the Cartwrights. That was about two hundred yards away. One was to the north – the Gibbonses. That was only a hundred yards away.

I was embarrassed to call on the Gibbonses. Old Ma Gibbons disliked me because I had once put a football through her front window and run away. She knew it was me – I have no idea how, since she wasn't actually at home when it happened. She had challenged me on the subject several times, insisting that I pay for the damage, but I always sulkily denied it. She was a heavy woman, with a thin, mean mouth and a way of looking at you that squeezed out shame like a smear of perspiration.

Although Ma Gibbons and her phone were closer, I ran to the Cartwrights' house. With every stride, I felt time sliding towards the irreversible. The house was fronted with a low brick wall, a rockery and a short concrete drive. There was a handwritten note stuck under the doorbell announcing that it was out of order. I could see, through a ridged glass panel set in the front door, the Union Jack they had framed on their hall wall. I could also see the outline of the red telephone on a small laminated shelf.

The door knocker was lightweight and cheap and jammed up with rust. It seemed to make no more noise than a pebble falling to the ground from a child's pocket, so I starting hammering on the glass panel with my fist. No one came.

I thought of breaking in, of smashing the glass. It would have been a rational thing to do. They would have forgiven me. I went so far as to pick up a lump of sandstone from the rockery with that intention in mind, but let it drop from my hand.

I didn't stop to consider how ironic it was that the custom and practice of politeness my mother had considered more paramount than any other virtue was now edging her towards a place where manners had no purchase. Instead, I turned and ran to the other end of the street, back past the rude block of Buthelezi House, trying not to visualize my mother stretched out on the kitchen floor. I guessed it was now more than five minutes since she had collapsed, and I had, effectively, done nothing. In fact, I had almost certainly made things worse by my incompetent attempts to give artificial respiration.

I bolted up Ma Gibbons' path and rang the bell. It produced a trembling and uncertain jangle rather than the more common *bing-bong*. She answered almost immediately. I don't suppose she was that old really, by today's standards – no more than sixty-five – but she was already, despite her size, baggy-skinned, white-haired and carved with canyons of wrinkles. She looked at me in astonishment, as if was I readying myself to attack her. Still in my pyjamas, my hair wild, my feet bare, I must have looked like a lunatic.

Once I had caught my breath and yanked out the bare facts of what had happened, she guided me into her front room, where she kept the phone. I was shaking so much that I dropped the receiver; she retrieved it from the floor and told me in a crisp tone to sit down. But I remained standing, shifting anxiously from foot to foot and hugging myself for comfort. She made the 999 call herself, only asking me to confirm the address and the spelling of my surname and of Buthelezi House. After she hung up, I refused her request for me to wait with her. She then said she would come with me to Buthelezi House, but I insisted that she stayed put. The bubble of time I felt stranded in seemed too private, the air too thin, to support another inhabitant, however well-meaning.

I returned to the flat, where my mother remained inert and in precisely the position in which I had abandoned her. There was nothing to do but wait. I sat down on a kitchen chair and tried to avoid looking at the space on the floor that she occupied. I understood that the second hand continued to orbit the face of the carriage clock on the windowsill above the stained-yellow sink with its rubber-nippled taps, but it seemed to be measuring nothing whatsoever. There was just my mother and me, suspended in a continuous, strange, present moment. My sense of helplessness was like an injury. I could hear my own breath, laboured, coming fast. It didn't sound like my breath at all. I risked a look at Evie. Her face was the colour of the sugar that was spilt on the floor.

After a while, my breathing returned to normal. My fear had consigned itself to a place of suspension. I had stopped shaking. Instead, I started to find it puzzling that this immutable presence, partially out of sight on the other side of the table, this continuation and source of my very self could behave in such an improbable fashion. I felt a flash of anger towards my mother, as if she had deliberately chosen to do this to inconvenience me. To embarrass me. I had no template for how to behave in such circumstances. In all honesty, I wanted to make myself a cup of hot chocolate, but it seemed disrespectful. It was also peculiar – I never drank hot chocolate, it was my father's particular treat. Yet I felt it would be obscurely comforting.

I shifted chairs and looked down on her, like a god. I felt myself becoming more and more motionless within – not out of calmness, but in a state of weird congealment, as if an epoxy had been added to a glue.

When the ambulance men arrived I remained sitting there, still wondering whether or not to make myself that cup of hot chocolate. There was nothing else on my mind: it was an unsolvable koan. When the doorbell rang, I remember wondering who it might be. I only realized that it was the ambulance when I became aware of the flashing blue light stroking the kitchen window.

The two medics didn't take long to work out what I, at some level, knew already, although they put on a small performance for my sake – chest compressions, an injection of something or other, mouth-to-mouth, even paddles to shock the heart back into function, which made my mother jump like a frog I had once seen on a dissection table when an electrical current was put through it.

One of the medics muttered, regretfully, that it was a shame they hadn't got there earlier. He looked not much older than me – a novice, I supposed. I remember asking him, while his more senior partner was distracted, how late was it? How late?

'A few minutes earlier, then . . . perhaps . . .'

He allowed the sentence to trail off when he saw his senior glaring at him reprovingly. The older man no doubt understood how many of the scenes he was called to held suspended within them the seeds of regret and self-punishment, interest on the inescapable debt of grief. The torments of decisions not taken, the revenge of the past on the present.

But now it was too late for me, just as it was too late for my mother. The koan was solved. I had killed her. My stupidity, my lack of decision, the ludicrous flight to the Cartwrights instead of Mother Gibbons had robbed my mother of any chance of survival.

She hadn't – it turned out – had a heart attack at all. She had been choking on the peanut butter and stale white bread – number one choking risk for adults, I later discovered – and had fainted from lack of oxygen, and only then suffered a coronary. I actually knew the Heimlich manoeuvre. If I had used it instead of trying to give her a mangled version of the kiss of life, I was sure I could have saved her.

They wheeled in a steel gurney and laid her gently on it, as if she could be made comfortable in some fashion. It was simply more theatre. I remember thinking that they might as well stuff her in a sack.

It was just after she had been loaded on to the trolley that my father arrived. Ma Gibbons must have phoned him. I hadn't thought to do it myself.

He was not numb and still in the way I had been. He didn't seem to notice I was even there. He became immediately hysterical. I had never seen him in anything like this condition before. He screamed and wept. He fell to his knees. Then he rose again, threw himself across my mother's body and had to be gently pulled away.

It disappointed me. It was no way to behave.

They found the Amontillado and offered him a glass. He knocked it back and demanded another. After the scene had played itself out – the quiet words of meaningless consolation, the request that he place himself 'safely' upon a seat –

the reality of the situation was clarified to me. The pile of matter on the trolley was simply that – a rapidly decaying heap of organic waste.

I remember wondering what caused decay. Was it the action of micro-organisms and bacteria? Or was there something implicit in the nature of organic matter that returned to dust by its own volition, a structure collapsing, like a building with its foundations removed falling in slow motion?

Then they took my mother away. Ray was still sobbing and calling her name. Shortly after she had gone, he fell into silence. He and I spent much of the following hours simply staring at the floor and not saying anything. Death snatches the words right out of your throat. Language shrinks and becomes too diminished to be of any use.

In the end I made myself a cup of hot chocolate. I remember how extraordinarily good it tasted.

Three

My father did not stage much of a recovery. Once the hysteria had faded, it appeared he had lost something essential to his proper functioning. He became withdrawn and monosyllabic. I never saw him eat anything after that, other than the occasional biscuit or dry piece of toast, more often than not charred. His grieving was appalling for me to behold, as if I had lost two parents rather than the one. But the feeling of grief I was waiting for never really arrived. If I felt anything at all, it was anger – overwhelming, inarticulable, directionless. If my father was reticent, I became stony and silent.

A few days after my mother's death, we went shopping for coffins, or 'caskets' as the funeral trade insisted on labelling them. This task struck me as obscene, but I couldn't quite bring myself to condemn my father to facing it alone. Even in his grief, he worried about being taken for a ride – 'They get people when they're at their most vulnerable' – so we visited several to see if we could get the 'best deal'.

The funeral directors we saw all seemed more or less out of the same mould – men, grave, with smiles forensically scoured to remove all trace of happiness. Solemn acceptance and quiet resolution seemed to be their stock-in-trade. At the first one we visited, we heard a sharp, brief burst of laughter from a back room. The man behind the counter ignored it. I couldn't help but imagine the backroom staff making jokes over the corpses – fooling about with the cosmetics they used to render the cadaver 'lifelike', or rearranging the anguished facial features into comic expressions.

I had entered some psychological space I had never encountered before – a place of suspension, of non-feeling, of robotic movements that merely signalled the presence of life, rather than vitally representing it. My father and I flicked through the catalogues of coffins in the way my mother used to pick through the Grattan catalogue to order winceyette pyjamas or 'authentic' Toby jugs. The colour reproduction in the second funeral director's catalogue was lurid – it reminded me of those Chinese-restaurant menus that illustrated the dishes with brazen photographs of flayed ducks and unholy intestinal parts.

We delayed the final choice until we made our third call, the Co-op funeral store. It was, unlike the other two, much more reminiscent of a practical, no-nonsense shop front. My father and my mother both trusted the Co-op because it was collectively owned and they were Labour voters – though Ray, I knew, had talked of switching because of 'all this union nonsense'. Evie tried to shop at the Co-op whenever she could and collected Co-op Dividend Stamps, which could be redeemed for a discount on goods. The stolidity of the brand appealed to my father, and he made approving noises as we entered: 'This is the sort of thing that's much more my mark.'

The man who greeted us was of the same stamp as the other two, but his suit was more informal – carbolic-soap grey rather than black – and his smile somewhat less mechanical. He didn't seem to feel the necessity to be unduly sombre – brisk and workmanlike was his pitch. I liked his face; it was that of a butcher anxious to show you some new batch of chops he had just got in fresh from the farm.

My father seemed reassured by his demeanour. His name was Flaherty, although there was nothing of the Irish in his accent. After we had gone through the pleasantries, condolences and so forth once again, we were offered the catalogue. On the first two occasions Ray had picked through the pages as if they were sacred, a book as holy as the Bible some anonymous vicar would be reading from when the actual ceremony took place.

Now, though, he was seasoned, and he flicked through purposefully, pausing over the cedar, the oak, the burnished teak. But it was clear that he was becoming exhausted by the whole process. He had no idea what to choose, it occurred to me – in fact he couldn't choose, because to do so was to acknowledge further that his wife was truly gone.

After he had considered, reconsidered and procrastinated for almost ten minutes, I noticed Flaherty furtively checking his watch, although he remained studiously polite. I leaned over to the page my father was on. He had been staring at it for some time. It contained the cheapest caskets – white pine, utilitarian, a good twenty per cent cheaper than anything else in the book.

'What do you think of these?' he said gently. It felt as if he was asking me to help choose a piece of expensive furniture for the front room.

I knew Ray was practically minded, and that a struggle was going on within him. His natural choice would be to go for the cheapest option, and yet I am sure he had a vague sense of wanting to honour Evie by making a gesture. I was beyond caring in any respect – I just wanted the funeral to be over so I could take a step away from death, get it past me, lined up in the rear-view mirror, shrinking from view.

I rested my finger on one of the cheapest models – the 'Standard'.

'That one looks all right.'

Ray momentarily looked doubtful, but I could tell he was pleased that I was acknowledging the practicalities of the situation. My mother had once confided to me that he had been of the same mind about her wedding dress: 'You only wear it once.' She had ended up walking down the aisle in a second-hand trousseau.

'Well,' said Ray, 'it's very plain.'

He looked up at Flaherty, whose corona of grey hair seemed itself to have expired, so inert was it when he nodded, as he did now.

'What do you think?'

'It's a very popular choice,' he replied. His voice was bland, but he was careful to insinuate the faintest grain of dis-appointment. This Co-op branch was not situated in a prosperous area – doubtless Flaherty longed for someone to splurge out and go for the Midnight Silver with dual-tone finish and silver crêpe interior.

'Is it solid pine?'

'No, it's a veneer.'

'Well, I don't suppose anyone will be able to tell.'

Flaherty said nothing.

'Pine's quite fashionable, isn't it? Lots of people I know are getting pine kitchens,' said Ray. 'It's quite the thing.'

Flaherty said nothing again.

'I don't know,' said Ray. He stared at the photo.

I knew I needed to speak what he was thinking, if only to get us out of there.

'She's gone, Dad. She won't know anything about it. She wouldn't have cared. You know what she always used to say: "Bury me in a paper bag if you like." She wasn't one for fanciness. She'd have worried about the cost.'

In fact, I remembered the air of sadness that came over Evie when she talked about her wedding dress; but Evie was gone. She would not be able to reminisce ruefully about her funeral.

'Do you think?' said Ray, looking at me pleadingly.

Flaherty's attention was wavering. Clearly there wasn't going to be a great deal of profit in this particular stiff. I noticed him glancing out back. I wondered again what horrors were held there behind the reassuring, wood-panelled vestibule.

'Do you . . .' Ray hesitated for a long time. I was wondering if he was going to be shamed into plumping for something more expensive after all.

'I'm not trying to be funny or anything. But do you accept Dividend Stamps?'

The expression on Flaherty's face never wavered. But he did wait for several seconds before answering, as if the question needed to be taken apart, examined, then put together again.

'I'm afraid not, sir. We are a quite separate concern from the supermarket chain.'

My mother had books of the stamps piled up at home. She always squirrelled them away but never got round to using them, hoping to save up for a big premium item. This would have certainly fitted the bill.

I almost left the shop, so visceral was my embarrassment. Instead I stared fixedly at a knot of wood on the floor. Ray seemed aware that he had committed a faux pas. Clearly trying to move the conversation along, he pointed blindly down at the catalogue again.

'The Standard. Does it come with the handles?'

'No, sir, I'm afraid the handles are extra. You have a choice – brass, chrome or steel.'

'Perhaps,' Ray was addressing me now, 'we could go for the Standard, um, thing and put some nice handles on it. You know. To jazz it up.'

Flaherty seemed very slightly encouraged by this turn in the conversation. He immediately suggested the solid brass handles, which were the most expensive by some good amount. He reached into a drawer and fetched one out.

'Hold it,' he said to my father. 'Feel the weight.'

Ray dutifully did so, lofting it up then bringing it down, as if he were competing in a 'guess the weight of the cake' competition at the local church fair. Then Flaherty hit him with the price. With all six handles, it was almost the price of another Standard, but this time my father, no doubt aware that he had violated some unwritten principle of bereavement with his request regarding the stamps, seemed determined on his course.

'We have to show some respect, don't you think, Adam? Let's have the brass handles. Shall we?'

He looked up at Flaherty.

'Good choice, sir,' Flaherty said quietly, replacing the

handle in his desk then scribbling with a pencil on a white blotter. 'A nice combination of styles. The practical and the decorative. It's a common election.'

Election. A weird Victorian term, which I supposed they used as part of a toolbox of arcane language, hoping it would elevate undertakers out of the crafts and into the professions.

'Well. That's it then.' Ray looked at me with an expression that somehow managed to simultaneously combine apology, anxiety, regret and relief.

Flaherty's smile – now more flagrantly mercantile – remained pasted in place as he totted up some figures on the blotter. He flipped it around to show my father.

'Will this be satisfactory?'

Ray stared at the figure long and hard.

'Does it include everything?' he said eventually.

'Gratuities for the pallbearers are sometimes proffered, but it is not compulsory. There is normally a pecuniary gesture towards the vicar who performs the service. You are C of E?'

Ray nodded.

'But apart from those small items, it represents the full cost.'

Still Ray hesitated.

'Of course, if it is beyond your budget—'

'No,' said Ray, a little too quickly. 'Something like this. It demands a certain . . .'

Ray struggled for the word. Flaherty stepped in.

'Gravitas.'

'Yes.'

Flaherty paused, as if wanting to make sure that Ray's level of commitment was not too fragile to survive an actual transaction. Finally he spoke.

'Then we're settled. There's just the matter of the deposit.'

Ray had clearly expected this. He reached to his inside jacket pocket and tugged out his chequebook, which he immediately fumbled and dropped on the floor. I picked it up and handed it to him. When he spoke again, his voice had changed, as if acknowledging that we now stood on the firmer ground of the commercial, rather than the spiritual, realm.

'How much?'

'Twenty per cent is customary. And if we could have the remainder within three working days?'

Ray scribbled briefly, then ripped out the cheque and handed it over. Flaherty took it and inspected it assiduously.

'I'm afraid you've dated it incorrectly, sir. Today is the twenty-seventh, not the twenty-sixth.'

'Does it matter?'

'It's important to pay attention to detail, we find.'

This seemed unnecessary, and I decided Flaherty was punishing Ray for choosing the Standard, even if he had splashed out on the brass handles. He took the cheque back, tore it in two, wrote another one and handed it to Flaherty, who inspected it again with a care that seemed largely theatrical.

'That's all in order. Thank you, sir.'

I watched as Ray wrote *Evie's coffin + brass handles* on the stub. The phone rang, and Flaherty picked it up. Immediately his voice changed and his face lost its equanimity and sheen of serenity.

'This isn't a good time. It's out in the shed. Behind the fertilizer. No, not the . . . the sack. The blue sacks. Yes. Goodbye.'

He put down the phone. His face was restored to its professional countenance. But he said nothing.

Our business was clearly concluded, but Ray hesitated all the same. I wondered what he was waiting for.

'Can I just ask? What if there is . . . I don't know . . . What if things aren't, don't turn out to be . . . satisfactory?'

For the first time, Flaherty sounded a note of impatience. Clearly the receipt of the cheque had relieved him of the need to be so dutifully civil.

'Are you asking if we have a money-back guarantee, sir?'

Ray flushed. 'I'm just not sure how these things work.'

'Any complaint would be very unusual. But of course, we are concerned that you will be satisfied, and that all due observances will be carried out efficiently and properly. Let me set your mind at rest about that. But there is a complaints procedure if you felt unhappy in any way.'

He reached into his drawer and brought out a glossy leaflet, the rough size of a business envelope. 'I hope you won't be needing it.' He smiled without warmth.

Ray looked at the leaflet, entirely beaten now.

'I'm sure I won't. Thank you for your help, Mr Flaherty. Come on, Adam,' he said to me sourly, clearly under the impression that he had been fleeced but powerless to do anything about it.

His head hung low, he walked out of the front door. He left the leaflet lying on the counter, and I saw Flaherty, with a satisfied air, return it to his drawer. He nodded to me, as much in dismissal as farewell, and I followed Ray out into the street.

Not many people turned up for the funeral. Evie was a shy woman who preferred work to socializing. She had cleaned other people's houses for small change in what spare time she had enjoyed, a solitary occupation in itself. An only child, her parents were dead. She had two cousins, both of whom she had long lost touch with. As with my father, extended family ties were considered extraneous to the nuclear unit.

Ray had elected for cremation rather than burial, and the funeral took place a week after our visit to Flaherty, in a light-industrial chapel on the outskirts of an anonymous satellite town skirting north-west London.

There were maybe twenty people sprinkled throughout the aisles, few of whom I recognized. Ma Gibbons was there, but I found it difficult to look at her. She was the closest thing I had to a witness to my shame. It was a chilly day for the season, and I shivered under a thin raincoat, having not wanted to ruin the effect of my one good suit – three-inch lapels, tucked at the waist, double vent – with the bulk of a sweater.

The vicar, a fat man with a pimple on his nose, was businesslike and inappropriately jocund. My father had briefed him about Evie's life, but it appeared he had transcribed some of his notes carelessly, describing Evie as an enthusiastic gardener (we didn't have a garden, although she had a collection of pot plants) and a pillar of the local operatic society (she occasionally attended Yiewsley and District Dramatic Society performances). My father sat blankly by my side as the priest delivered platitudes about resting in the hands of God, the shadow of death, rods and staff, lying in green pastures etc, etc.

The coffin looked ill-judged, both cheap and gaudy simultaneously. The expensive handles confessed the tackiness of the pine veneer, and I sat, chilly and distracted, despairing over the statement the casket made about the value of my mother's life. I could hear whispering during the service, and

I imagined that each of congregation was judging the ceremony as lacking in both taste and sufficient capitalization.

At one point I heard a latecomer arriving, the timpani of
their shoes puncturing the grainy, maudlin background drone
of the pre-recorded organ. I looked round and saw Henry,
brandishing, like a processional torch, a bunch of flowers –
a bouquet of simple sweet peas. My mother always loved the
quiet delicacy of sweet peas more than any other bloom.
How had he known that? In his other hand he carried a dark,
bone-and-silver-topped walking cane.

He was, as before, tanned to perfection, the colour of
nutmeg. He wore a pure black two-piece suit, cut close to his
rangy frame. It was expensive-looking but slightly shot around
the edges at the collar. His shirt was sparkling blue-white. No
tie, open top button, burnished ebony leather shoes that I
knew my father would register as hand-made. He looked out
of place – although he seemed perfectly at ease. Other people
had turned and were staring at him, wondering how this ele-
gant creature had lost its way and stumbled into this maimed,
bargain-basement ceremony. Henry caught my eye and gave
me a carefully modulated smile, pitched somewhere between
sympathy and familial affection.

A few minutes after Henry's arrival, the box was consigned to the flames. I watched like a wax dummy as the pine
and brass monstrosity disappeared, while my father choked
out tears. Then, with the gasp and whine of the sourest-yet
organ music, Ray and I took our places at the exit from the
chapel and the mourners began to file out. Ray shook their
hands one by one as they left and exchanged a few muttered
words. Then we stood outside in the cold among the sparse
flowers that decorated a concrete plot allocated for tributes
to Evie.

31

Henry laid his flowers among the few other scrappy offerings, eclipsing them. Then – to my astonishment – he fell to his knees and kissed the ground. After remaining in this posture for several seconds, he took a vial of something out of his pocket, uncorked it and sprinkled the contents on the blooms.

He bowed down again, forehead touching the concrete. Then, he rose gracefully in a single movement. I saw a tiny chip of gravel embedded in his forehead. Ray stared at him. Henry held his arms out to Ray, as he had on his visit to our flat. This time, Ray somehow seemed to fall forward, and Henry enfolded him. Ray gave way to sobs, Henry supporting his weight, his legs moving apart in order to keep his balance. The other mourners averted their eyes, as if the time for sobbing had ended when they had left the chapel, and now the protocol of grief was being subverted.

Eventually Ray peeled himself from the buttress of his brother.

'Thanks for coming, Henry.'

'I'm sorry I was late, Raymond. Well, to tell you the truth, I wasn't late really. I was standing just outside. I struggle with religious ceremonies, I'm afraid. Thought I'd slip in for the final . . . consignment. I hope you'll forgive me.'

Ray nodded.

'The casket was perfect,' he said, as if sensing Ray's insecurities.

'Thank you.' My father looked genuinely lightened by this comment.

'Raymond, I want you to know that if there's any way I can help over the coming weeks and months, I will do so. These are not empty words. These are words spoken in all sincerity and full intent. Please write to me if there is something.

I am not on the telephone, as you know, but I will be there for you.'

Something struck true in Henry's words, and I sensed that Ray, like me, was comforted by them.

Then Henry looked at me.

'Hey, stupid,' he said lugubriously.

'Hey.'

'You should come and see me. At the boat. In Somerset.'

'Maybe.'

He looked at me askance, clearly doubting that I would do any such thing.

'What did you sprinkle on the flowers?' I asked.

'Water blessed by the Dalai Lama.'

Ray looked sceptical. 'Where did you get that?'

'He gave it to me,' Henry said simply. 'Raymond, I'm sorry, but I can't stay for the Scotch eggs and finger buffet. I've got a meeting in town about my book, and it can't wait. They're already annoyed with me keeping them waiting by coming to this in the first place. Business, you know. Hard heads, cold hearts. But I hope you know my thoughts are with you and will remain with you.'

Ray said he understood. Henry hugged him once more, shook my hand and tousled my hair. That was the last I heard of him for several more months.

Four

Shortly after the funeral I began to spend a lot of my time wandering the avenues and crescents of Yiewsley in the evening, half-heartedly trying to sniff out mischief. I idly vandalized road signs and kicked cans at stray cats. Most dramatically, I was caught joyriding a car – an Austin Princess, still smelling of fresh seat leather – that had been left unlocked in the street adjacent to ours. The owner – who had momentarily nipped inside his house, I later discovered, to retrieve a tin of driving sweets – had left the keys in the ignition. I just took the car without a second thought. My father had taught me to drive, around the back of an abandoned gasworks, but I had never driven on a road.

The owner saw me juddering away – I hadn't quite mastered the exigencies of the clutch – and immediately phoned the police. They were on the scene within minutes, when I had put only a couple of streets' distance between myself and the scene of the crime. I panicked, and didn't have the sense to stop. There followed a brief and farcical car chase. I crashed into the post of a creosoted fence after thirty seconds, denting the Princess and banging my head on the windscreen badly enough to need hospital attention. I ended up in front of the magistrates, with the probability of juvenile detention. But my mother's death, and a carefully elaborated head bandage, worked in my favour, and they let me off with a caution and a large fine, which my father had no choice but to settle, not without bitterness.

It was early July. It was apparent to Ray that I had lost the ability to care about anything. In June, immediately after my mother's death, I had failed to turn up for my History exam, out of raw apathy. Once again, my bereavement got me off the hook – on compassionate grounds my school offered me the opportunity to retake it in September, a prospect that depressed me more than my automatic failure. The two A levels I had completed shortly before my mother died, English and Physics, I felt were doomed to poor grades anyway. Furthermore, I had no plans to go to university, simply because nobody I knew – other than Henry – ever had. I would take a year off, then busk it. I had not the faintest idea what I wanted to do for a living, but I assumed something would turn up. My aspirations were pitched higher than Ray's and the shoe shop, but not massively so.

My father, who was struggling to cope with the demands of his job through the dislocations of his grief, told me plainly that he couldn't deal with me any more. The car theft, the flunked A level, most of all my surly and uncommunicative attitude, came as an intolerable surplus burden on top of his attempts to cope with the loss of Evie and his new, onerous role as a single parent. I was beyond making my standard response to being criticized – that my father was being self-ish. Neither was I capable of registering the selfishness that I was displaying towards him. I had lost all interest in both of us.

Then – as with the sweet peas, as if he had intuited it – a letter arrived from Uncle Henry, reasserting the sincerity of his offer to do anything he could to help. Duly prompted, my father immediately wrote back to him and asked – without checking with me first – whether I could go and stay with him on the boat for the summer.

Henry phoned the shoe shop the day Ray's letter arrived in Somerset to say that I would be welcome. He gave his address and told my father to bring me down right away that weekend. He lived alone on the houseboat; there was no schizophrenic ballet dancer. There wasn't much to do where he lived, Henry said, but he was sure that he and I would find something to amuse ourselves.

Ray informed me that I should pack up my things on Saturday. He would drive me to Henry's on Sunday. After that weekend, school was finished for the summer.

Ray would immediately return to London, and I wouldn't see him, or Buthelezi House, again until the autumn. I would have a chance to revise for my History A level, which I would then resit.

I made no resistance. Any course I chose – or was compelled to take – would, I was convinced, have the same lack of significant consequence.

On the Saturday I packed, neither raising objection nor showing any enthusiasm. Most of my possessions fitted easily enough into my nylon sports holdall and a couple of plastic supermarket bags. There were six pairs of Y-fronts, a pair of brown Speedo swimming trunks, some cut-off Wranglers, patched, bleached and faded. There were several washed-out T-shirts which had long ago lost their shape, some of them bearing the names of bands I liked or slogans of which I approved. One bore an image of Hollywood killer Charles Manson with I AM ONLY WHAT YOU MADE ME. I AM ONLY A REFLECTION OF YOU inscribed beneath, in letters that appeared to drip blood.

An ancient, battered, green-painted suitcase, steel with rivets, held a couple of bulky towels and a lump of cheap soap. Also Converse basketball boots, black socks disfigured by bobbles, some unattractively fresh brown leather sandals that my dad had got on staff discount from the shop.

I put a canvas military-style jacket and a bum freezer with a fur collar on top of the pile. I also had a Slazenger shoulder bag for bits and pieces – a Swiss Army knife, a transistor radio, a bag of spearmint chews and a copy of *ZigZag* magazine. There was also a wooden apple crate, which had once held Cox's Orange Pippins, containing a selection of my favourite LPs – Jackson Browne, Tim Hardin, Leonard Cohen, and a few others of a likewise introspective and lugubrious nature. Set against these melancholics were a number of heavy-metal albums, including *In-A-Gadda-Da-Vida* by Iron Butterfly, the first Black Sabbath album, MC5's *Kick Out the Jams*, and *Deep Purple in Rock*. There was a small portable record player, with chipboard case, vinyl-covered, with a hinged lid and a broken catch. I sealed it shut with Sellotape.

Other than basic toiletries – a bottle of Eau Sauvage after-shave my mother had bought me for Christmas a couple of years back, plus toothpaste and a ragged toothbrush – that was more or less it. I also had my most prized possession, a spick pair of yellow-lensed aviator-style Foster Grants, which lent me the essence, so I believed at the time, of a seasoned veteran of Laurel Canyon in the Hollywood Hills rather than an ordinary teenage slob from the London exurbs.

After much lobbying by my father, I agreed to pack my revision notes and History textbooks – although I had little intention of applying myself to them. My entrenched list-lessness was apparent in the food stains on my clothes; the slouch of my shoulders; the silent, accusatory contortions of my mouth. My examination materials sat lumpen, a jumble in a single plastic bag, the corner of one History primer pen-etrating the thin polythene like an unwelcome fact piercing an untenable theory.

The journey to Uncle Henry's houseboat took nearly four hours. The temperature stood at eighty-three degrees and when we stopped for a roadside picnic – trestle table set up in a lay-by, carbon monoxide from passing juggernauts spic-ing our luncheon-meat sandwiches – I noted that there was no wind whatsoever, other than displaced air from speeding traffic.

The boat was moored on a tributary of a tributary of the River Severn, some ten miles or so outside Bristol. Ray and I passed the time more or less in silence. At one point he tried to engage me in a game of red car / blue car, but the competition expired from lack of engagement on my part after several minutes. I can't remember anything else about the journey except the smell of the car – a mud-coloured five-year-old Ford Anglia, already spawning carbuncles of rust at the wheel arches. My father, who had also become somewhat careless and dilatory of late, had inadvertently left a half-eaten banana under the passenger seat for several days. He had removed it before we set off, but the interior continued to reek of the sweet, decaying pulp throughout the overheated, rickety journey. The windows were open to cool the interior – and purge it of the odour – so the sound of the air pushing past rendered conversation difficult. Not that we had anything to say to one another in the first place.

Finding the boat was not easy. Henry had posted Ray a small, hand-drawn map, written on the back of a 'Visit the West Country' holiday postcard which featured on the front a yokel dressed in sackcloth sitting on a farmyard gate, chewing straw and holding a stone bottle of Somerset cider. The map appeared to have little connection with the actual topography we were experiencing. We turned off the main road, as suggested by the diagram, then on to a B road, then on to a back road, then a mile down what was little more than a dirt track. Any confidence that we could possibly be in the right place drained away. There was no sign of habitation of any kind.

The rough land we were travelling across – the Anglia creaking and complaining and Ray looking anxious about what effect the terrain was having on the crankshaft – gave way to a small but dense wood looming in front of us. Then the wood was above us, forming a carapace. The vegetation was growing wilder by the yard, looping out from the trees as if intent on discouraging strangers.

It seemed that we were destined to come to a dead end – the track becoming narrower and narrower, the wood and brush thickening exponentially – but then, just as my father was about to back up and retrace our path, we burst through a row of overhanging trees, one of which scraped the roof of the Anglia with a ratcheting sound that made my father wince and curse. We found ourselves facing an isolated riverbank. Moored flush against the bank was a houseboat, bobbing slightly in the gentle swell of the water. Parked ten yards in front of us was Henry's Karmann Ghia.

The wooden boat was constructed on two levels, with sides roughly painted in what I thought of as English green, since it was the dark-seaweed hue of sheds and wooden gates and front doors throughout rural England. Three round porthole-style windows, with horizontal sash divisions bisecting them, were set on the lower level. There were two smaller portholes at the first-floor level. At the prow, a hand-painted legend in Chinese-style script announced the name of the boat – *Ho Koji*.

The roof of the upper storey seemed to be set slightly at an angle, presumably in order to facilitate the run-off of rain-water. This gave the boat a rickety, off-centre air. There was a decorative crenellated awning attached as a fringe to the first-floor-level base, also green, but punctuated with alter-nating leaves of white. The aft of the boat, at its furthermost point, where the cabin and steering wheel might be located on a sea-going craft, held two rectangular windows, which faced us as we sat regarding the boat silently. The car, now unventilated by passing air, heated up quickly to an uncom-fortable level, and I climbed out, my trousers stickily unpeeling from the vinyl seat. Ray continued to sit behind the steering wheel, the motor still running, staring, as if unable to take in his brother's unconventional living arrange-ments. I don't know what he had expected – pebbledash, perhaps, or carriage lamps.

The front door, centred between the two rectangular windows, sat behind a small deck which supported two large ceramic pots containing delicate, red-leafed trees – which

Henry later identified as Japanese acers – on either side. The door was intricately carved with birds and flowers, and painted a livid purple which clashed somewhat with the serenity of the surrounding green gloss. Somehow the whole construction had the feel of a gypsy caravan, although it was much larger than any caravan I had ever seen. Both stern and aft were squared off – it clearly wasn't a boat that was built for river cruising. There was a sun terrace on the higher level, framed by a white rail at waist height. A lounger was stretched out on it, the canvas material decorated with wide blue and white deckchair stripes. A ragged, nubby white towel was draped over the angled back.

The feeling of the boat was homely. Although I couldn't think of it as beautiful – it was too blunt and squat for that, and the paint was flaking badly in places – it fitted into the surroundings very naturally, snugly negotiating the space connecting land and water. Another white metal rail, which appeared to be newly painted, since it was much brighter than its yellowing counterpart at the upper level, stretched around the entrance deck, with a gap where the gangplank was attached. The gangplank was set at a right-angle, a short stretch out over the water, then a longer section leading off to the left on to the boat, creating an L shape. There was a single metal chimney protruding from the roof.

'Not exactly the *QE2*, is it?' said Ray.

He finally killed the engine, exited the car and stretched, with a yawn that I think was meant to convey to me how unimpressed he was by his brother's strange choice of lodgings. He looked uneasily around him, and then spoke briskly, as if he wanted to get my transplantation over and done with as quickly as possible.

'Here we are. Get your things.'

I didn't move, and continued to take in the scene. Along the patch of dried grass that ran in a wide rectangular strip abutting the mooring were scattered an array of objects – a rusted metal barbecue, a rattan chair, a few beanbags partly protected by a plastic cover on stilts, and a large rubber mat. There was what appeared to be a generator, which was a relief – I had been concerned that there might not be any electricity.

A few paperbacks were baking on the ground. One had the intriguing title of *The Electric Kool-Aid Acid Test*, and there was another larger book, about the area of an LP cover, called *An Index of Possibilities*. It seemed to be some kind of popular-science book. There were the remains of a log fire, which was faintly smouldering, and an empty packet of Smith's cheese and onion crisps. I could smell ashes and grass cuttings and, perhaps, the river, slightly rotten and fresh at the same time.

Ray was at the boot, pulling out my steel suitcase, the sports holdall and my green shoulder bag.

I hauled out my revision books and notes from the back seat and laid them on the grass. I removed my apple box of LPs. I was worried they might have warped in the heat. The plastic bag full of ice I had carefully rested on top of them had long since melted. I emptied the waste water on to the ground, then anxiously took out a disc to check – The Incredible String Band's *Strangely Strange But Oddly Normal*. I held the record at a steady horizon. It appeared to have survived the journey intact. I gently lifted out my portable record player, unstuck the Sellotape and confirmed that the needle hadn't been damaged in transit.

I decided to check if Henry was actually in the boat. I would have expected him to hear the car pulling in and come to welcome us, but there was no sign of life. I approached the boat and peered through the first porthole I came to.

Uncle Henry was sitting cross-legged on a futon. He had spectacles on, round and wire-framed like Mahatma Gandhi's. He was naked. His body was wiry and brown with a little pot belly. His eyes were open and he was absolutely still. I tapped gently on the window with my fingernails, but there was no response.

My father was already crossing the gangway, carrying the suitcase in one hand and my holdall in the other. It was very quiet. The only sound I was aware of was the slight lapping of water against the hull. Under the waterline, it was patched with green slime. Ray started calling out.

'The charabanc has arrived. Where's the welcoming committee?'

There was no answer. My father put down my bags on the front deck, then noticed me staring through the window.

'Is he in there?' A note of irritation sounded in his voice.

I gestured for him to come and join me. He looked flustered. There were vast sweat patches mapping his armpits.

Ray peered through the window. His face ruptured in distaste.

'For Christ's sake. He could at least have made himself decent.'

He knocked on the glass with his car keys. Henry did not move or react in any way. He gave the appearance of being dead, except that his pot belly could be seen very slowly expanding and contracting with his breath. Beneath his midriff, his cock was substantial. Perhaps this was another reason for my father's irritation.

My father knocked again, more firmly this time. Some light returned to Henry's eyes, which had been fixed and blank. After a couple of moments, his shoulders dropped slightly and his eyes began to move, though his head remained still. His torso relaxed slightly. His eyes focused and his head swivelled slowly in our direction.

Showing no embarrassment or surprise, his face broke into a wide smile, displaying his small, even, rather dirty teeth. He rose from his position and stretched, as if nothing could be more normal than sitting naked apparently enjoying an out-of-body experience. He stood still for another moment, facing us, as if inviting us to admire his physique.

'He should put his wedding tackle away at least,' muttered Ray. 'Not much to boast about if you ask me,' he added sourly.

Henry left the cabin via a door to his left. After about thirty seconds he reappeared at the front deck, with a clean white loincloth wrapped loosely around his hips and his spectacles removed. He beckoned and we crossed the gangplank to join him. Ray marched purposefully while I loped behind.

'Raymond. Adam.'

He reached his arms out for my father and this time, despite the precedent of the funeral, my father shrank away. Being hugged by a largely naked man, even if it was his brother, was clearly too much for him to stomach. Henry held his shoulders instead, at arms' length. Ray stood there, rigid. After several seconds, Henry allowed my father out of his grip. He looked past Ray and his gaze fell on me. He winked.

'The real business of the visit,' Henry said. He smiled his terrific smile. 'Hey, stupid.'

'Stupid yourself,' I said casually.

'Can I help unload?' He ignored the bags on the deck and started striding across the gangplank. Ray and I followed him. On reaching the bank, instead of picking up any bags, he immediately delved into my box of records. He flicked through them, nodding silently and occasionally tut-tutting. My father went towards the gangplank, carrying my suitcase and sports holdall.

'Grim stuff here,' Henry said. 'Music to slit your wrists to. Or to listen to whilst strafing innocent passers-by. Shame we don't have a record player.'

Before I could tell him that I'd brought my own, he smiled.

'Only kidding, stupid. We've got a hi-fi that can break the sound barrier. Fifty-watt Wharfedale speakers. Put your heavy-metal thrash on and see how that sounds. Different world entirely. The bass can shatter tectonic plates.'

He picked up the box of records and made his way towards the deck, while my father sat waiting with the rest of the luggage, unsure whether or not to enter. I slung my Slazenger bag over my shoulder, balanced my revision materials on top of the record player, and followed Henry.

'What shall I do with these?' said Ray, brandishing my suitcase and sports holdall.

'Put them in Adam's room. It's the one with the orange door decorated with crescent moons. Directly up the stairs and right in front of you.'

Henry led us into the interior. I followed, close behind Henry's naked brown back. His buttocks were clearly visible either side of the loincloth. They were as brown as the rest of him.

We entered the main cabin, which, to my surprise, was wall-to-wall carpeted with thick white pile, within the soiled forest of which I could see cigarette burns and several tea or coffee stains. There was a slightly raised platform to the right of me, on which sat a small, unvarnished, rectangular wooden table with four battered iron folding chairs. On the table was a roughly cast green-glazed ceramic tea set, which my father would have designated 'ethnic' since the cups had no handles or saucers and the glaze was unfinished. To the right of the table there was a small galley area, which comprised a sink with a single tap, a draining-board and a Calor gas hob and grill. Under the portholes on the opposite side was a seating area, simply some low storage cupboards with flat cushions placed on top of them. As Henry had promised, there was a music system in the far left-hand corner, with speakers the size of filing cabinets.

There was an astonishing number of books piled into the space, some arrayed on makeshift bookshelves, others sitting in teetering piles on the floor. A brief inspection revealed few novels among the collection. It was largely philosophy, psychology and anthropology. An orange-embroidered kilim hung across one of the walls, depicting, in stitch, an elephant and rider.

Henry started fumbling with his loincloth, which was apparently in danger of coming undone. My father was breathing heavily. Instead of following Henry's instructions to take my things upstairs, he put the bags down, grunted and pointed to a paisley-patterned cotton robe that lay in a pile on the floor. Henry made a good-natured apology about losing track of 'the way things are done', dropped the loincloth to reveal his genitals again, and put on the robe.

Now he was decent, he tried to hug my father for a second time. Ray acceded, but remained stiff, his arms pressed against his sides, his eyes sliding from side to side in their sockets. Then he pulled away.

'Jesus, Henry. Why are you always grabbing people?'

'Sorry, Raymond. You just seemed lonely.'

'I'm not lonely.'

'I'm sure the loss of Evie must still weigh on you very heavily.'

'Why have you always got to talk that way? Like you were broadcasting on the wireless.'

Henry shrugged, and his gaze alighted on me again. I somehow wished he would hug me too, but he simply held out a hand. I shook it.

Ray busied himself with the bags again.

'You've had a long journey. Settle down for a moment. I'll muster a brew.'

My father, who was clearly tired, stopped fussing with the luggage and settled himself down at the table, looking incongruous and uncomfortable in his permanent-press suit trousers, grey easy-iron rayon shirt and staff-discount Hush Puppies. His thin socks were visible beneath the cuff of his trouser legs. Above one of the socks I noticed a little stripe of pale flesh, bumpy like chicken skin, the sight of which somehow made me sad.

Henry offered him a choice of herbal teas 'from California' – camomile, peppermint or liquorice 'yogi tea'. Ray requested 'a common-or-garden cup of char'. I asked for coffee, which, instead of being ladled out of a jar as was invariably the case in Buthelezi House, Henry carefully prepared using a stovetop Italian-style *moka* and beans which he ground in an old-fashioned mill. Having delivered the drinks, he lit a cigarette from a packet of twenty Lucky Strike, then joined us at the table.

The porthole windows were open, as was the front door. A warm breeze explored the room. A large brown duck waddled through the door, gave a single quack and made a beeline for my father, who recoiled anxiously. Then the duck – which had a yellow plastic tag attached to one of its legs – altered course and marched in martial style around the carpet as if it had something pressing to do. It snapped once or twice at my father.

'That's Ginsberg,' said Henry. 'He sometimes comes and pays a visit if he has nothing better to do. I consider him to be my lucky mascot.'

'What's his bloody problem?' said Ray, eyeing the duck carefully as if it might rush him.

'He seems friendly enough to me,' I said.

Henry shrugged. 'He has his good days and bad days, like all of us.'

'What are you talking about, Henry? He's a duck, not some tortured soul. Anyway how do you know it's not just any old duck?'

'Because he has a ring round his leg. Something to do with conservation. As for him being a tortured soul, on the contrary: it seems to me that Ginsberg is very much at one with himself.'

'You really do come out with some cobblers.'

'Is he anxious? Is he hungry? Does he have regrets about the past? Or worries about the future?'

'Probably not, since he's got a brain about the size of a bloody pea.'

Ginsberg eyed my father with what I felt certain was a degree of hostility. He gave one more plaintive quack, then, still purposeful, waddled out of the front door, his rear end swinging like a chorus girl's.

My father, visibly relieved, took a sip of his tea. I saw him making a face as it occurred to him that it was not Typhoo at all. I had noticed the packet – it was a breakfast blend from Fortnum & Mason.

Then Ray started to talk. It was as if the duck had shocked

him into action. He was the most garrulous I had seen him by far since my mother had died.

After talking about the onerousness of his work at the shop, the progress or otherwise of my studies and the chronic back pain he suffered as a result of bending so much to fit his customers' shoes to their feet, he began, almost as if he had run out of other things to say, to talk of the funeral. How it had been a disappointment, how the vicar had barely known anything about my mother, how he wished he'd chosen a more appropriate casket. It was out of character for him – but there was something in the atmosphere on that boat that made people do surprising things, I later learned.

Also, the place appeared to intimidate him with its threat of peace. The boat seemed held in a corona of deep silence, nothing like the suburban pastiche of quiet, which was perpetually overlaid by a soundscape of cars, planes, voices and distant transistor radios. Henry listened attentively, occasionally stealing a glance at me. Despite how impressed I was with what I had seen of the boat and its furnishings, I was determined to remain surly. My coffee tasted black and sweet and earthy, and it made my heart beat fast.

My father gulped down his tea, shifting continually in his chair. Henry sat very still and watched him. He had grown a small goatee beard since the last time I'd seen him. It suited him. Everything suited Henry.

My father suddenly rose and turned to me. He seemed uncertain as to what to say. Then he touched me on the shoulder, nodded and turned towards the door.

'I ought to be going.'

'But I haven't shown you round the boat,' said Henry.

'A boat's a boat,' said Ray. 'Thanks for the tea.'

'There's no need to be rude, Dad.'

'That's enough from you. I'll not be taking any lessons in manners from *you*.'

Henry looked mildly across at me. 'It's OK. I don't mind.'

I made no more protest. In all honesty, I was desperate for Ray to leave.

Ray turned back to Henry. He looked faintly chastened.

'Henry. Look. I appreciate this. I do. You've been gone a long time. I suppose I'm not sure I'm quite used to you popping up again. But listen. I'm grateful. Really.'

He reached in his pocket and drew out a thin roll of ten-pound notes.

'This is to see Adam through the summer. I hope it's enough.'

'Dad. Why can't you just give it to me?'

Henry threw me a glance that required – no, requested – my silence. He took the money and put it in the pocket of his robe.

'I'll make sure he budgets wisely, Raymond, don't worry.'

'OK, then.' He turned to me. 'See? Your Uncle Henry agrees.'

I said nothing. There was an awkward pause, then Ray rested his hand on my shoulder. I wasn't sure how to respond. After a few moments, I felt its weight lift, and Ray headed towards the front door. Neither Henry nor I moved. Ray turned again before he left the room, as if to say something. His mouth opened, but no words emerged. He snapped it closed again and nodded, twice, as if that settled everything. I raised a hand briefly in farewell.

'Say goodbye to your dad,' said Henry, surprisingly sharply.

'Goodbye, Dad,' I said. I looked at him standing in the doorway, forlorn.

'Look after yourself, kiddo. Good luck, Henry.'

'*Adiós*, Ray.'

Then he was gone. After thirty seconds, I heard the car start. There was the squeal of tyres, followed by the sound of the motor fading into the distance. Ginsberg reappeared, raised his head as if to acknowledge the new status quo, then waddled briskly out again.

Henry came and sat back at the table with me. He reached into his pocket and handed me the wad of notes. I pocketed them.

'Thanks.'

'People should be free to make their own mistakes,' said Henry.

'Really?'

'A cornerstone of my philosophy. "The fool who persists in his folly will become wise." Blake.'

'Blake who?'

My coffee was almost drained. I remained determined to be unimpressed. We sat in silence, finishing our dregs. Henry offered me a Lucky. I took it and he lit it for me. He smiled, as if he considered some kind of deal to have been struck. I smiled too, for a different reason, silently sealing a pact with myself that I wasn't about to be Henry's stooge, or his disciple. He was part of the adult world and as such was not to be trusted, however particular an example of the species he considered himself to be. Adults always let you down, with their parade of good intentions, their self-sabotage, their brutal, unheralded transience.

'Shall I show you round the rest of the boat?'

'A boat's a boat,' I said, deadpan.

Henry laughed. I rose and followed him towards the stern. In the centre of the boat was the small staircase leading up to the second level. We walked past that to the two rooms beyond it, one on either side of a small passageway. Henry opened the doorway to his right, to reveal an interior that was little bigger than a cupboard. There was a single mattress on the floor, a few blankets and a chest of drawers. It was stifling. The room, however, acquired an atmosphere of romance from the large round porthole that looked out over the river.

'This is the spare room. I have the occasional visitor.'

The room opposite, which overlooked the reach, was somewhat larger and altogether more pleasant. It was likewise dominated by a porthole, and contained a trestle table and an adjustable office chair. The table surface was almost entirely obscured by scraps of paper, and in the middle of the mess was a sturdy old black Remington typewriter. There was also a chrome filing cabinet, a multi-storey paper tray and a pin-board covered from border to border with scribbled notes, receipts, letters, snapshots – Indian temples, beaches at sunset – and ticket stubs.

'This is my office. And this . . .' Henry reached over to a drawer in the desk and pulled out a large pile of A4 papers, 'is my book. This is what I do every day. I'm near the end now.'

'What's it about?'

'Everything,' said Henry, and put the manuscript back into the drawer.

He led me up the staircase to the upper level, which was smaller than the lower one, and contained only two bedrooms, Henry's on one side and mine on the other, as well as a tiny loo-cum-shower-room. There was also an entrance to the sun deck, where I could see the nubby towel on the back of the lounger moving in the breeze.

Henry's room was full of intriguing objects: jade Buddhas, Japanese watercolours, a ceremonial sword and an ink and pen set – 'For calligraphy,' he explained. There was a silk screen, which served no obvious purpose. His bed had a painted headboard which showed a snake consuming its own tail, and was covered with a large green embroidered coverlet, the sheen of which suggested silk.

My room overlooked the river through a square window. The bed was a single, with an iron bedstead and a continental quilt with a plain white cover. There was a pillow with a matching coverlet. There were two folded towels on the bed and a purple beanbag on the floor. The floor itself was laid with battered cork tiles. There was a small wardrobe, a chest of drawers and a tiny pine desk with a sloping lid that looked as if it had been salvaged from a schoolroom. A matching chair stood in front of it. Adjacent to the desk was a sink with an unframed mirror over it. The room had little in the way of decoration, but it was full of light, and somehow profoundly friendly. I liked it, and thanked Henry for it. He told me I was welcome.

We fetched up what there was of my luggage. Henry finished the cigarette he was smoking, apologised to me, and said that he knew it appeared terribly inhospitable, but he had set himself a very strict work schedule and needed to stick to it, despite my arrival. He promised to make up for it later in the evening. He asked if I could amuse myself for a couple of hours while settling in and allow him to complete his work for that day. Then he left, without waiting for an answer, tugging on his beard with one hand and blithely scratching his buttocks through the material of his robe with the other.

I started to put my possessions into the drawers and the

wardrobe. After a minute or so, I could hear the clatter of his typing from the office downstairs. The typing was as repetitive and irritating as the birdsong that I could hear outside my window. I wanted to feel happy, but I felt afraid – not of Henry, but of boredom, and nothingness, and the slow, dead tug of water against a vessel that could never be launched.

I lay down on the bed and drifted into sleep.

Five

W hen I woke, there were rich, unfamiliar smells per-
meating the air. They were spicy and exotic. This
made me feel nervous. I had been brought up on plain food.
My mother rarely stretched herself imaginatively beyond
spaghetti bolognese and my father, after her death, had never
offered me anything other than toast-related snacks, pre-
cooked pies, chops and plain boiled veg.

Outside, the first gutterings of dusk were encroaching on
the aerosol blue of the sky. It seemed I had slept for several
hours. I could hear Henry clunking around in the galley. The
odd molecule of Calor Gas drifted up the staircase, remind-
ing me of the camping holidays my parents had compelled
me to participate in when I was a child. The sulphurous, fart-
like smell brought back thoughts of wind and rain, cold
showers in the morning and long walks across chilly fields
and stony beaches in the afternoons.

I pumped some cold water from the tank and splashed my

face. In the light reflected from the river, I looked different from the image that was presented to me every morning in Buthelezi House. I saw myself as raw, as if a layer of skin had been stripped from my face. I looked young. I never thought of myself that way any more.

The clunking stopped and a few seconds later, Uncle Henry appeared at the doorway. He was wearing faded jeans, a T-shirt with the emblazoned words FILLMORE EAST and a pair of battered brown open-toed leather sandals. His hair was slicked back behind his ears. In his hand was a tumbler of red wine, which he held out towards me. I was confused that it was in a tumbler. In my experience, wine always came served in a stemmed glass, and was never offered to anyone under eighteen.

I took it and downed it in a swig. I didn't say thank you. Henry nodded, as if acknowledging something too obvious to be spoken, and informed me that dinner would be ready in about twenty minutes. Then he left the room.

Half an hour passed. The sun had fallen very low. There was a deep, hazy dusk. I was reluctant to leave my room. The existence of other people in the world seemed an imposition. I looked through the window at the dark water, and dreamed of slipping under it.

I heard Henry's warm, sandpapery voice calling up to me. I rose, still in bare feet, and slouched my way downstairs into the main room. It was very warm. The table was laid with deep-red 'ethnic' ceramic kitchenware.

'Moroccan,' said Henry without turning round, as if he had sensed the question in my gaze.

There were silver knives and forks that bore hallmarks and the patina of age. There was a crystal wine goblet in front of one place, and a tumbler in front of the other. Remaining silent, I duly sat down in front of the water glass. Henry informed me politely that I was sitting in the wrong place – he was the one who was drinking water.

He brought over an earthenware pot and started to dole out the food. I know now that it was Thai green curry, though I had no idea at the time. I registered that there were leaves in it, and stared it at grimly. Henry served out his own portion. He replaced the cooking pots, sat down opposite me and raised his glass in a toast. I rather awkwardly raised my wineglass.

It occurred to me some twenty minutes later – through the haze of several more glasses of wine – that Uncle Henry might be queer. My prejudices informed me that queers liked cooking and wine and art. He was childless and unmarried. My father talked of him as a womanizer, but I had no reason to think my father's information in any way reliable. He had invited me, a seventeen-year-old boy, on to his boat for the whole summer with no obvious motive, other than a professed compassion and out of a supposed respect for a family connection that he had shown no traces of previously in his life. The attempts to win me over – giving me Ray's money, offering me cigarettes and red wine – suddenly appeared to me as suspect.

As I sat there, I became uncomfortably convinced that he was going to try and take advantage of me. I shifted uneasily on my chair, and stared at the French loaf I had been picking at in lieu of eating my supper.

Henry indicated with a wave of his hand that I should eat. He had finished his meal and I had barely touched mine. I noticed that his fingers were very long and delicate, displaying several elaborate rings, more evidence in my mind, now, of his homosexuality. I shook my head. I said I didn't much

like it. He asked me how I knew I didn't like it when I hadn't
tried it. It was one of those trick questions my parents used
to ask me when I was a kid. I didn't answer.

I swigged at my wine again. I suddenly felt unprotected,
and in a strange place where I did not know the rules.

'Which team do you play for?' I said, slurring slightly.

'I beg your pardon?'

'Are you that way inclined?' I said, struggling to find a way
of putting it delicately. I was vaguely aware that I was lifting
these euphemisms from sitcoms I had watched. 'I don't particularly mind if you are. I just want to set the record straight.'

'Which way inclined is that?' Henry raised an eyebrow. He
clearly knew what I was talking about and was teasing me.
The knowing expression on his face sent a bolt of irritation
through me.

'What I'm asking is: are you queer?'

I immediately regretted the brutality of the question. But
Henry simply took a swig of his water and smiled at me,
apparently unconcerned by my rudeness. He made no reply.
This annoyed me more than his teasing.

Convinced now, on the basis of no evidence whatsoever,
that Henry was, as I thought of it then, a sexual pervert, I
rose, went back to my room and sat mutely on the bed. I felt
very hungry and I had to admit that the smell of the food was
actually extremely good. But I wasn't prepared to surrender,
although I had no idea what it was I would be surrendering
to, or where the lines of the battle had been drawn.

Just before I fell asleep, I heard Henry call to me from outside the door.

'Goodnight, stupid.'

'Stupid yourself,' I muttered, this time not loud enough
for him to hear.

Six

The first few days I spent on the *Ho Koji* were unremarkable. I was bored in Buthelezi House and I was bored on the boat.

My History revision books sat in a pile in the corner, still untouched in their plastic supermarket bag. I passed the time dozing, listening to music or reading pulp in one form or another – I liked science fiction and Henry had found a pile of DC and Marvel comics somewhere and dumped them on my floor. I read a lot of Superman adventures. It struck me at one point as significant that green Kryptonite, the only thing that could kill Superman, was actually a piece of his home planet that had broken off and floated into space.

His own home was the only thing that could destroy him.

During that first week, Henry made no special attempt to accommodate or entertain me. He was neither hostile nor particularly convivial. He ventured a few exploratory queries about school, friends and so on, but he didn't press very hard when I proved consistently reticent. I was determined not to display any positive signals that might encourage him in my seduction.

The days were long – and there was no television to watch in the evening. Henry showed me the larder and the fridge, both of which were well appointed with eggs, cheese, bread, butter and all the staples. I was left to fend for myself.

To pass the time, I sunbathed on the upper deck during those first, hot days. It was a pleasant enough kind of boredom. There was no requirement for any activity here – Henry seemed to expect nothing of me at all except that I remain reasonably clean and tidy. One of my few virtues was that I was someone who liked order and almost instinctively cleared up after myself.

Henry, on the other hand, was clean but messy. I often found myself picking up his detritus – scraps of paper, fountain pens, even laundry – from the floor and placing it out of sight. Also, he snored at night, so loudly I could hear him, the walls between the rooms being thin. He smoked heavily, both pipe and cigarettes, so that even with the windows and doors open the place reeked of tobacco.

We quickly settled into a routine, with barely a word being spoken between us. I would rise mid-morning, around ten o'clock. I had always been able to sleep for long periods without any trouble.

By the time I made my way into the main cabin, Henry would have been up for hours, clacking away at his typewriter and coming to the end of his first pack of Luckies. He would beam at me vaguely if I looked into his office, and make a gentle attempt to engage me in conversation, which I usually rebuffed.

I would fix myself some coffee, help myself to one of his cigarettes – there were several cartons of 200 stacked under the bench seats – and make myself a couple of slices of toast. Then I would put on my Speedos and go and stretch out on the sun deck, where I had decided to build up a record-breaking suntan. I slathered myself with coconut oil, given to me by Henry. It offered me no protection from the sun, and I burned myself quite badly on the first day. But I persevered. Although I was gangly and thin – and, partly as a consequence of this, a virgin – I was not beyond teenage vanity, nor its shadow, insecurity.

On the fourth day, as I was settling into a kind of timeless zone that made the boredom palatable, Henry appeared on the deck where I was stretched out in the full heat of the sun, even though my nose and back were already red and peeling. I immediately assumed that he was ogling me, but then I heard a woman's voice from behind him, mellow, with a slight American flavour.

'So this is the kid, right?'

A young woman appeared from behind Henry. She had long, straight, chestnut hair halfway down to her waist, a galaxy of heavy freckles decorating her improbably symmetrical and tanned features, and a pair of blue jeans indistinguishable in style from Henry's. She was wearing a yellow scoop-neck blouse with long, flared sleeves. She was small – maybe five foot two – stick-slim and golden like dreams, and not so much older than me. Early twenties, I guessed. Her hair kept falling across her face, and she kept pushing it back behind her ears, where it would never stay. She looked vaguely familiar. She also looked like Ali McGraw. Maybe that was it.

I covered myself with a towel.

She smiled and held out her hand. 'Hello. I'm Strawberry.'

I sat up and took her hand. She pulled it back and inspected it.

'Ew.'

'Sorry. I'm afraid it's a bit slick. From the tanning oil.'

I handed her my towel and she carefully wiped her hand, concentrating on the space between the fingers. I felt embarrassed.

'Your name is really Strawberry?'

'As in the fruit.'

'That's an unusual name.'

'Do you like it?'

'Sure. I suppose. My name's much more boring. I'm Adam. Adam Templeton.'

'I don't have a surname,' she said. 'I had it changed by law. It's just Strawberry. Or to be precise, since the passport authorities insisted on something like a surname, Strawberry Shortcake. But I think that's just my full first name'.

She giggled in a way that made me think she was even younger than I had guessed.

'That's a joke?'

'No, that really is my legal name. I mean, sure it's a joke, but a joke on the passport squares. The government. You know?'

'So what was your name before?'

'Nothing interesting. Susan, actually. Strawberry's much better, isn't it? Always gets a conversation going.'

Her voice was cultured despite the American twang. She had an air of powerful self-possession, laced with a certain obscure fragility.

Having offered my towel to Strawberry, my body was

exposed again. I thought I saw Henry gazing at me, and started to pull on my jeans.

Strawberry looked at Henry and began to laugh.

'What's so funny?' I asked.

'You are,' she said.

'Me? You think *I'm* funny? With your name?'

'Oh, don't be a sour lemon. I'm not laughing *at* you. I just think it's funny that you think Henry's a fag,' she said, still smiling.

So this was what the visit was about.

'He's not. I know that for certain. From my own *personal* experience.'

She kissed Henry, and flung her arms around his neck.

Henry smiled at me and said, 'I thought you'd be more comfortable if you knew.'

When I came down from the roof, an hour or two after Henry's theatrical attempt to offer proof of his heterosexuality, I went to my room and put Nick Drake's *Five Leaves Left* album on. His voice hung suspended in sadness like a skeleton leaf on a cold winter pond. I lay there in my room until the late afternoon, floating with the leaf, when I became aware of a gentle knocking at my door.

I ignored it at first, having been embarrassed by the double-act on the sun deck. My feelings of vague hostility towards Henry had not been allayed. It had seemed that he was mocking me. Also I felt humiliated that my admittedly absurd presumption had been proved wrong so forcefully. The knocking continued. Then I heard the sound of a woman's voice.

'Adam?'

I uttered a sullen acknowledgement. The door inched open. A sliver of a face appeared. Shining, burnished. The hinge creaked as the door completed its parabola. Strawberry was standing there, smiling lazily, her left leg bent slightly so that she stood just off centre. Her head, too, was cocked to one side. The effect was inviting without being necessarily sexual. I could smell patchouli oil, cloves and something else. Iron? Old pennies?

I blushed and avoided eye contact. She had changed. She was now wearing a simple white linen dress, embroidered with a fine pink and blue looped pattern across the bust and, it seemed, nothing much underneath. I could see the caramel darkness of her nipples through the material. No shoes. She was carrying two of the green ceramic cups from downstairs.

She gave a small cough, which quickly developed into something more serious – a hacking rasp that shook her tiny frame. Her body was underdeveloped – I hadn't realized how much so when I had first seen her. Her calves and thighs, exposed beneath her buttocks – where in fact, there was barely any curve – seemed to be no more than the circumference of a sturdy table leg. 'Spindly' was the word that crossed my mind. It made her seem vulnerable, even in her beauty.

The coughing was so extreme that I thought she was going to drop the cups. Then, as suddenly as it had arrived, the fit ended. She had tears in her eyes, presumably from the seizure, which she was unable to wipe away because of the cups in her hand. She held one of them out to me. I took it, tearing my gaze away from her body, and nodded acknowledgement.

'Coffee,' she said. 'Instant. Not that tar water Henry cooks up.'

She wiped the teardrops from her face with her free hand. 'I sort of like Henry's coffee,' I answered.

'I only drink green tea. You get it in health-food stores in the States. And spring water. Or rainwater. I'm very strict. Green tea helps to remove impurities. The pollution is every-where. Invisible rain. Even here we're not safe. Right out here in the boonies, that shit still comes down. That's why I get these terrible coughs. Charged particles. Radiation. You know about the radiation? But it's better here than in the Smoke. It feels clean. Even if, really, it's not. You know?'

I didn't know how to respond, so I didn't answer. I expected her to withdraw, but she didn't move. She adjusted her posture slightly, leaning forward as if inviting herself in further. She sipped her tea, leaving a trail of moisture on her ghostly lips, whose paleness contrasted sharply with the rest of her body. It occurred to me then that she was waiting for an invitation to sit down. I was slouched on my bed. On the wall above it, a large poster of Jerry Garcia of The Grateful Dead, in mid-solo, was stuck with drawing-pins at four cor-ners: bearded, ecstatic, the neck of his red guitar pointing to heaven.

The only place to sit, other than the severe chair at my desk, was the rumpled and stained purple beanbag. I nodded faintly towards it. Delicately she sat, cross-legged. Despite myself, my eyes darted towards the inner apex of her thighs. She noticed – I saw the slight raise of an eyebrow – and I immediately looked away. But I had time to take in that she was wearing slight, filmy pants, stained slightly with some-thing dark.

She didn't speak again for some time. Perhaps a whole minute passed. She gazed out towards the window, as if I weren't even there. I was worried that I had offended her by the intemperance of my gaze. Disconcerted, I asked her if she wanted something. She shook her head, the wings of her long brown hair like thin curtains in a breeze, but remained silent, apparently staring at the slight movement of the trees outside the window. A big white bird – an egret? – swooped down from one of the branches and snapped up something small with its beak. I shifted my position on the bed uneasily, but could think of nothing else to say.

Eventually, after about two or three minutes, she spoke – so quietly that I had to strain to hear her.

'What do you think of Henry?'

'I'm not sure yet.'

'You must think something.'

'He's very different from my father.'

'He really isn't a faggot, you know. Far from it.'

'I get it.'

She looked at me directly for the first time.

'He's on a very strange journey. A long road. You know? Sometimes I think he's like . . . ' – she glanced down at my pile of comics – '. . . Superman. No, that's not it. Atticus Finch. You know Atticus Finch? I don't know. That sort of guy. And he is. He's really a trip. Like no one else. But inside. There's . . . I don't know. He wants to be something. But he isn't really it. Do you see what I mean?'

The question didn't seem to require an answer. She took a sip of her green tea.

'Have you ever tried it?' She held the tea out to me.

I shook my head.

'Go ahead. You should. It has remarkable properties. I have nine, ten cups a day. It cleans you out. Of course if you do it properly – Henry does this sometimes – you're meant to whisk it for ages. But I just sling the leaves in and pour on hot water. It's very lazy of me. Yeah. I hate the way I'm such a slob.'

She looked suddenly depressed. Then she propelled the tea an inch closer.

'Go on. I dare you.'

I took the cup. Our fingers momentarily touched, and I felt a thrill. Then her hand withdrew and I sipped the tea.

'It's horrible.'

Strawberry laughed – a tinkly, silvery jingle.

'It's good for you.'

'It tastes like medicine. Or wood bark. Bitter. Maybe you should put sugar in it.'

'Sugar is poison. It's like, I don't know – honestly, you should read about it. There was this piece in the *Village Voice*. You know the *Voice?*'

'I've heard of it.'

'Oh, it's like, the bible and all. Greenwich Village. You know, in New York? I lived there awhile. Not literally though. Not "the gospel". It just tells the truth, you know? Real stuff, *real* stuff. Not this bullshit government propaganda.'

She frowned fiercely as she pronounced the word 'bullshit', as if she was suddenly very angry.

'Anyway, the big sugar corporations, I mean from the eighteenth, or was it the nineteenth century? – shit, I can't remember – have peddled this to the people to make bucks. It's like a whole thing. Conspiracy. Same old, same old. Fucking everyone over. I feel sorry for them, actually. To be that greedy. All the same, they got the whole Western world hooked. Ask Pattern. He told me all about it. What was it built on? Slave labour. That's right. You know? Anyway, I just take honey sometimes. You know, from bees? That's OK. It's different.'

'Who's Patton?'

'Pattern, not Patton. Patton was a fucking general. Pattern's more like an annoying Boy Scout.'

I was having trouble following her, but I remembered a few facts from my science lessons.

'Actually, chemically, honey is more or less the same as sugar.'

'That's what they teach you in school, right?'

'Well, yes.'

'Yeah. And who pays the schoolteachers? The government, right? And who controls the government?'

I shook my head.

'Think about it.'

Strawberry stood up, smiled at me and held out her hand for my empty cup. 'How was the coffee?'

'OK. Not great.'

'Shit. You really are Henry's nephew, aren't you? You like your poison pure. Intense. Well, maybe that's why he's so fucked up. All those toxins.'

'Henry's fucked up?'

'Everyone's fucked up.'

She paused, and her face changed again, as if her internal self was resetting in the space of a moment. Having been playful, she looked sad again.

'You'll let me know if anything happens, won't you? I mean, if he stops being . . . all right.'

I nodded as if I understood her completely. She seemed to take my acknowledgement as confirmation that I had fully appreciated her concerns. Her sadness slipped away again, and she smiled gratefully.

'He's been good to me.'

'Has he?'

Now she leaned forward. What followed came out in a torrent.

'I was so strung out. Everything you could name. Coke, hash, DMT, acid. Not to mention sex. Can you believe it? That's pollution, right there. That's *right*. You know? He took me in. Came and got me out of the Valley. Once they got me back here – him and Troy, between them, they put me straight. Henry doesn't like Troy – of course he doesn't. Perhaps he's jealous, I guess. But Troy taught me where else to go after I'd left where I was. What I'm into now is such a positive place. I'm working on art. Not figurative, you know. It comes from the inside. It's like feeling on paper. Like giving form to thought. Like Pollock, you know? I'm teaching myself yoga. Yeah. Shows you how to breathe.'

'I already know how to breathe.'

She ignored me.

'I've started this macrobiotic diet. I found out about it in LA. I met the guy who devised it. Kenzaburo Suzuki? You know about macrobiotics? Amazing. Really. It's helping me. I got this book, *Macrobiotics and the Zen Way*. Grains and green tea. That was it for me. Some raw vegetables. Fruit, if it's properly grown and properly washed. Really clean. It has to be clean.'

'Who's Troy?'

'Yeah, right, he's this guy. Lives in Bristol. I hang at his place sometimes. That's why I haven't seen you before.'

'Where are you when you're not at Troy's?'

'I have a little place further down the reach. A few hundred yards away.'

'You *live* here?'

'On Henry's land. Like I say, he's very kind to me. You should come visit.'

'Sure. Nothing else to do.'

'Anyway. Thank you. No, really. Thank you, Adam. You're a beautiful person. I think you could really hear what I was saying. People speak but they don't hear. You're different. Open.'

She bent and kissed me on the cheek, close to the mouth. Her breath was acidic.

'I should be going home. Well, I call it home. It's . . . Henry calls it a shed, but I like to think of it as a cabin. You know he wanted me to move in here? On the boat? Yeah. You got my room. He's worried about me. I guess we worry about each other. But I need my freedom. "The refuge of the roads". You know? Or of the fields, or something. Well anyway . . .'

She seemed to have finally run out of words. She gave a little bow and left the room.

The fragrance of patchouli oil and cloves dissipated. I breathed in the air deeply, as if to retain a few particles of her within myself.

The other smell – the iron/old-penny trace – lingered. It was, it then occurred to me, the smell of blood.

Seven

Over the following days, I saw little of Henry. Strawberry did not reappear. I was continuing to feel bored and restless. My lack of interest in anything at all did not even feel like a weight. A weight would have been tangible, but this was simply an absence. All the same, I had begun listlessly to attend to my studies, out of a vague sense of commitment to some undisclosed future, and a terror of ending up with Ray in the shoe shop.

I once more made a lackadaisical attempt to unpick the causes and consequences of the First World War. Was it German aggression? Was it larger, global forces, pent up after sixty years of peace – some kind of collective blood lust?

Or did history turn on a sixpence – on a million million sixpences? Brute, uncontrollable forces, an infinitude of tiny human decisions and an unknowable amount of blind chance. Yet I was required to pretend that there existed these invisible abstractions labelled 'causes' that explained it all, that made the past happen as it happened, when it happened. It made no sense to me, but I put that down to the fact that I was too stupid to work it out.

I had hoped that Henry would have laid on some diversions for me, knowing that I was to be with him for the whole summer. But all he did was pound away on his Remington most of the day, sending tattoos of keyboard clacks skipping across the water. The *taptaptap, ching, taptaptap* irritated me, but I was powerless to do anything about it other than turn my music up to a level that would slightly muffle it. However, the sharpness of the taps always found their way through the prophylactic of the drum, bass, vocal and guitar with which I tried to insulate my room.

He offered me food intermittently – lentils, salads, bread as thick, rough and brown as a solution of sandpaper and flour, and something called falafel – all of which I refused. I existed on a diet of baked beans, frankfurters from a tin, and chocolate digestives. He disappeared most afternoons in the Karmann Ghia. There was a small town – Lexham – about five miles away. Henry always offered me a lift there, which I stubbornly refused, out of motivations that were obscure to me. I suppose I equated the acceptance of generosity with the imposition of a duty.

Henry owned a sturdy sit-up-and-beg pushbike that it was possible to navigate through the baked brown Somerset fields. One afternoon after I had been there a week, following Henry's departure to do some shopping, I set off on the bike to the town.

I took a grip on the ancient machine – it had the heft of a butcher's boy's delivery bike, old and heavy and without gears – and began pedalling across the fields towards the road

that would take me into Lexham. Lexham had a population –
according to the road sign that announced it – of 5031.

I felt physically good despite my sloth and the makeshift
nature of my processed-food diet. My tan had come along
well, and although I wasn't a particularly handsome boy, I
wasn't fat, or spotty. I was just unbearably average. After a
few minutes' cycling I took my T-shirt off – thin and red
with flared sleeves and a tie-dye design in the shape of a
circle across the chest – and pedalled furiously against the
restraining gravity of my body and the bike, so that a breeze
would make itself felt on my hair and skin. My cut-off jeans
stretched at the seams and incubated sweat. It momentarily occurred to me that this part of England was radiant
with beauty. There were tumbling expanses of deeply green
fields, punctuated with constellations of daisies and but-
tercups and grazed by flocks of sheep and herds of cows
whose only purpose seemed decorative. Under other circumstances, I hypothesized, I would have felt happy.

When I reached the town, after forty-five minutes of hard
pedalling, the sweat I had worked up left me parched. I leaned
the bike against a drystone wall and inspected my surroundings. Lexham was the very epitome of a small English
provincial town at that time – marinated in ancient monotony.
The houses – which I could not date, merely characterize as
'old' – were, for the most part, laid out in terraces. There
were several detached cottages with thatched roofs. On the
fringes were a few clumps of modern grey council houses, all
of them pebbledashed and stark.

At the centre there was a square, overlooked by a clock set
in a short tower. Clustered around the square was a collection of shops, among them a newsagent, a post office, a
supermarket, a greengrocer and a butcher. There were three

pubs visible. Those inhabitants that I saw — it was pretty deserted — were elderly, the women with Toni home perms and blue and pink rinses, the men in golf sweaters and polished shoes. They looked at me — inasmuch as they deigned to notice me at all — with either indifference or suspicion. I cast around for Henry's car but it was nowhere to be seen.

My vision was tinted by the amber Foster Grants I was wearing. They made everything seem washed with gold, or sepia. There was an old stone drinking-fountain underneath the clock tower. I pushed the worn brass button and a stream of cold water emerged from the spout. I splashed myself in the face, forgetting to take off my sunglasses and misting my lenses. I removed them, hoping that no one had noticed my gaucheness, wiped them with my T-shirt and replaced them. I drank from the spout — the water tasted of nothing. I took a cigarette out of a pack from the pocket of my jeans. They had been crushed and bent during the ride. I lit up and took a deep draught. The sensation of smoke in my mouth and lungs was noxious, but I persisted anyway, determined that this emblem of adulthood should be mastered, like my tenuous attempts to grow a moustache, which had yielded so far only a light furze, largely invisible without a magnifying mirror.

I took a stroll around the town centre. I still failed to spot anyone younger than about thirty, other than a few squabbling little kids with sticky faces who stared at me as if I was a freak. It only took me half an hour to explore the place entirely, finding nothing of interest.

I made my way to the newsagent. At ground level was a fly poster announcing SOMERSET FOREST FIRES — LATEST. Above the door were green panels advertising Woodbines. On the wall above, an enamel hoarding with the *News of the World* logo. The window held a pinboard stuck with dozens of ads — for char ladies, second-hand garden furniture, a bring-and-buy cake sale, a giant-vegetable competition.

Inside, the counter was attended by a cheerful old biddy with gap teeth, a red scarf tied round her head and a matching nose like a radish. I bought a fresh packet of cigarettes. On a rotating magazine rack they had a few copies of old Marvel comics and I discovered an issue of *Dr Strange* I hadn't read. I handed over the money for it. I still had my shirt off, but the old lady seemed oblivious to my outlaw status. She greeted me warmly, asked me if the weather was hot enough for me, and handed me my change. I mumbled a thank you and, adopting my best swagger, made my way out of the shop.

It was mid-afternoon. There was an off-licence selling locally made cider, and I bought a bottle. I doubted that the slightly drunken man with a checked flat cap and a bottle of pale ale in his hand sitting on the other side of the counter believed I was eighteen, but he was clearly happy to take any money he could get. Then I sat on one of two green wooden benches on either side of the water fountain under the clock. I finished the cider off, smoked another cigarette and lay down on the struts. My head began to swim with the heat and the effects of the cider, which was almost viscous, very strong, and actually smelled of apples, unlike the mass-produced equivalent I bought in London.

I fell asleep. Almost immediately — or so it seemed — I was woken by the sound of giggling. Opening my eyes enough to let in a crescent of light, I saw that there were two girls about my age sitting on the bench opposite, glancing at me then looking away and at one another, then glancing at me again.

One was attractive, the other plain. They were dressed similarly — both in bib-and-brace overalls, although one was blue denim and one was white cotton. Overalls had, the previous year, made the transition from the garage forecourt to the arena of street fashion. The length of their hair was identical, down to their shoulders, and they wore short-sleeved T-shirts under the overalls. The attractive one wore the blue outfit, with black plimsolls, the plainer one what looked like school shoes, black, buckled and with a low heel.

It was the plain one in white who noticed that I had peered out between my lids, and whispered something to her friend. I sat up and yawned. The attractive one wasn't intimidatingly beautiful like Strawberry – her nose was snubby, slightly upended at the tip, almost porcine, and her brown hair was frizzed at the end. Whether it was styled that way or a product of split ends, I wasn't sure. Her mouth was generous, at all four points of the compass, and her eyes, which held a glint of salacity, contained a promise that somehow you felt she would honour, under the right circumstances. The plain one wasn't objectively that much plainer, although she was perhaps fifteen pounds heavier and ungainly. But there was a certain limp quality about her, an air of apology mixed with pique, that drained her – to my eyes at least – of any appeal. She took a pack of menthol cigarettes out of her pocket and lit one. She came over to where I was sitting and offered me the pack. She smelled of fairgrounds – candy floss, sawdust and cheap hamburgers. I shook my head. She shrugged and resumed her seat on the bench.

I was about to get up and walk somewhere – anywhere – when the plain one, having taken a single puff on her cigarette, spoke. I noticed that she was also chewing a wad of gum which was visible, pink, when she opened her mouth.

'Are you a hippy? Is that it, then? One of those hairies, is it?'

Her voice was distinctively West Country rural, with twangs and boings quite unlike the suffocated impersonation of received pronunciation that we spoke in Yiewsley. It had a soft enough timbre, but with a whine and a taunt buried in it that set my teeth on edge.

'No,' I replied.

Now the attractive one spoke. Her voice was different from her friend's – more or less classless, but well modulated, with the regional accent schooled out.

'There have been sightings,' she said.

'Of freaks,' said the other one, meaningfully. 'And weirdos.'

'Makes the locals nervous.'

'All the cauliflowers are up in arms. Worried about drug pushers. You're not a drug pusher, are you?'

'"Cauliflowers"?' I said.

'The white hair,' said the well-spoken one. 'That's what we call the oldies. Cauliflowers.'

'There's a hippy that lives on a boat near here,' said the plain one. 'An old bloke. Old for a hippy, anyway. Yellow teeth.'

'He's my uncle,' I replied, tucking my stomach in slightly. It was bulging over my too-tight cut-offs.

This announcement brought forth coos of amazement.

'You been to his boat?' the plain one said.

'I'm living on it. For the summer. I'm down from London.'

'Like for a holiday?' said the other one.

'It doesn't much feel like one.'

'Are you bored?' said Blue Boiler Suit.

I nodded, and looked for my Foster Grants. I realized that I had been sleeping on them. I put them on, sensing immediately that they were slightly out of true.

'Here, they're all wonky,' said Blue Boiler Suit. She took a step forward and adjusted them so they sat more evenly. It felt intimate, but I wasn't quite sure how to escape, or even if I wanted to. She smelled of Imperial Leather soap.

'They don't like it round here,' said Blue Boiler Suit. 'The boat. They think it's an eyesore. Also they say it attracts wrong sorts. They've got a petition up to get rid of it. I wouldn't make yourself too comfortable. Council want him out.'

'You seem to know a lot about it.'

'My dad's on the council. Why are you here anyway?'

'My mother died.'

This remark surprised me as much as it did them. I hadn't talked about my mother to anyone. I immediately regretted it. The pretty one looked at the plain one in bewilderment.

'I'm sorry,' she said.

I shrugged as if it didn't matter. 'My dad thought it would be good for me to get away for a while.'

Blue Boiler Suit nodded. White Boiler Suit picked her nose. It appeared she had already lost interest. She spotted someone across the street and waved. Blue Boiler Suit, however, took a step closer to me.

'Actually, that's not quite true,' I heard myself saying. 'He couldn't cope with me. I stole a car, see. Ran it into a wall. Got arrested. It was pretty bad. Yeah.'

Blue Boiler Suit regarded me steadily. It was as if she had aged years in a moment, or changed emotional gear somehow. Instead of being a silly adolescent, she seemed suddenly adult, and genuinely concerned. Meanwhile, White Boiler Suit had started to drift off in the direction of the person she had spotted, leaving the two of us alone.

'Arrested?' said the remaining girl.

'It's all right,' I muttered. 'They let me off. Said I was grieving or some such rubbish.'

'Well, weren't you?'

'I don't know,' I said. I had presumed until that moment that it was just a convenient excuse. Now it occurred to me that of course I *had* been grieving, and that it actually did somewhat explain my behaviour, even mitigate it to a degree. The thought came as a relief, although the relief was from the chill of a light shadow that stood at the edges of a much deeper, darker umbra.

'My name's Ash,' said the girl, toying with the buckles on the straps that kept the front panel of her suit attached to the back.

'Adam Templeton.'

'OK. Well, Adam Templeton, I might see you around. It's a pretty small world around here. Lilliput.'

'Sure.'

She turned and followed her friend in the direction of the post office, pausing once to glance back and give me a small wave, which I half-heartedly returned, before she rejoined her friend and a third girl roughly the same age.

It was yet another scrap of narrative without meaning or consequence. Since my mother had died, I had mentally categorized all events in this fashion – disconnected, purposeless, isolated and leading to nothing in particular.

I bought another bottle of cider from the man in the flat cap, who seemed to have sobered up slightly, because this time he asked my age. However, he accepted my lie without demur and handed over the bottle. I briskly necked the contents and fell asleep again. When I woke, I had a headache. The town centre was deserted and the sun was setting. There were no lights on the bike. I started to worry that I would run out of daylight. Shakily — the cider had made me feel drowsy and somewhat nauseous — I took a last swig of water from the fountain, mounted the bike and headed back towards the boat.

I cycled as hard as I could, but by the time I got to the track through the trees, the light had gone. From what little there was, I could see cracks in the dry ground, like veins and roots pushing out, like scattered bones. I started to make my way towards the mooring as a complete darkness descended with a discomfiting rapidity. I began to feel slightly anxious, although rationally I was in no danger. I could just about feel the relative smoothness of the dirt track under the wheels, but there was little else to guide me. There were no stars, no moon.

I was not used to such blackness and was beginning to panic. Apart from the not very realistic possibility that I would get lost, my imagination started to play up. What kind of animals were there in these woods? What kind of people? The darkness made me feel naked, and vulnerable.

I dismounted the bike — the going was getting too heavy, and I was scared of colliding with something I couldn't see. I dropped it and started to run — at a jog at first, then faster. I could hear creaking noises — presumably branches in the wind. Animals moved in the undergrowth. In the distance I heard a cry like a baby being throttled. I imagined it was a mating fox, but still, it was an uncanny sound.

I felt something strike me in the face, and I fell back, clutching at my cheeks. It was clear from the sticky wetness there that I had been cut. Even as it dawned on me that I had simply walked into a sharp branch, I felt a nausea of terror rise up in me. I could hear the screeching of a bird that I

didn't recognize, and sudden movements in the under-
growth. Almost crying now, I started walking again in what
I hoped was the right direction. But I was lost, somehow, lost
and blind in the dark. The howling of the fox continued, and
I could feel my hand wet with blood. I had no idea how badly
I might have cut myself.

I hit what appeared to be a hedge of some sort, which
proved to be impenetrable. I turned and started back the way
I'd come, where I thought I had left the bike, but I couldn't
see it.

I saw a light coming towards me. Instead of reassuring me,
it frightened me further. Why was there a light in the middle
of this darkness? Who or what was behind it? The fox wailed
again. I pressed myself against a tree, as if it might make me
safer from whatever was out there.

I could hear footfall across dry leaves now. I felt like running, but I had no idea where to run. I held my breath. Then
I heard a voice.

'Adam?'

I jumped from behind the tree into the beam of a torch.
It was Henry.

I was panting, my chest heaving with relief, mixed almost
immediately with shame. I had been scared – of nothing, I
now realized.

'The dark in the countryside takes a little getting used to.
I should have given you a flashlight,' Henry said mildly. 'The
boat's over here. Only a few hundred yards.'

There was no hint of mockery in his voice. He just seemed
pleased to see me. I followed him silently back to the boat.
It was, sure enough, no more than a two-minute walk, albeit
through the blackness of the wood. The *Ho Koji* glowed wel-
comingly in the darkness. As I got closer, I could smell the

scent of cooking – herbs and meat and wine. I was immensely grateful that he wasn't making a fuss.

When we entered, Henry turned to me. His stance was open, as if he expected me to hug him. I almost did, but somehow Ray's words came back to me and acted as a brake. *Why are you always grabbing people, Henry?* Instead, I slumped on to the bench under the porthole. Henry just smiled again, and asked me if I wanted some food. I nodded. He served me up something I had never tasted before, which turned out to be boeuf bourgignon.

I stared at it, but this time without resentment. Then I picked up the spoon he had given me and wolfed it down hungrily, consuming it in great gulps. It tasted very good. Henry poured me a glass of red wine and I drank that too, with gusto, despite the remnants of my hangover.

We sat in silence through the meal together, but it was a silence that, for the first time, contained an element of truce. Henry did nothing to force the point – neither stretching for conversation nor remarking on my uncharacteristic acceptance of his meal. After a while, he simply rose and bade me goodnight. A few minutes later, I could hear the sound of his typewriter keys once more, but this time, instead of irritating me, I found it comforting, like the introduction of punctuation into a sprawling, formless sentence.

Eight

The next day, I awoke late even by my standards – around 11 a.m. Henry's office door was open, so I glanced in. He was sitting as usual at the table, punching the keys on his Remington, wearing only a pair of underpants. *Clack, clack, ching.* He stopped typing and started fussing with the ribbon, cursing mildly in an American vernacular – 'Goshdarnit goddam helluva pieceashit.' Sensing me at the door, he stopped, looked up, gave me a friendly nod and, having apparently fixed the problem, resumed typing. It was clear he was focused on what he was doing and wanted no interruption.

I made myself a cup of coffee – Henry-style, thick and black with drumlins of sugar – and returned to my room. I resentfully eyeballed the pile of school textbooks, scribbled-in notepads and dummy exam papers that reproached me from the plastic bag in the corner.

It was too overcast to sunbathe. I didn't feel like going into town again. I had hardly lifted a finger to work on my retake since I had arrived at the boat, supposing that I would eventually find myself 'in the mood'. But I began to realize that such a mood was unlikely to manifest itself without my lowering the barricades of determined indolence. I picked up the textbook that happened to be sticking out of the top of the bag, opened it and began to read. Negotiating each sentence was like ascending a steep hill with a heavy backpack and a painful stitch in the abdomen.

The causes of the Great War were listed and annotated with numbers in a summary section at the end of the book. I decided to make a start by trying to memorize the list. I picked up a biro, took out a blank notebook and began copying them, in the hope that it might give me some material to regurgitate when I reached the examination room.

Britain and Germany were involved in a naval competition. The scramble for Africa. The system of alliances. The ideology of nationalism among the great powers. Instability in the Balkans caused by the collapse of the Ottoman Empire and the liberation movements of smaller proto-nations. The assassination of Archduke Franz Ferdinand. This latter, I dutifully read, was the spark that brought on the whole conflagration.

Henry appeared at my open door, a cigarette burned down to the filter in his hand. He was now dressed in what appeared to be a Japanese kimono. The sleeves could easily have held half-a-dozen arms.

'Studying?'

'Trying.'

'What's the topic?'

'First World War.'

'"Lions led by donkeys." All that jazz.'

I put the book down, yawning. Henry squatted beside me, picked the book up and began flicking casually through it.

'What do you make of it?' he asked.

'What does anyone make of it? It happened. There's a list of why it happened. Now I have to learn it.'

'Why do think you have to learn it?' said Henry. 'Other than to pass the exam.'

'Is there another reason?'

'Presumably.'

I paused for a moment, and took a sip of my coffee. It had cooled and now tasted vaguely medicinal.

'So that it never happens again,' I said.

'That's the theory. That's the point of history. So they say.'

'I suppose so.'

'Do you believe that?'

'I suppose.'

Henry nodded, put down the book. Then he seemed to dismiss the subject.

'I'm going into town in half an hour or so. Want a lift? We could get a cake at the tea shop. You might see your new friend.'

'Which new friend is that?'

'Ashley.'

'Who's Ashley?'

'Ashley Toshack. Known around these parts as Ash.'

I tried and failed to look unsurprised.

'I'm afraid this is a small place. I know her father rather well. The Very Reverend Wesley Toshack. Vicar of this parish. Also a property developer, councillor and all-round pillar of the community. Upstanding man. Or so it's said. We have some lively discussions. I bumped into him in Lexham yesterday, right before I set off home. He mentioned that his daughter had met my nephew. I have no idea why he felt it was sufficiently interesting to warrant a mention, but doubtless there was some deeper motive behind it.'

'Perhaps it's because the council want you off the boat.'

Now it was Henry's turn to be taken aback.

'You know about that?'

'I'm afraid this is a small place.'

'*Touché*.'

'Are they going to throw you off?'

'They've started a petition. But I've heard nothing from the council. And actually, the main threat is not from the council but the church commissioners. They own the land, as a matter of fact. The council are in cahoots. They're biding their time. Anyway, I'm resourceful, I know my way around the law. Trouble is, all this wrangling is keeping me away from my book. It's so time-consuming.'

'What would happen if they succeeded in getting you out?'

Henry looked surprised, as if he had never considered this possibility.

'They won't. They have no grounds. Typically enough, they're brandishing the cudgel of morality. Toshack and his brigade of "concerned local citizens" have spent a lot of time combing through the small print of my lease, and discovered somewhere on page gazillion, subsection nine hundred and ninety-one, clause F, paragraph four – or something like that – that it demands I behave in a "lawful and upright manner" and "conduct myself at all times with due decorum and appropriate responsibility".

'Just because I've had a few parties down here – which the locals naturally assume quickly develop into drug-addled orgies – they think they can sling me out. But they have no evidence whatsoever. The police have raided on more than one occasion – again, no doubt thanks to Toshack – but have found nothing other than a few empty cases of, admittedly poor-quality, wine.'

'Is Ash on her dad's side? She didn't seem like much of a puritan to me.'

'Ashley is bored. Everyone's bored around here. Most of them have forgotten how bored they are, though.'

'So I'm not alone.'

'Oh no. You are very much participating in the local zeitgeist, so to speak. But be careful. You'd be surprised what they do in order to ease the weight of all that piled-up tedium. Particularly the young ones.'

'Is that some kind of warning?'

'I don't know much about Ash. She probably not so bad really. Some of the boys around here call her "Ash the Pash". She's quite widely fancied.'

'She's pretty.'

'More than that. A red-hot chilli pepper. But don't get any ideas. She's a Bible basher. Just likes to play it down. Very keen on her father. Quite the daddy's girl. Mother died six, seven years ago. They're close. And Wesley is not my biggest fan, so Ashley probably lines up on his side.'

'Why? What did you do? Apart from live on a houseboat.'

'The worst thing a man can do to another man around here.'

'What's that?'

'Made him feel foolish. And, as I said, he doesn't like some of the company I attract. I think that was the real reason he buttonholed me. To truffle-hunt for information. I'm having a bit of an, um, *event* down here in a couple of weeks, and he's hoping we're all going to be dancing naked around the campfire and handing out peyote to minors. Chance would be a fine thing! He'd love that, because it would give him further grounds for litigation. But I know the rules, and I'll stick by them.'

'What if they did get enough evidence to throw you off?'

Henry stared out of the window. His eyes took on a faraway look.

'I would have nothing, I suppose. This is the only home I have. I can't just sail it away and moor it somewhere else. Moorings are hard to find, and expensive. Plus I'm sure this old bucket would sink if you tried to take it anywhere.'

'My father always told me you had plenty of money.'

'Raymond thinks I'm Daddy Warbucks. That's because I have a few old friends in the banking business, and I can raise loans easily enough. Have done in the past, and always made them pay. So my credit is good. But in terms of real cash, I've got next to nothing. I can live here because there are no expenses. I mean, the insurance is fierce – because the *Ho Koji* is made of wood they say it's a fire risk, which I suppose is fair enough – but other than that, since I own the lease on the land, there is nothing to pay apart from the peppercorn ground rent. I live on my wits and what practical skills I have. Also Strawberry sometimes gives me a few coins for letting her sleep in the cabin.'

'I've not seen anything of her recently.'

'She's been staying in Bristol with Troy for a while, but she'll be back. Sometimes she earns a little money – busking or waitressing. She always tries to give something to me. Which I accept largely so that she doesn't feel indebted to me. But it's all hand to mouth.'

'How about the Karmann?'

'A gift from a friend. Well, not so much a gift. The man owed me money and he didn't have any, so he gave me the car. Which was worth about a quarter of his debt. Still, it was better than nothing. Talking of Strawberry – I understand she dropped in to see you the other day.'

'Yes.'

'Something of a compliment. She's usually slow to "reach out" – as they like to say in California. What did you make of her?'

'She's too thin.'

'Anything else?'

'She smelled of blood.'

'Probably that time of month. She doesn't believe in tampons or sanitary towels. Uses moss or leaves or something. Anything that comes to hand. Tree bark, I shouldn't wonder. Unsanitary towels, I call them. She just bleeds. Lets it return to the earth. Claims that menstrual blood is good for the soil.'

I felt discomfited by this revelation. I had very little knowledge of female anatomy or biological processes. My mother and father had never talked about it, and such matters were not mentioned at school or addressed on television.

'Anything else?'

'She looks like she'd break easily.'

'Now there you're entirely wrong. Strawberry is very, very strong. She has the most remarkable will-power. Nothing will divert her from her path once she's set on it. I admire her greatly, although I certainly don't agree with all her choices. But then, mistakes are a kind of fertilizer for good decisions, which will come as the seasons change. The thing is to keep moving forward. The Zen masters say, "Go left or go right, but don't dither."'

He checked his watch.

'On the subject of dithering, I need to be going, and I still have to get changed. Are you coming?'

'I'm meant to be studying.'

'Who was it said, "History is bunk"?'

'Henry Ford.'

'There you are. From the great man's mouth. Your lift leaves in five minutes, if you want it.'

This time, I wasn't difficult to convince. I pulled on my baseball boots. When Henry reappeared he was wearing white linen pyjamas – 'everyday wear in Rishikesh'. I followed him out on to the deck and over to the Karmann Ghia. When we reached it, I felt Henry's hand resting on my shoulder.

'Can you drive?'

'No. Well – I can. I just don't have a licence. I've driven my dad's Anglia round the local gasworks, though. And I stole a car once after my mum died and crashed it.'

I hoped Henry would be intrigued by this and eager to hear the story of my escapades, but he remained impassive. It occurred to me that Ray had probably told him all about my exploits anyway.

'Why don't you give the Ghia a spin?'

'You're kidding.'

'Not at all.'

'It's illegal.'

'That didn't stop you before, apparently. Anyway, it's not illegal in my field. I own the lease on everything from here to the fence.' He gestured towards the enclosed perimeter, maybe half a mile away. 'Beyond that, guess who the land belongs to?

'The government? The Church?'

'You're close. Wesley Toshack. God knows how many acres he's bought up around here. I'm like a little sore, a pimple on the chin of his empire. He doesn't like it. Cut off his access to the river, where all the most valuable land is.'

'Valuable for what?'

'House-building. This stretch I hold the lease on is one of the few patches of soil on the river suitable for construction. For some weird topographic reason, this part of the river seems immune from floods. He could make a fortune if he could get hold of the land. And there would be nothing to stop him if the lease was rendered invalid. He's tried to buy me up several times. That's why he never quite gets round to threatening me. Because he thinks he can schmooze me. But I won't sell. It's my home. Also there's the matter of Strawberry.'

'What's Strawberry got to do with it?'

'As I said, she lives here. She has nowhere else to go. And I've kind of adopted her. She visits Troy, but that's on his good will. See that patch of trees? Standing a little higher than the rest?' He pointed to a line of beech trees around a quarter of a mile from the mooring. 'Behind that is her little shack. No running water or electricity. Really just a shed. But it's dry, and livable in the summer. There's a bed in there, and a primus stove for cooking and heating water. Strawberry's been ensconced there since the spring – that's when she came over from America. I keep asking her to come and stay on the boat. It's very isolated out there. But as I said, she's stubborn. She wants to get back to nature, she says. If my boat isn't back to nature, I don't know what is. Not close enough for her, though. She cultivates a vegetable garden, although all it's produced so far is a couple of potatoes, a carrot and a handful of radishes. So much for the properties of menstrual blood on the soil.

'She sits in there and reads or meditates. Plays pat-a-cake with the ducks or fondles the trees. I've heard her talk to the flowers. God knows what she was saying. Really. Good kid, though. Smart in her way. But she's a fruitcake. Guess it comes from growing up in California. The fruitcake state.'

I was only half listening, so enthralled was I by the prospect of driving the car. I climbed into the driving seat. I understood that manipulating the clutch was the hardest part, so I felt with my feet for it. But there were only two pedals.

'It's an automatic,' said Henry. 'Just an accelerator and a brake.'

I pressed my foot gently on the accelerator. The car lurched forward. Henry laughed as we both flew backwards. I tried again, more gently. This time, the car inched ahead.

I moved the wheel to the left slightly, and the car began to move towards the field gate. I pressed the accelerator again. We started to move at about five miles an hour. Without asking for any permission from Henry, I began to accelerate. He said nothing. All he did was reach up and crank a handle above our head. The sun roof creaked open. Air and light poured through the gap.

I stopped in front of the gate. Henry got out. I expected him to take over, but he simply opened the gate so that I could manoeuvre the car on to the empty track. Henry shut the gate behind him and climbed back into the passenger seat. We were off his land. I glanced at him, still presuming he was going to take over. But he said nothing, just looked straight ahead.

Surprised by both my recklessness and Uncle Henry's indifference, I pushed the accelerator a little harder. Now we were moving along at twenty miles per hour. Henry began to hum a tune to himself. I recognized it as an old song, Donovan's 'Sunshine Superman'.

It was several minutes before we saw another car. I had reached the road proper and needed to give way. A blue Ford

Escort drove cautiously across our path. I raised a hand in acknowledgement, enjoying the gesture for its premonition of the privileges of adulthood.

The country road stretched away in front of us. A warm rush of wind splayed my hair in front of my eyes, and I found enough confidence to brush it away, leaving me momentarily one-handed on the wheel. Henry remained unconcerned. He seemed to believe absolutely that I was able to drive, and his belief somehow made it possible.

He reached over and put a cassette on the 8-track. It was something from the early sixties – 'Surfin' Bird' by The Trashmen.

I did something I hadn't done for years. I let out a whoop. Henry began to join in the chorus.

'*Papa ooma mow mow, papa ooma mow mow . . .*'

I couldn't help but join in. Together we made a ragged harmony.

I saw a pigeon in the road in front of us. It stared at us insolently. As we closed in, it didn't move. It was too late to brake. I was certain I was going to hit it. Panicked, I swung and crashed into a small, shallow ditch at the side of the road.

Henry and I rocked forward and back again with the impact. Neither of us was wearing a seatbelt, but the ditch I had deposited the Karmann Ghia in was soft and grassy, cushioning the impact. 'Surfin' Bird' continued jauntily, if unsteadily. Henry remained silent. The motor had cut. I waited for the inevitable explosion of anger.

'Sorry,' I muttered. 'The pigeon. I didn't see it in time.'

I had heard glass smashing as we made impact; and some

other sound, harsh, grating, had seemed to suggest that metal had been bent and paint had been scraped.

Henry still didn't say anything. Instead, he indicated for me to move over. I climbed awkwardly out of the car – the door was obstructed by the wall of the ditch – and he took my place. He started the motor. It seemed to be running smoothly. He put the gearbox into reverse and eased the car back on to the soft shoulder of the road. From where I stood, I could see that a headlight had been shattered and bent out of shape, and the chrome bumper was contorted into almost a right-angle at the end where it had struck the verge.

Henry, leaving the car idling, moved back into the passenger seat. Then he nodded to me to resume my place behind the steering wheel.

I got back into the driving seat and looked once at Henry, who nodded. Amazed at his insouciance, I started the car moving again. A new track had begun, 'Louie Louie' by The Kingsmen. The sun and wind once more in my face, I could see Lexham approaching in the distance.

'Nice of you to be so concerned about the pigeon,' said Henry. It was the first time he had spoken since the car had veered off the road. It sounded not, as I expected, that he was controlling his temper, but that he was utterly unconcerned by the damage I had done to his beautiful car.

'Aren't you angry?' I turned towards him briefly.

'Keep your eyes on the road.'

'But . . .'

'I have no right to be angry. It's my responsibility, not yours. Why should you know how to drive? You didn't ask me, I asked you.'

'But I messed your car up.'

'That's the past. Nothing I can do about it now.'

I considered this. What he said made a lot of sense. But it was hard to imagine my father, for instance, taking a similarly philosophical point of view had I pranged his Anglia.

'So you find it pretty boring down here,' said Henry.

'Sometimes,' I admitted.

'If you're sufficiently bored, I've got a thing on Saturday. In Bristol. You might want to come.'

'What sort of "thing"?'

'It's called the Mind, Heart, Body and Spirit Fayre. They've held it for the last five years. I usually put in an appearance. Mostly rubbish and nutcases, but there's space for some serious stuff. I like to think of myself in that category. I'll have a stall. It's relatively painless. You could help. I'd pay you.'

'What would I have to do?'

'Nothing much. Keep me company. Hold the stall while I go for a cup of coffee. Help me load and unload. You might meet some interesting people. Don't worry if you don't want to do it. I can manage by myself.'

I felt the weight of duty on me, a weight I had experienced every day at Buthelezi House. I said nothing.

'Strawberry will probably show up. She likes you. She told me so. She does a bit of singing. Picks up a few coins. And she reads palms. Badly, so far as I can ascertain. But it's all simple fun.'

Still I said nothing.

'I don't want you to do it for me. Honestly. I don't care. But I was rather hoping Strawberry and you might find something in common. I think she's lonely, though she would never admit it.'

'She only lives a few hundred yards away.'

'She's proud. Likes to believe she's self-sufficient. Nobody's

95

self-sufficient, though, are they? Anyway, it's no big deal. Forget about it.'

He seemed genuinely unconcerned and I could tell he wouldn't hold it against me if I decided not to come.

'Can I think about it?'

'Certainly. You might even find it interesting. Sometimes I think you are capable of finding things interesting. Other than yourself, that is.'

The sting of the implied criticism must have shown in my face, because Henry held his hand up, palm towards me.

'I don't mean to put you down. I still find myself the most fascinating thing in the world. There's nothing wrong with self-absorption. It's the only first-hand experience we have of what people are like. But I like to make room for other matters too. Only because it pleases me, you understand. Not out of politeness, or duty.'

Nine

We were reaching the outskirts of Lexham and a few cars were spotting the roads. The crash had left me nervous and uncertain, but Henry's confident, untroubled face reassured me. I knew there was a free car park 200 yards along on the left – it was just beyond the bench I'd stopped to sleep on the last time I visited. Closing down the final stretch, I pulled into the car park, stopped the car and turned off the engine. The exhaust gave a cough, then a bang, then expired. Henry reached up and began to turn the handle to close the roof.

'I'll pay for the damage,' I said suddenly, not knowing how or where I would get the money, whether my father's cash would cover it.

Henry shrugged. 'It's not necessary.'

He pulled himself out of the car, carrying a plain hemp shopping bag. He strolled round to my side and opened the door for me. I got out and handed him the keys. Without bothering to lock the car, he started walking towards the newsagent that I had shopped in before.

My shoelaces were undone. As I bent down to retie them, my face close to the lace holes, the smell of canvas in my nostrils, a thought struck me.

'I wonder if should call my father?'

'That's a good idea, Adam. I'm sure Raymond would appreciate it.'

Henry gestured towards a phone box directly across the road.

I made my way to the box, then realized I had no change. I managed to catch Henry's eye. I rubbed my fingers and thumb together to indicate the need for cash. He crossed the road to join me. He took out a few coins from his pocket and handed them to me.

I shut myself in while Henry waited outside. I dialled the number of the shoe shop.

The phone rang three times, and then I heard my father's voice at the other end. It was his shop voice – slightly more pinched than his home voice, and perhaps a shade up the social scale.

'Dolcis, Yiewsley.'

'Hello, Dad. It's Adam.'

'Who?'

'It's your son. The apple of your eye.'

'Adam?'

'Yes. Adam.'

'Oh. Right. Just a minute . . .'

He shouted something to someone in the shop. There was a few seconds' pause, then he spoke again into the receiver.

'Adam.'

'How are you, Dad?'

'I'm very glad you've called. Only . . . only I'm very busy. The shop is busy.'

I could hear no noise at all in the background, and yet the phone, I knew, was located right on the shop counter.

'I just wanted to know . . . to see . . . that you were . . .'

I ran out of words.

'Adam. I can't . . . This line is bad. Are you . . .'

The line at my end was perfectly clear.

'It's OK, Dad. It's OK if you're busy. I'll call again later.'

'Look. Are you all right? Is everything OK? Do you need anything?'

I felt something give way inside myself. Without saying goodbye, I put the receiver back on the cradle. I stood there staring at it until I felt the door of the box open and Henry's hand fall on my shoulder.

'It's all right,' said Henry.

He put his other hand on my other shoulder. I twisted out of his grasp and turned to face him.

'Get off! I'm not a kid!'

I turned back to the telephone, hoping Henry would leave me alone. I wiped my cheek with the back of my sleeve. When I turned again, Henry was still there.

'There's no need to explain.'

I followed him, grateful now, a step behind. I was a little embarrassed by his outfit, but no one took any notice. Plainly the locals were used to Henry's eccentricities. So I took up position next to him and we walked, our strides matching, until we reached the store.

Henry bought some paper, five pens, some files, paper cups, a typewriter ribbon and carbon paper. Then we went to the greengrocer. Celery, carrots, lettuce, apples, a pomegranate.

'The pomegranate is very important. At least Strawberry thinks so. Protects against some *juju* or other. I ordered it from the owner specially,' said Henry.

Tomatoes, lemons and cucumbers went into a second, plastic shopping bag. I didn't offer to carry it, but Henry held it out to me anyway. I took it reluctantly. An only child, I had been spoiled by Evie and was unused to making any effort when an adult was around to do the work for me.

'That's a lot' I said, feeling the weight of the bag.

'Strawberry gets through this stuff at an alarming rate. She eats it, drinks it, purées it, juices it, crushes it. She probably sleeps with it.'

I risked a joke. 'No strawberries?'

'She hates them. Says the seeds are like fruit acne.'

'Is the rest of this stuff for her?

'Most of it. Although she is somewhat suspicious of the sugar in fruit.'

Next we visited a grocery and bought baked beans, cornflakes, ham, tinned peaches, a loaf of brown bread, butter, sugar, tea and a bottle of R. White's cream soda for me.

'I only buy staples here,' said Henry. 'Most of the fresh food is of such dismal quality. The British have no respect whatsoever for what they put in their mouths and bodies. Much the same as the Americans. Of course, Strawberry's taken it too far, but there's some sense in her stance. Processed this, frozen that, canned the other. There's a delicatessen in Bristol, and a good butcher, which we can do much better at, and it's reasonably priced as such places go.'

His voice was louder than most of the voices around us. It seemed that he was untroubled by self-consciousness. Two women – who comprised the rest of the queue – exchanged glances, partly amused, faintly hostile.

We left the shop, passing the church, St Jude's, and a 'public notices' board. I glanced at the cards and posters pinned there. One stood out from the rest.

VIBRATIONS, POLARITIES
AND THE SECRET UNITY OF OPPOSITES

Eastern Wisdom in Everyday Life
Dr Henry Templeton DPhil (Cantab) talks
on the mysteries of Chinese, Japanese and Indian
thought and how they can teach us about
understanding and acceptance

Come one, come all.
Leave your prejudices at the door

Doors open 7 p.m. at the *Ho Koji*,
Eastern Reach, Lexham
Voluntary contribution of £1
Drinks and refreshments will be served

Then there was a map, showing the way to the boat and the date. It was happening the Saturday after next.

'This is the thing you mentioned, the event?'

'It is the thing, yes. I'm surprised the poster is still up there. Usually some local yokel tears it down.'

'Looks OK.' Though in fact I thought it looked pretty boring. Marketing clearly wasn't Henry's strong point.

'Thank you.'

'Are you looking forward to it?'

'I don't really look forward to things,' he said. 'It's as foolish an emotion as regret.'

'You can't help how you feel.'

'Oh, you can. Absolutely.'

Henry found a bench, sat on it, took out a Lucky and offered me one. I accepted it and sat next to him. I opened the cream soda, which frothed violently out of the bottle.

As I raised it to drink, a torrent of bubbles still erupting out of the neck and running down my chin, I felt the touch of a hand on my back. I didn't react but continued drinking. This was a lesson I was trying to learn from Henry. Act as if nothing has happened. That was how you got to be cool. I harboured this ambition more than anything else, but it had always seemed a remote possibility. People from Yiewsley simply weren't.

'Hello, Ashley,' said Henry, without looking round. 'How's Jesus's little sunbeam?'

I felt her hand lift. She moved from behind us and into view. She had had her hair cut. It now sprang in a tight curly bob, stopping short of her neck. The split ends had gone. Her hair was auburn, rather than the simple brown I had earlier registered, with tones of red. The new cut suited her, making all her features, which were generous in the first place, seem lusher, larger, more inviting. Her eyelids were painted with pale blue eyeshadow. She smiled, showing a gap in her teeth. I remembered that when I studied Chaucer's Wife of Bath for A level, this was meant to suggest a propensity for lewdness.

'No wonder people have difficulty with you, Henry,' said Ash.

'I was only making a polite enquiry.'

'My father's the vicar, not me.'

'I would have thought you and the reverend were pretty closely aligned.'

'We have very different beliefs about the way things go, actually.'

Without asking permission, Ash sat down between us. I could feel the slightest touch of her thigh against mine.

'Lovely day,' she said. 'Again. I'm getting tired of lovely days. Sometimes I just want a good thunderstorm. Or some snow.'

'That's quite a remote meteorological possibility,' replied Henry. 'Last time I looked the thermometer was pushing ninety.'

I got the impression he wanted to get away from Ash, that he found her presence oppressive. I, on the other hand, was impressed by her self-confidence and her readiness to verbally tangle with Henry.

'How's your nephew?'

She didn't look at me as she said this.

'He just smashed up my car,' said Henry. 'The little tyke.'

'You *didn't*.'

Ash turned to me now. Her eyes had widened slightly. They were no colour I had ever seen before, some colour without a name. Sea green, blue, brown and purple all mixed together. Like some sort of imaginary coral.

I nodded and stared at the ground. I couldn't think of a thing to say. It occurred to me how much women frightened me. The intimation of sex imbued them with a near supernatural power.

'It was my fault,' said Henry. 'He can't drive. I talked him into it.'

'I can't believe you could be that irresponsible, Henry,' said Ash, apparently seriously. 'Someone could have been killed. Actually, come to think of it, I *can* believe you might be that reckless. It's all "anything goes" with you.'

'Better that than "nothing is allowed". Except what the Good Book tells them. Anyway, it could have been me who was killed. That would have suited a lot of people, I suppose.'

'What are you getting at?' said Ash.

'How are things at the church?' said Henry.

'Why don't you come down and find out? My father was asking about you the other day. He thinks you're an interesting case.'

'Wesley claims to think everyone is an interesting case. He's just extraordinarily interested in people, isn't he? What they get up to. What they should and shouldn't be doing.'

'He says he'd like to talk to you again.'

'I would only offend him again. Anyway, we talked only yesterday.'

'I doubt you'd offend him. He's forgiven you your little trick.'

'We disagree on a number of fundamental issues. Not only theological.'

'Disagreement's normal.'

'He's hounding me.'

'He's trying to reflect the views of the community.'

'The community can be extraordinarily tiresome.'

I had finally thought of something to say.

'What did you do,' I asked Henry, 'that was so offensive?'

'He set fire to a bible. In my father's church,' said Ash quickly, before Henry had a chance to answer.

'You make it sound like an act of terrorism. I was just trying to demonstrate a point. It was a misjudgement. I didn't mean to upset anybody. I put it out right away.'

'Yes,' she said, bone dry. 'You were very placatory.'

'You set fire to a bible?' I said.

'On my father's pulpit,' said Ash, her eyes widening again. I thought of muscles loosening and contracting.

'Wesley had asked me to make a guest appearance, so to speak – in the spirit of ecumenicalism. He knew I had a doctorate in Divinity, so he invited me to make a brief address on "alternative approaches to Christianity".'

'I always thought you were some kind of Buddhist.'

'Not at all. In fact I am a supporter of the central message of Christianity. I just don't much like the way the Church presents it. Diktats from the Big Boss and his tiresome son.'

'Half the congregation walked out. Half of that number haven't come back again,' said Ash.

'What were you trying to prove?' I asked.

'That it's not the words that matter. It's the spirit.'

'You're a show-off. You liked the dramatic effect,' said Ash.

The atmosphere was tightening. Henry, usually impeccably calm, seemed to be very slightly irritated. His body had tensed up. I decided it was time to try and shift the focus of the conversation.

'What's it like having a vicar for a father?'

She turned to me. She ran her left hand lightly down one side of her body. The gesture could have passed for innocent if it wasn't for her eyes. They narrowed. Her gaze became direct. The light in them had changed from a flinty, wry curiosity to something more brazen. Her voice dropped a tone.

'Do I look like a vicar's daughter?'

'No.'

'What do I look like?' she said.

'I don't know. Normal?'

'You'd be surprised,' she said, smiling archly. 'I'm really not as normal as you think.'

'You look like the Devil's own work to me,' said Henry, half under his breath, as he took a final puff on his cigarette before stubbing it out on the pavement. 'Come on, Adam. We need to go.'

'Do you have to?' said Ash. I wasn't sure if she was being genuine, or mocking.

'No, we don't have to,' said Henry. 'We just want to.'

'*You* just want to,' I said.

'If you like. Yes.'

He started making his way back towards the car. Ash watched him go, then turned to me.

'Sorry,' I said. 'He's my transport.'

'Try not to smash the car up again. You shouldn't make a habit of it.'

I followed Henry at a clip, without turning back to Ash. I fancied I could feel her eyes on my back. When I caught up with him, I was breathing heavily.

'Did you have to be so rude?'

'I'm not necessarily a fan of excessive politeness. Certainly one should respect others. But there is a point where the need for authenticity trumps the need for civility.'

He stopped for a moment, and turned to me.

'She somehow always manages to get under my skin, that girl. There's something about her that unnerves me. A vague whiff of fanaticism. And I'm not that easily unnerved.'

He continued striding towards the car, now only a few yards off.

'What did you mean by that? Calling her the Devil's work?'

I caught up with him as he reached the car. Henry climbed into the driver's seat. It seemed he had bestowed enough freedom and responsibility on me for the day.

'What must I have been thinking? She's a saint. Isn't that apparent? Like her father. Very much the one to uphold standards.'

'Isn't that a good thing?'

'There's nothing more dangerous than a saint,' said Henry. 'The road to hell is paved with good intentions.'

'Meaning?'

'Meaning the reason for most of the unhappiness in the world is guilt. This is Wesley Toshack's stock-in-trade. His daughter is a strong advocate for the family business.'

'But surely—'

'Most of the evil in the world has been done by people who thought they were doing good. Robespierre, Cromwell, Torquemada, Lenin, you name it. Even the war that you are so conscientiously studying, or not, was fought out of principles of honour. Pol Pot is only the latest example. They want the world to be cleansed of all its impurities, you see. Give me a man who just wants territory and women and riches over a man who wants to make the world a better place every time.'

'Wesley Toshack is like Robespierre?'

'It's a matter of degree. He'd be like Robespierre if he had the chance. He'd probably have a finger in the tumbril business as well and consider it a good honest profit.'

Henry cut the conversation short by shuffling through his 8-track cartridge collection, selecting one and clicking the player on. It was some weird folk-rock thing by a duo called Judy Henske and Jerry Yester. They were singing a song about Aldebaran.

'What's Aldebaran?'

'A star in the constellation of Taurus.'

'Taurus?'

'The bull of heaven. Closely associated with Inanna, the Sumerian goddess of sexual love, fertility and warfare.'

'Oh.'

'I thought it would be appropriate.'

'Whatever that means.'

'Think about it.'

As we headed back towards the boat, the melancholic psy-chedelia pumping through the speakers, Henry asked me what I made of the lyrics. I was unable to answer, for I hadn't heard any of them. Just one word pulsed through my head, obliterating everything else.

Ash. Ash. Ash.

Ten

On the Saturday, I woke early. I had agreed to help Henry prepare for the Fayre in Bristol. He was already down in the galley, swilling hot water in the teapot to warm it before adding the leaves and sporting a natty suit – steel blue, single vent, narrow lapels, straight leg and a chalk pin-stripe. His hair was carefully brushed and secured in a knot at the back.

We took breakfast, then loaded up the boot of the car with posters, books, flyers and badges. The badges read, WHO ARE YOU? I pinned one to my jumper.

'What about Strawberry? Is she coming?'

'She's already in Bristol. She slept over with Troy.'

'Is he her boyfriend?'

'I don't think Strawberry does the boyfriend thing any more. She finds the whole business of bodies a bit messy. I think she just wants to be pure air. Or water. To melt, thaw, and resolve herself into a dew.'

'But I thought . . .'

'You thought she and I were lovers? No, it's not that at all. I hope the fact that we haven't slept together isn't going to reignite your suspicion that I'm going to creep up on you in the middle of the night and use you as my catamite.'

'What's a catamite?'

'A catamite is the passive partner in anal intercourse.'

When we arrived in Bristol, we parked in the grounds of what I assumed was a deconsecrated church, since it had a spire but no stained glass in the windows. It was still only 8.30 a.m. Henry maneouvred the Karmann Ghia into a spot between a VW Kombi and a Land Rover.

I caught the scent of hashish, and followed it to its source. I saw a man with a halo of frizzy black hair, a red headband keeping it in place, a white cheesecloth shirt and blue hip-hugging trousers ballooning out into flares that had been expanded by triangles of patterned cloth. He held the joint in his mouth while he took a large bundle of posters out of the back of a battered Citroën Dyane. He had a circle of red cotton tied around his wrist. He began to walk towards us.

'Hi, Hank. Where y'at?' he drawled, in a voice that sounded transatlantic, but with a slight English twang. Henry held out a hand to greet him.

'Troy.'

Troy ignored the outstretched hand, put down the posters on the bonnet of the Karmann Ghia and embraced Henry. Henry – the grabber, as my father would have it – appeared not so keen on being grabbed. His face registered distaste, possibly because smoke from the joint was seeping into his face.

'You're going to get yourself arrested.'

'Toke?' Troy removed the sodden stub from his mouth and held it out to Henry.

'No thanks.'

He waved it in my direction. I shook my head.

'Who's the teenybopper?'

'My nephew.'

'Is that so? He looks worried.'

'I'm not surprised, with you waving that thing around.'

'If the filth do turn up he'll make a good patsy, by the look of him. Innocent face. He'll get off light. Three months, tops, minimum security.' He gave me a big grin, and took another toke.

'Is Strawberry here?' said Henry.

'Somewhere.'

'She stayed with you last night?'

Troy dropped the stub of the joint and ground it with his foot.

'She stayed with me. But she didn't stay *with* me. So don't start coming over all caveman.'

'Strawberry does what Strawberry does.'

'Ain't that the truth?'

Troy picked up one of his posters and inspected it. It was a blown-up image of Farrah Fawcett from *Charlie's Angels*.

'Bit mainstream, wouldn't you say?' asked Henry.

'Got to move with the times. This stuff sells.'

'That's the main thing. Right?'

'That's not the main thing. That *is* the thing.'

'And are the crystals generating the required spectrum of healing vibrations for your credulous patrons?'

Troy was examining another poster. It depicted a variety of coloured stones, with prices underneath. They struck me as startlingly expensive. At the top, set in a wobbly, bloated typeface, were the words TROY PALOMINO'S WORLD OF CRYSTALS.

'They certainly appear to be. Get lots of repeat orders. People love this shit. The bloodstone is red hot right now.' He licked his finger, touched it to the photograph of the bloodstone and made a *tsssss* sound, as if it were singeing his finger. 'Scorchin'. Can't get enough. Gives you sex energy. Libido, man.' He winked at me. 'How 'bout you, Hank? What you selling?'

'I'm not really selling anything as such.'

'Cool.' He looked puzzled. 'What?'

'I'm just trying to . . .'

Henry paused for a moment, as if he was suddenly unsure of what it was he was trying to do.

'I'm just trying to make people think a little bit differently.'

'Consciousness expansion. That's a solid growth area.'

'There's no money in it.'

Troy laughed, without malice.

'You always were an idealist, Hank. I'll give you that. Listen, you've got dough, right?'

'I do have access to funds. Some friends who would trust me with a small amount of business capital.'

'If you ever want to turn that small amount of capital into a rocket in your pocket, we should talk. With some capitalization, this business could let rip.'

Troy made his back towards his Citroën. He began to unload trays of coloured stones. They were elegantly presented, in individual polished-glass containers. Although they were only rocks, the way they were displayed made them seem precious.

'Presentation. It's all that counts any more,' said Henry. 'The proliferation of *maya* continues apace.'

He began to walk towards the entrance. I followed.

'What's *maya*?' I asked.

'Things as they seem. As opposed to things as they are.'

A beggar sat by the church doorway – an old-style tramp, by the look of him: elderly, with a massive, filthy beard through which pink wet lips poked like some kind of sea anemone stranded in a hay bale. His trousers were knotted with rope. Next to him was a battered pushchair supporting a chaotic pile of what were presumably his possessions. He reached out a hand for some money, fixing us with his blood-shot eyes.

Henry bustled past him, ignoring him completely. I was taken aback. For some reason, I had assumed Henry was the sort of man who would give money to beggars. He caught my glance.

'"And though I bestow all my goods to feed the poor, and though I give my body to be burned, and have not charity, it profiteth me nothing."'

I said I didn't understand.

Henry looked at me. Then he took a pound note out and dropped it on the floor in front of the beggar.

'Am I a good person now?'

He walked into the hall. I followed him, stepping over the legs of the tramp, who appeared to be indifferent to Henry's donation. He still hadn't picked up the pound note.

Inside, the space was around a third of the size of a football pitch. The ceiling was pitched, with high windows. The floor was scratched parquet. I estimated there were about thirty stalls set up. Several transistor radios competed with one another to provide a patchwork soundtrack, embroidering the air with messy, mashed-up voices, rhythms and melodies.

A strong smell of incense hung in a low cloud, mingling with the faint odour of wood varnish. Stallholders were gathering to register at a table to the left of the entrance, and Henry joined them. Everyone seemed to know him and greeted him, hugged him or shook his hand.

I strolled among the stalls. Psychic numerology. Electromagnetic balancing. Back massagers in the shape of dolphins. Cassettes of whalesong. Stalls selling second-hand records. One table was devoted entirely to a magazine called *Shrew*. It was attended by a smiling, pleasant-looking woman, with sharp eyes. I guessed she was in her mid-thirties, wearing a shapeless olive-coloured blouson dress. At the far end of the hall, furthest from the door, was a small stage where an amp and a mike stand were being set up.

Most of the exhibitors were wearing colourful, casual clothes of one kind or another, with an American or Indian influence. With his slicked-back long hair and his smart, well-cut suit, Henry stood out as genuinely unconventional. I joined him at the registration desk, where a drably dressed middle-aged man — fawn trousers and a chunky cream V-neck cardigan over a brown shirt with a fraying collar — sat writing in a large, black leather-bound ledger.

'Name?' said the man, without looking up.

'Dr Henry Templeton.'

The man scanned the book until he located Henry's name. He looked up for the first time. He didn't smile, and made no eye contact, although he glanced at me briefly and dismissively.

'Become What You Have?'

'Become What You Are. Your handwriting is terrible.'

'Stall A17. One pound fifty, less your deposit. That's one pound.'

Henry handed over a five-pound note. The man held the note up to the light, placed it meticulously into a chamber in a cash box and handed Henry his change. Then he began making out a receipt.

'Why has it gone up in price?' asked Henry.

'Demand and supply. If you don't want the stall, I'll give you your deposit back. There's plenty of others who will take it, even now. There's people waiting outside on the off-chance.'

'It seems greedy.'

'I'll tell you what, old butty. You become what you are, and I'll stay what I am. OK? And what I am is someone who charges one pound fifty for a table.'

The man handed the receipt indifferently to Henry, along with a mimeographed map showing the whereabouts of his allotted stall. Henry folded the receipt briskly into the shape of a plane and sent it flying towards the ceiling.

'Everything's going up,' he said. 'See how the hot air carries it.'

He checked the map, and we started making our way towards the far left-hand side of the hall. We passed about twenty stalls on the way to our spot. Troy's World of Crystals was already set up. He had arranged for the tray to be under-lit, so the translucent and semi-translucent stones seemed to glow.

We passed the *Shrew* stall. Henry nodded to the woman with sharp eyes.

'That's Vanya,' he said to me. Then, 'Stick it to the man, Van.'

'The men,' said Vanya.

'That's right,' said Henry. 'The men. They did it. They made the mess.'

'And the women are right here after them with the dust-pan and brush.'

'Oh yes.'

'And the incinerator,' she added, without smiling.

Some outfit called the Aetherius Society was next to us. A bald, pink-eyed, rather vacant-looking man in a suit that looked ten years out of date raised a hand at Henry as we passed.

'What's the Aetherius Society?' I asked Henry as we began to unpack our stuff.

'They believe Jesus came to Earth from Mars.'

'Seriously, though?'

'I am being serious. Quite a lot of the people here are powerfully deluded. Nevertheless, I like them rather more than the ones who are here simply to make money.'

He began to stack up the books we had hauled over. I scanned the titles. *Tractatus Logico-Philosophicus* by Ludwig Wittgenstein, of whom I had vaguely heard. Several books by Carl Jung, among them *Memories, Dreams, Reflections*. There were Joseph Campbell, Aldous Huxley, G. K. Chesterton and St Augustine, Richard Brautigan and Allen Ginsberg.

I continued stacking the books on the table while Henry went back to the car, this time returning with a collapsed steel frame and some canvas, out of which he constructed a small, upright booth, just about large enough for two people. There was a door-size flap at the front. He had also brought two small folding chairs, which he placed within the booth. After he had set it up to his satisfaction, he emerged, closing the flap behind him, and pinned an A4 sign on the outside that read PHILOSOPHER FOR HIRE — PAY WHAT YOU THINK I'M WORTH.

'What would you hope to be paid?'

'I would hope that whoever came into my little marquee came out feeling they had enjoyed a different kind of wealth.'

'What are we here for? If not to make money?'

'Ah. The Troy Palamino Paradox. We're here to try and help people to look at their lives in a different way. We're providing a service. I only ever ask for voluntary contributions.'

'Doesn't that strike you as unrealistic?'

'Oh, let's all be realistic. Have a look around the world and see how that's working out. This is the way it's all going, Adam. The way people were thinking a few years ago – they were reimagining the world. Now it's reverting. The old patterns are reasserting themselves. Perhaps it is human nature after all. I expect this will be my last time here. Troy's right: I'm a relic.'

He stood stock still, as if trying to incorporate this perception of himself into some internal map. Then he sighed, appeared to relax, and started helping me arrange books on the table.

There were poster reproductions of work by artists, most of whom I had never heard of – Georgia O'Keeffe, Willem de Kooning, Frank Stella, Jackson Pollock. There were books of photographs – Robert Frank, Garry Winogrand, Diane Arbus. These were all expensive, although Henry claimed they sold at the same price he bought them for. Some of the cheaper books were offered on free loan.

Customers were now making their way down the aisles, mainly in clumps of two or three. After a few minutes a lone woman approached us. She had a daffy look about her – slightly too-wide eyes, slightly too-parted lips – and hair that curled into infantile ringlets at the ends. She examined our stock silently, with a smile glued on her face.

'Have you got any books about angels?'

Henry looked puzzled. 'You mean like the ones on top of the Christmas tree?'

'Guardian angels,' said the woman. 'I want to know how I can get in touch with mine.'

'That's quite a conundrum,' said Henry.

'I've heard there are ways.'

'You might want to try this.'

He held up a book on anthropology and mythology – *The Hero With A Thousand Faces* by Joseph Campbell.

The woman took it and flicked through a few pages.

'It's actually excellent, and written with admirable clarity. You can have it for free. Just send it back to me when you've finished with it.'

She shook her head and returned the book to the pile.

'Have you read a book called *Jonathan Livingston Seagull*?'

'I'm afraid I have.'

'Do you have a copy?'

'I think you might be better off at an ornithologist's.'

Her smile, for the first time, disappeared. 'You're not going to do much business with that kind of attitude.' She began to move away. 'You're a freak.'

'Thank you,' said Henry genially.

A few moments later, a man who looked to be in his mid-twenties occupied the space where the woman had been. He wore a combat jacket, army trousers, Doc Marten boots and a khaki T-shirt. From one of his belt loops hung a Swiss Army knife and a hefty set of keys. His hair was cut very short, which, along with the duds, gave him a martial air, as if he was preparing to engineer a coup there and then and sequester Henry's books for the greater good. He had a full Zapata moustache that stretched to the line of his jaw.

Henry nodded towards him.

'Hello, Pattern.'

'Who's the kid?' said the man, gesturing in my direction.

'Adam, this is Pattern.'

'I've heard about you,' I said.

'Really?' said Pattern, looking edgy. 'Who from?'

'Strawberry.'

'Oh, yeah,' said Pattern. 'Sweet kid. Nut job.'

He looked down at the stall.

'Why do you keep coming, Henry? Your shit is so out there. Have you ever come across something called the real world?'

'Why do *you* keep coming, Pattern?'

'Because there's work to be done.'

'I'm sure that's true. A portion of pious outrage is no doubt our birthright. If only it weren't for all that tiresome false consciousness keeping the man on the Clapham omnibus in chains. But what is one to do?'

Pattern seemed oblivious to Henry's flagrant sarcasm.

'Read this, Henry.'

He handed Henry a leaflet, then gave one to me.

It showed a pig decorated with stars and stripes. Four guns were pointed at the pig by unknown assailants. Along the barrel of each gun was a motto: GET OUT OF THE GHETTO, GET OUT OF LATIN AMERICA, GET OUT OF ASIA, GET OUT OF AFRICA. The pig was cowering. Underneath was the legend *March Against America: Bristol Town Hall, Saturday 27 July, 11 p.m. Free food. Pink Fairies. Free music.*

'I thought you might want to get down from your ivory tower and get involved in something that actually might make a difference, for once in your privileged, complacent and largely useless life.'

'It's not really my territory.'

'What *is* your territory, Henry? What use are you?'

He was smiling and Henry was smiling back. It seemed they had a well-practised routine.

'Let's just say I have a different approach to these things.'

'You need to get angry.'

'According to you, everyone needs to get angry. Your manifesto seems to be for an angrier world.'

'There's plenty to get angry about.'

'I'm not really sure that helps anyone. How's Moo?'

'Why do you want to know about Moo?'

'I'm asking out of politeness. You don't have to answer.'

Pattern paused, as if weighing the consequences of giving out sensitive information. He nodded towards the stage at the far end of the hall.

'She's over there.'

I followed Pattern's glance. A rather overweight young woman with greasy brown hair and wearing a long floral frock was arguing with a middle-aged man while trying to give him a pamphlet.

'How long has she got to go?'

'Oh, that. Yeah. That's not going to happen.'

'Oh dear. I'm sorry to hear that. What happened? Was there some sort of mishap?'

'Not really. We made a choice.'

'You did what?'

'Wouldn't want to bring a child into a world like this.'

Moo looked up from her discussion with the middle-aged man and noticed Henry staring at her. She smiled and waved, then returned to her customer, who was examining a book with a fist and a gun depicted on the cover.

'Moo agreed?'

'Moo sees my point of view.'

'Did you bully her into it? Poor woman. She should try someone with a little more paternal instinct.'

'What would you know about that?'

'More than you might think.' There was now a note of irritation in Henry's voice.

Pattern smiled.

'You see what I mean about getting angry, Henry? It's good energy.'

Eleven

Pattern turned his back and walked towards his stall. Moo made another faint wave. Although Pattern was dressed for the army, his walk was anything but military, with a long, loping stride that gave a slight rubbery bounce to his walk.

'Why is he called Pattern?'

'Because he believes everything has a pattern. Usually controlled by malign forces.'

'It doesn't sound all that implausible.'

'Life isn't like that, Adam. Life doesn't have a pattern. Not one we can map, anyway.'

I was sitting next to Henry behind the table. There was now a steady flow of people entering the hall.

'It's going to be a busy day,' he said.

He was wrong. Most of the other stalls, even the Aetherius Society, got medium-to-heavy footfall as the morning rolled by. We, on the other hand, received few visitors. People wandered into the orbit of the stall and wandered off again, looking thoughtful, or amiable, but finally unengaged. They seemed confused by what it was that Henry was offering. Five or six books were borrowed. Henry took no money, simply pointed out that donations were welcome. A few entered his philosophy tent, mainly with a larky attitude, but none of them left anything but small change for the privilege.

A fat man with a large red beard and rectangular wire spectacles had arrived at the stall and was picking indifferently through the books.

'Can I interest you in a session in my philosophy tent?'

'Sounds a laugh. 'Ow much is it?'

'It's absolutely free. Unless you want to make a contribution.'

'I don't know. What sort of contribution?'

'Whatever you like. Or nothing at all.'

The man looked suspicious.

'I don't get it.'

'You pay what you want.'

'Oh, right then. No, I don't reckon so.'

'Aren't you curious about life?'

'It all comes out in the wash, doesn't it?'

Without waiting for a reply, he put down the book he had been inspecting. I noticed that he had jam on his fingers – I recalled seeing him at the Women's Institute stall, helping himself to Victoria sponge. He left smears all over the expensive copy of Elliott Erwitt photographs.

'Not much happening,' said Henry. 'It's odd. The fact I'm not charging anything for my books or my services seems to convince people that they can't possibly be worth having. Human nature is highly perverse, don't you think?'

'Maybe it's you that's perverse.'

'It has been said before, I must confess.'

A few more minutes passed, silently. Henry nodded towards the tent.

'Do you want a go?'

'In the tent? Why? I can ask you what I want when I'm at the boat.'

'It's different. The nature of the space transforms the relationship.'

'Hello, Henry.'

I turned and recognized Moo, Pattern's wife or girlfriend, I wasn't sure which. Although she was solidly built, with a strong face and a commanding presence, she gave off a faint aura of anxiety. She nodded towards the tent.

'Henry, could you spare a few minutes with me?'

'Certainly.'

Relieved, I stayed in my place behind the stall. I had no desire to spill my guts to Henry. After a few minutes, I could hear sobbing coming from the tent. It got more plaintive, until it broke down into almost uncontrollable wailing. People began to stare.

Embarrassed, I left the stall and went to pretend to use the lavatories. When I returned Moo had gone.

'What was wrong with her?' I asked.

'The same as what's wrong with most people,' said Henry. 'She doesn't believe she's worth anything.'

At around 2 p.m., while the rest of the market was still booming, Henry, clearly discouraged, began to pack up.

'Can't we at least wait until the music starts?' I said.

There was some movement by the stage — sound checks, a man shifting speakers and tapping microphones. To my surprise, I saw Strawberry walk up on to the stage, cradling a scratched and beaten acoustic guitar like a sickly baby. There was a flutter of applause. She acknowledged her audience, then tried to say a few words into the microphone, but was immediately sabotaged by brutal feedback. An engineer dabbled with some cables, and she tried again. This time the PA rang clear.

She did not speak again, simply went straight into the song. Her voice was shadowy, not much more than a sketch at the lower registers, but gutsy, violent, broken and sharp like a dropped crystal glass on the bigger notes. I didn't recognize the song – Henry informed me that it was by Jacques Brel, 'Ne Me Quitte Pas'. Like many *chansons* it did a lot of grandstanding, shading into melodrama at the crescendos, aching with loss in the troughs. As the song reached its conclusion I thought I saw a minuscule tear work slowly down Strawberry's cheek. There was a moment's silence before applause began to roll across the room.

Strawberry didn't smile. In fact, she seemed distressed. She just nodded and left the stage. Henry made his way in her direction, and after a while brought her back with him. She seemed to have regained her composure.

'Oh! Adam!' She reached across and kissed me on the cheek. Her lips felt waxy and warm. There was still a track on her face, where the left eye had been weeping. 'I'm so flattered that you came to see me.'

Before I had a chance to blurt that I hadn't come to see her, Henry interrupted. 'I think everyone here would have happily made the trip just to see that performance.'

'It's a hobby. Something anyone could do, given a bit of practice.'

'You're wrong,' objected Henry.

'Am I?'

She looked almost pathetically hopeful, as if what I first took to be false modesty was in fact genuine, and acute, self-doubt.

'Self-effacement is a nice quality, Strawberry. But you shouldn't deny your gift.'

'Ahh, you're biased.' But she was clearly pleased.

'Adam and I are just leaving. I find this place depressing. It's like the remnants of a past time – or the hideous vernix of one that is newly born.'

'Why does it always sound like you're spouting shit from a book?'

She looked around her at the hall. It was bustling.

'Are you coming with us?' said Henry.

'I promised Troy I'd hang out with some friends this evening. I'll be back at the shack after that for a while, probably tomorrow.'

'Are things OK there? Is he behaving himself?'

Strawberry strummed a few melodramatic chords on the guitar – *de, de, DAH*.

'Don't be silly, Henry.'

She was so thin I imagined her to be translucent under her cotton shift. Her words were punctuated, as when I had met her on the boat, by small, skipping coughs.

'Perhaps you would agree to see a doctor for that cough?' said Henry.

Strawberry ignored him and turned to me.

'Why don't you drop in and see me tomorrow? I'll show you my cabin. I have some little Greek pastries someone gave me that I can't eat because of the sugar, and they are apparently quite fucking yum for those in the grip of that particular addiction.'

'As long as I don't have to drink any green tea.'

'I've got some of the ordinary stuff for those who like to hit the tannin mainline. So that's a date?'

'I guess.'

'Henry, you going to swing by with the boy?'

'See how it goes.'

With that, we said farewell and made our way towards the exit. I was excited to go and visit her, although not out of any sexual promise. Despite her beauty, her frailty rendered her more or less neuter. The fact that she had called me 'boy' rankled. She wasn't that much older than me – although I had to admit there was something about her character that seemed, if not ancient, then wizened.

Outside, a group of about twenty protesters had gathered, brandishing placards. STOP THE PORN FESTIVAL, said one. CHRISTIAN MOTHERS AGAINST ABORTION, said another. MARIJUANA KILLS, said a third. Henry ignored them and made his way towards the Karmann Ghia, carrying a heavy tea chest full of books. I made to follow him, but then I noticed Ash standing under the Christian Mothers Against Abortion banner.

She caught my eye. I felt that to go over and talk to her would somehow be a betrayal of Henry. But at the same time it seemed rude not to say hello. I walked over and she separated herself from the group.

'What are you doing here?' I had to raise my voice to make myself heard over the singing.

'Helping my father out.'

She nodded in the direction of a wide, tall man, built like a sturdy Victorian wardrobe, with wiry pepper-and-salt hair and a corrugated face. He stood at the forefront of the protesters, fiddling impatiently with a megaphone, which tweeted and squawked as if protesting at its treatment. He was wearing a clerical dog collar to top off an outfit of black clerical vestments.

'Are you part of . . . this?'

I looked around at the protesters. Ash was by far the youngest one there.

'My father likes it if I come along. It passes the time. Lexham gets kind of boring – anything for a day out.'

I looked over to where Henry was packing up the car.

'I have to go. I'm helping Henry.'

'Shame.'

Her lips drew back to reveal a glimpse of those lascivious gap teeth, a flash of provocative, Pantone-scale eyes.

'It is. Obviously, I'd like to stay and shout at people going in. Is that what passes for entertainment round these parts?'

'It's less fun than it sounds. Listen . . .' She paused, as if carefully considering options. 'Perhaps you'd like to come and see me? Later in the week? Just to pass the time? We could kick up a bit of dust in the village? We could carry banners and intimidate passers-by with slogans.'

I looked around at the car again. Henry was looking up, scanning for me. I took a step away from Ash.

'If your dad doesn't mind.'

I glanced at her Wesley Toshack. He had fixed the megaphone and was bellowing into it – complaining, from what I could make out through the distortion, that the church building, although deconsecrated, should not be used for the purposes of promoting 'drug culture' and 'free love'.

'He's not as scary as he looks,' said Ash.

'He looks livid.'

'He's caught a touch of the sun.'

Another flash of her eyes.

'Just to pass the time. Sure.'

'Monday? At the clock?'

'The day after. Tuesday.'

'About noon, then.'

I held up a hand to say farewell, and she reached out and touched her finger on my palm. This time she didn't smile, but looked serious. As if the contract we had sealed was momentous.

I turned and walked towards the car. Henry was looking faintly irritable.

'Where have you been?'

'I was checking out the zoo.'

'You see what I mean about Ash the Pash?'

So he had noticed after all.

'What? That she's a "red-hot chilli pepper"?'

'That she's a zealot.'

'Just trying to please her dad, I think.'

Henry regarded the thin corona of protesters surrounding Wesley Toshack, all singing together now, a thin, gruelly rendition of 'We Shall Overcome'.

'I don't know who are the most lame, the protesters or those protested against. This is a two-ring circus. Are you going to help me load up the rest of this stuff? Or are your hormones too occupied with other matters?'

It took a couple more trips to finish loading the car. I was about to climb in when I saw Strawberry approaching across the car park. She waved and picked up her pace. Henry started the engine.

'Adam. I'm going to do another song. Do you want to stay and hear it?'

'I'm meant to be going back with Henry.'

Henry revved the motor.

'We're all going back to Troy's after the Fayre. Why don't

you come with? You can stay over. Crash on the couch. I
checked with Troy. It's fine.'

I looked at Henry. He shrugged.

'Troy's only staying here for another hour or so. I'll introduce you to some people. What do you say?'

'All right.'

She grabbed my hand and squeezed it feebly.

'Good. Come on. I'm due on stage. My audience awaits.
Catch you on the flipside, Henry.'

'OK,' said Henry, with an air of slight weariness. He
turned to me. 'If you need to get back, there's a bus to
Lexham from Bristol on the hour.'

She led me back towards the hall. I turned to wave goodbye, but Henry was already driving away.

Inside, Strawberry moved towards the stage, still limply
holding my hand. Just before we reached it, she turned
towards the stall selling *Shrew* magazine.

'Hey, Vanya, could you look after the boy for a few minutes? If you can bear that much testosterone messing with
your oestrogen.'

Vanya was taking some change in return for one of the
magazines. She didn't look up.

'"The boy"?'

'Adam. He's staying with Henry down at the boat. His
nephew.'

Now she threw me a glance.

'Makes no difference to me.'

'Great. Listen, you coming down to Troy's later?'

'I might drop by. Yeah.'

Strawberry let go of my hand, and Vanya beckoned me
behind her table. Strawberry mounted the stage and picked
up her guitar. I sat on a single upright chair to Vanya's left.

Strawberry hit the first few chords of a song that I recognized as 'Freedom' by Richie Havens.

Vanya handed me a copy of *Shrew*.

'Here. Educate yourself.'

I took the magazine and started to flick through it. It was badly printed, and contained headlines like END HUMAN SACRIFICE – DON'T GET MARRIED, WOMEN'S MOVEMENT AT THE CROSSROADS, THE NEW WAR AGAINST WOMEN.

Strawberry was getting carried away with 'Freedom', her voice cracking again.

Vanya sat down next to me. She smiled. She had a certain odd, contradictory atmosphere to her – an earth-mothery aura of concern and indiscriminate warmth mixed with an undertow of thoroughgoing, scattergun resentment.

'So what do you think of it?'

'Um.'

'You can be honest.'

'Everyone seems kind of pissed off.'

'Do you know much about the women's liberation movement?'

'Not really.'

'Any of the articles in there catch your attention?'

'One of them said that all men were rapists.'

'Who knows what's buried in the hearts of men?'

'Even so. *All* of them?'

'Not every article reflects the views of the management.'

'Is that you?'

'I'm part of the collective. Would you like a cup of tea or something?'

'No thanks.'

'Biscuit?'

'No thanks.'

'Do you masturbate?'

I stared at the floor and picked at my fingernail with my front teeth. I hoped I wasn't blushing too obviously.

'Of course you masturbate. You're a . . . what? Fifteen-year-old boy?'

'Seventeen.'

'What do you think about when you masturbate?'

'I . . .'

'Don't worry. I'm all in favour of masturbation. It's universal. I'm just asking what you masturbate *to*.'

'Isn't it obvious?' I muttered into a space somewhere in front of my chest.

'Then why won't you tell me?'

'Women.'

'What kind of women?'

'Ones without any clothes on.'

At that moment Strawberry appeared, clutching her guitar. I hadn't even noticed her stop singing, but I became aware of the faint after-smattering of applause.

Vanya looked up and smiled innocently, as if we had been discussing gardening or cake recipes.

'You're talented, Straws.'

'Have you been giving the boy a hard time?'

Vanya gave me a soft look.

'I've been yanking his chain a little. Makes a change from him yanking his own.' She prodded my arm playfully with her index finger. 'Have I been giving you a hard time, Adam?'

I shook my head.

'He's a bit shy, isn't he?'

'He has hidden depths, I'm sure. Listen, Troy and I are setting off now. Come on, Adam. See you at the square, Van.'

'You know, you should make some recordings or something. Wasn't Troy going to make some introductions? He's connected, isn't he?'

'He says he is. But then, he says a lot of stuff.'

Troy appeared behind the stall, lugging a box of crystals.

'I say a lot of stuff? About what?'

'Whatever you say stuff about. I mean, you're not short of opinions,' said Strawberry.

'He's a bullshitter,' said Vanya, throwing a rolled-up scrap of paper at his head, which bounced, like a pebble on a trampoline, off the halo of his hair. 'Olympic-standard.'

'Get knotted, you old dyke,' said Troy affectionately. 'You coming with?'

'I'll be there later, I guess. And I'm not a dyke, you fairy.'

'See you later, Van. Sorry there won't be any muff-hunting. Only Pattern and Adam.'

'And Strawberry,' said Vanya.

'You ain't going to get Strawberry munching at the Axminster, dear. She's *entirely* post-sexual.'

Twelve

Troy's home was a one-bedroom flat in a Regency square, with a very large front room – maybe twenty-five feet long and nearly that much across – put together beautifully. Every single object – statuettes, vases, clocks, gongs and chimes – seemed to be in precisely the right place. There were abstract oil paintings on the wall, one of them just uninterrupted brown covering the canvas from corner to corner. The floors were plain varnished boards, which in those days was radical. There were rich, dark-patterned rugs that smelled of citrus fruit. There was no television, neither was there an overhead light suspended from the plaster ceiling rose. Evening sun was coming through the high windows that overlooked the square. The sashes were open, admitting a mild breeze into the room.

There were two immense three-seater sofas – one red, one dark blue – both upholstered in velvet plush and decorated with vividly embroidered scatter cushions. There was a coffee table with intricately carved legs that, Troy informed us, had recently arrived from Kashmir, and a hanging on the wall dyed in a pattern that showed white roses against a pink background. There were a couple of dining chairs, and a few large cushions on the floor.

I had been there for about an hour, and was slowly beginning to unbend. The conversations at the Fayre had left me uncomfortable. These were clearly people who didn't mind saying what they felt, and this was the opposite of the convention in Yiewsley. Being asked whether or not I masturbated was bad enough, but the fact that Troy was unashamedly homosexual discomfited me even more. My experience of gay people came entirely from the television – Larry Grayson or John Inman. Troy was nothing like this stereotype. He was powerfully built, with a six o'clock shadow on his garden-trowel chin and muscles that rippled through his T-shirt. Although he did occasionally lapse into rather arch forms of speech – describing himself sometimes in the feminine – there was nothing particularly mincing or camp about him.

I was loafing on one of the floor cushions, sipping on a glass of not very well chilled white wine. Strawberry was reading Troy's palm on one of the sofas, while Pattern and Vanya were arguing animatedly on the other. Pattern was starting to raise his voice. Vanya got up with a look of distaste on her face and walked over to me. She carried a half-drunk bottle of wine with her.

'How you doing, boy?' She lowered herself down on to a cushion beside me.

'As soon as you start losing the argument you just walk away, don't you, Vanya?' Pattern snapped from the sofa.

'That's not why I'm walking away, Pattern. I'm walking

away because I'm bored with your rantings and because I've decided that Adam has been ignored quite long enough. He's come all the way from – where is it?'

'Yiewsley.'

'Yiewsley. Wherever that is. And hardly anyone has talked to him since he's arrived.'

'I'm OK,' I mumbled.

'Funny that you were overcome with empathy at the exact moment that you couldn't sustain your point any more. So you walked away. It's what you do,' said Pattern.

'Oh, how *female* of her,' said Troy drily, without looking up from his palm, where Strawberry was tracing a line with her finger.

'You said it,' said Pattern.

'What do you know about females, Pattern?' said Vanya. 'You've only had one girlfriend since you were fifteen.'

'Therefore. I know the mindset.'

'On a sample size of one.'

Vanya turned her attention to me.

'Do you find me attractive, Adam?'

'Am I allowed to?'

'I'm not really a lesbian, you know. Troy is just using his sledgehammer wit.'

'I know.'

'I'm not flirting with you either. You're still a kid.'

'Everyone keeps saying that. Like being a bit younger than everyone else makes me some kind of simpleton.'

'I didn't mean that.'

'I'm not bothered.'

'I'm sorry about that interrogation earlier about your personal habits. I was bored and cranky. I get like that when I've got nothing else to do. It was rude of me. I had no right.'

'It's OK.'

Troy got up from the sofa.

'I'm going to have a VERY long life,' he announced.

He put a record on his state-of-the-art Bang & Olufsen stereo. The Stooges.

Pattern sat smoking on the sofa, twitching his leg up and down, agitated.

Vanya leaned over and spoke, quite loudly over the music, into my ear. 'What do you think of Strawberry?'

'I've never met anyone like her. In fact . . .'

'I can't hear you.'

'I said I've never met anyone like Strawberry. I've never met anyone like the rest of you, either. I'm not used to people like you.'

'How so?'

I tried to work it out.

'None of you seem ashamed.'

'Why should we be ashamed?'

'No reason. But people act like they are.'

'Do you? Feel ashamed?'

I wanted to say, 'All the time.' Instead I shrugged.

'Do we make you uncomfortable?'

'A bit. But it's sort of interesting.'

Vanya took a packet marked MAHAWATT out of her pocket and extracted a long, thin, black cigarette. She lit it and blew a cloud of smoke in my direction. It had the faint tang of liquorice. She blew another cloud in the direction of Strawberry.

'I get worried about her.'

'She seems a little undernourished,' I said.

Vanya nodded. 'No shit. And that's just her body. No part of her seems to be able to receive nourishment. She's like a clam. All closed up and chilly and salty inside.'

'She seems friendly enough.'

'Friendly has nothing to do with it.'

'Maybe that's the way she is because she's American.'

'Yeah, they're friendly folk,' called Pattern from the sofa. 'Ask the Viet Cong.'

'Keep your nose out of it, Pattern.'

'What part of America does Troy come from?' I said.

Vanya laughed. 'Troy? He's not American.'

'Canada then.'

'He's from Stoke-on-Trent. And his name isn't Troy. It's Jonathan. Jonathan Swindles.'

'Jonathan Swindles?'

'Perfect, isn't it? Dickens himself, et cetera.'

'I would never have guessed.'

'He talks the talk, I'll give you that. He has quite the spiel. Strawberry says you couldn't tell. But he worked as a local-radio DJ for a while. In Stafford, I think. It was the thing to have an American accent. So Jonathan got himself one. And then got himself an American name too. Very resourceful fag. It helps sell those silly rocks.'

'But Strawberry *is* American, right?'

'Oh yeah. Born right there in Loopyland on the West Coast.'

Vanya took another sip of the wine. She suddenly seemed angry.

'Do you know what happened to her? Do you know what they did to her?'

The conversation, as so often since I had arrived, was taking a turn that was too grown-up, too far out of my field of experience. I stayed silent. There was a small fleck of spittle on Vanya's lip. Her eyes looked wild.

'Well? Do you know?'

I said I didn't.

Vanya's eyes looked bleary. It occurred to me that she was quite seriously drunk.

'It was a real thing what they did to her. Really something. I don't know. What the fuck is wrong with people?'

Just then Pattern flopped down on the floor between us.

'What I'm saying is, Vanya – what I was trying to say – is that class is the fundamental *lodestone*, the most significant indicator of power. How the man on the hill maintains hegemonic—'

'"The man". Look, Pattern. I don't wish to be rude. Well, I do, actually. Just leave us alone, will you?'

'It's capital, Vanya. You're being naive. It's money. It's always money.'

'People who think it's always money are always overly interested in money themselves. You're pissed off because you're poor.'

'You're trivial. You're playing your games fighting against housework and ironing while Indochina is burning. We sit and do nothing. You're guilty.'

'So are you, then.'

'We all are.'

'What am I responsible for specifically, other than not catching the next plane out to Saigon with my trusty cutlass?'

'Apathy and smugness. You're smug because your daddy left you a pile when he checked out, and your husband has a paying job. Which is more than you do.'

'You're married?' I said, trying to defuse what was threatening to turn into a serious breach of the good feeling in the room.

'Why shouldn't I be?' said Vanya.

'She married a plumber.' Pattern. 'It was a political decision. Otherwise known as slumming it.'

'I happen to love Tony.'

'When he's not down the pub or at the footie.'

'There are cultural differences.'

'Like him knocking you about.'

'I told you, I walked into a double-glazed French door. Talking of political decisions, I heard that you and Moo decided not to go ahead with the kid.'

'Yeah. It was one of those things.'

'Moo was on board?'

'More or less. I figured we shouldn't be going around having kids if both us aren't completely into it.'

'*You* figured. Pattern, no couple are ever both completely into it, or anything else. You've just got to take the plunge and hope for the best.'

'What would you know about it, Van?'

Vanya's eyes clouded.

'We've tried.'

The music suddenly cut off. Strawberry, who was drinking soda water with lemon in it, stood up.

'Come on – let's dance! The frug. You know? The mashed potato. The boogaloo!' The Stooges were powering into their anthem of disenchantment, '1969'.

Nobody moved, but Strawberry launched into a frenzied series of movements that resembled less dancing, more an epileptic fit. Her arms and legs were all angles. There was no fluidity to it. If it expressed anything at all, it wasn't music, but confusion and anger.

After a few seconds, she toppled over on to the floor. She started laughing – not a healthy laugh. Then she rose and adopted an actorly pose, a pose that affected nobility and almost convinced.

'Life is beautiful.'

'Amen,' said Troy.

'For you, maybe,' muttered Pattern.

Strawberry's body seemed to slump.

'I want to go to bed.'

'It's only nine o'clock,' said Pattern.

'I'm tired.'

'You're always tired. You're going to stay tired until you start eating some proper food. All that macrobiotic shit is just another scheme dreamed up for fleecing the gullible.'

'I'm sure you're an example to us all, Pattern, when it comes to non-gullibility.'

'You're making yourself sick, baby.'

'Thanks for the insight, Patty-cake. Anyway, sorry to be a wet rag. Vanya. Adam. You can choose which couch you want. I think the blue one is nicer.'

I thought the party was going to fade out then, but five minutes later Strawberry changed her mind. Just as suddenly as she had decided to go to bed, she emerged from the bed-room in Troy's oversized pyjamas and announced that she'd got a second wind. I could see through to the bedroom where she had been changing. The bed was huge, easily big enough for Troy and Strawberry to sleep without even touching.

Troy went to the cupboard and started searching for some-thing, while Pattern fiddled with the music system. Having selected a Kevin Coyne album, he came and sat down next to me. Vanya had headed off to the kitchen to refill her glass.

'Adam, right?'

'That's right.'

'Adam from Yiewsley. So what are you going to do when you leave school, Adam from Yiewsley?'

'I'm not sure. Worst comes to the worst, I can get a job in my old man's shoe shop.'

'How's that working out for him?'

'Not great, I guess.'

'How about your mum?'

'She's dead. She died a few months ago.'

'That's tough.'

'I thought I might go into computers.'

'Technology, man. They're replacing the humans day by day. Twenty years, ain't going to be any fucking jobs. You know what the future is? Mass unemployment. Or nuclear war. Add up to the same thing. We're all fucked.'

'Anyone played the dice game?' said Troy.

'The what?' said Strawberry.

'Haven't you read *The Dice Man*? Luke Rhinehart?' said Vanya. 'It's about some guy who throws a die then goes upstairs and rapes his neighbour because the die tells him to. Sort of a male-fantasy novel.'

'You're missing the underlying theme of the book, Van,' said Troy. 'What if you lived your life randomly? That's the question he's exploring. Perhaps it would free you.'

'I think throwing the die sounds like a fun idea,' said Strawberry brightly.

'Let's give it a kick. My life is pretty random anyway,' said Pattern.

'OK, this is the way we're going to do it,' said Troy. 'We come up with a set of options—'

'How many?' said Pattern.

'Six – obviously. Idiot. Then we each throw the die and we have to follow the challenges.'

'Like kiss-or-dare,' I said.

'Sort of.'

'What kind of options?' asked Vanya.

'OK, well,' said Troy. 'One of them could be, say, go down to the Handy Gandhi on the corner in your pants.'

'Shit, man, I ain't doing that,' said Pattern. 'And don't call it that, you fucking racist.'

'I'm a homo. I'm allowed prejudices.'

'Let's lighten it then,' said Vanya. 'Option one, kiss Troy. A proper kiss.'

'Oooh,' said Troy. 'Pattern, this could be your lucky day.'

'Let me check that die. It's got to be loaded.'

'Like *you're* my dreamboat. You wish, darling,' said Troy. 'What about you, Straws? What options?'

'Drink piss.'

Everyone laughed.

'You're kidding – right?'

'Not at all. I do it all the time. It's a health thing. It's good for you.'

'Disgusting,' said Troy.

'You'd be surprised. Chill it down a bit with ice, it's OK.'

'Whose piss?' said Pattern.

'Your own. Troy's if you like.'

'He's not having any of mine. It's vintage. Year of forty-nine. Anyway, it's on the list,' said Troy. 'Four more to go. How about a soft option? You've got to have some hope. Adam?'

'Um. I don't know. Suck someone's toe.'

More laughter.

'That's a good one.'

'How's that a soft option?' said Pattern.

'Depends whose toe you want to suck,' said Vanya. 'Don't suppose anyone will be getting in line for yours.'

Pattern took off his sock. 'Nothing wrong with those babies.'

There was a strong Parmesan smell in the room. Strawberry and Vanya made retching noises.

'OK, that's three. Three more to go.'

'Putting ice cubes up your ass,' said Troy. 'Old junkie trick for waking yourself up after an OD. Sounds kinda fun.'

Pattern suggested the men dressing in women's clothes, but then decided there was no equivalent trial for the women. So he changed it to eating six cream crackers within ninety seconds. Since there were only five of us, Troy offered the final option – stripping down to your underwear then walking around clucking like a chicken for thirty seconds.

Vanya threw first, then Pattern. Disappointingly – from the point of view of the spectators at least – both threw a number four, eating mouthfuls of cream crackers. The task proved entirely impossible, but entertaining to watch. Vanya gave up after about twenty seconds, but Pattern set out with a real determination to complete the task, chewing manically and throwing his head back in order to get the mush down his throat. It still defeated him in the end. There were crumbs and lumps of half-masticated goo all over the floor by the time he'd finished. It was making me uncomfortable – calling up memories of my mother's choking fit. It was over soon enough. I hoped no one else would throw a four.

Troy went next. He threw a two: drink piss. Everyone whooped and clucked – none of us believing for a moment, I suspect, that he would try. But immediately he stood up, grabbed a glass – a small one – and headed for the bathroom. All the time he was in there we were laughing, convinced that he was just bluffing. But sure enough, he came back with some yellow liquid.

'You want to smell? To authenticate?' he said, waving the glass in front of our faces, one by one.

'You're not really going to,' said Pattern.

'It's fine,' said Strawberry.

Instead of answering, Troy went to the fridge and took out some ice cubes. Removing a rolling pin from the drawer, he crushed the ice. Then he produced a cocktail shaker, poured the yellow liquid in with the crushed ice and shook it.

'Can I add anything?' He looked at Strawberry.

'Why not?'

He poured some lime juice, vodka and chilled tonic water into the shaker. In the end there was something like half a pint there.

'Down the hatch.'

He opened his throat and downed it in one. We all whooped. He slammed the glass down on the table.

'That's one for the cocktail book. A piss martini.'

We were all doubled up with laughter now.

'How did it taste?' spluttered Pattern.

Troy looked thoughtful, and licked his lips.

'Absolutely fucking horrible.'

Everyone started laughing again. Pattern slapped Troy on the back. Strawberry gave him a kiss on the cheek. Vanya shook her head in astonishment.

'Now nobody can go back on their dare. Not after that,' said Troy.

I was beginning to feel acutely apprehensive. My turn was still to go and, clearly, to back out now would seem cowardly.

It was Strawberry first, though. She got the option to suck someone's toe. She looked around at us one by one.

'OK. Well, Pattern's out of the running, obviously. Ain't sucking no Limburger. Troy, I don't think he'd get the full effect. Gay toes are different. Vanya, let's have a look.'

Vanya removed her shoe – a small black plimsoll – and revealed a set of perfectly pretty small toes.

'Dry skin in between. Could be a fungal infection. Adam?'

I took off my left baseball boot. My foot was unremarkable, my toes more so. However, I had recently cut the nails, so they looked neat. And they were tanned, and powdered from this morning. I thought they looked like pretty good toes.

Strawberry got up, found a clean cloth near the sink, then rinsed it in hot water.

'OK, Adam. Lay back.'

She got down on all fours and started coming towards me.

Vanya said, 'Is this your big fantasy, Adam?'

'The kid's a foot man,' said Pattern. 'A foot freak. A pedi-phile.'

I closed my eyes. I was embarrassed, but also excited. First I felt the cloth rubbing me in each crack and crevice. This seemed to go on for some time.

'Why don't you just dip it in Dettol, Straws?' said Pattern.

'I don't like impurities.'

'If there's any germs left on those tootsies they've got to be getting their last rites.'

'OK, maybe that's enough.'

There was a silence. Then I felt Strawberry's lips close around my big toe. I could feel her little teeth nipping at it. She moved her mouth back and forward.

'Remind you of something?' said Troy.

'No,' I lied.

'Maybe you should try the little toe, to make it a more, um, analogous experience for Adam,' said Vanya.

Strawberry disengaged her mouth.

'I don't have to do all of them, do I? Not that I mind, Adam. But it does feel a bit unhygienic.'

'It tickles,' I said. 'Really tickles.'

'Otherwise, I'm enjoying it more than I thought I would,' said Strawberry. 'I'll just do one more.'

She took my little toe in her mouth and began sucking it in and out. I felt myself, to my horror, stiffen under my trousers. She began to moan theatrically, and everyone started laughing again. I desperately wanted her to stop now, so that my excitement didn't become visible.

'OK. That's my limit.'

'Hark at her,' said Troy, pointing to my groin. 'She's a big boy now.'

Vanya squealed with laughter.

'It just tickles,' I said feebly.

Strawberry took her mouth away.

'Thanks, Adam. I think I discovered a new experience. Much better than I expected.'

'Any time,' I said, attempting to restore my cool, but my voice came out cracked and overstimulated. Strawberry went to the sink and drank a glass of water. I heard her gargle briefly.

'OK, one more to go,' said Troy. 'Adam, you've had your fun. Time for you to put out.'

I anxiously picked up the die, weighing it in one hand. I dreaded drinking the piss. So when I saw it wasn't a two, I felt immediately relieved.

'What's a one?' I said.

Troy puckered. 'Guess, sweetheart.'

I quickly leaned over and pecked him on the cheek.

A round of boos immediately ensued. 'Cheat' and 'Not fair' and 'Cop-out' rang in the air.

'Not like that, sweetheart,' said Troy. 'Like this.'

He grabbed me on both sides of the face, pulling it towards him, and before I had a chance to do anything about it, he pushed his tongue into my mouth.

Without even thinking about it, I bit down.

'FUCK!' Troy pulled back from me, rubbing his sleeve against his tongue. 'Shit. I'm fucking bleeding.' His voice had lost its American twang and now sounded vaguely Brum.

'Come on, Troy,' said Vanya. 'That was rape. *He* was meant to kiss *you*, not the other way round.'

'Shit, man, I'd have bit down harder,' said Pattern.

I could taste Troy's blood in my mouth.

'He caught me by surprise.'

Troy was examining the blood on his finger. I saw Strawberry put her hand on his arm, as if to restrain him.

'Troy, he just got a shock.'

Troy flexed his shoulders back and forth, took a tissue out of his pocket and wiped his finger clean. He stared at me, and for a moment I thought he was going to fling the tissue at me. But then he seemed to relax back into himself. He dabbed at his mouth once, then delicately placed the tissue in a bin that sat by the sofa.

'OK.' I heard him sucking on his tongue and swallowing. 'I guess I didn't really give him a chance. No hard feelings, Adam.'

He put out a hand and I took it. Then he pulled my hand to his lips and kissed it.

'So are you going to do it properly?' he said. 'You know. With you being the man?'

'Come on, Troy,' said Pattern. 'You've had your tongue in his mouth. He's traumatized enough as it is. Kid's only seventeen. Give him a break.'

'He's confused,' said Vanya. 'Strawberry's just been plating his toe, and suddenly he's Truman Capote.'

'I'll let you off, kid,' said Troy. 'But you don't know what you're missing. So – another round?'

'Once blood is shed, time comes to change games. Who wants to do the weejee board?' said Vanya.

There was a chorus of approval. Troy went to a cupboard and returned carrying a wooden board with an alphabet painted in a circle around its edge.

'I don't know, Troy,' said Strawberry. 'Ouija's a head-fuck.'

'Well, this girl's game for it,' said Troy.

He placed the board on the coffee table. Vanya clapped her hands. Pattern sneered. Strawberry looked uncertain. I took my place next to Vanya. Dusk had fallen, and Troy started to light candles around the room.

Thirteen

'I want to talk to Jim Morrison,' said Vanya.

'Only he's not dead,' said Pattern. 'No one ever saw his body.'

'That should make it easier, then,' said Vanya. 'Anyone you want to talk to, Strawberry?'

'Can you get through to God?'

'Now he *is* dead,' said Pattern, deftly fingering a rollie.

'What would you ask him?' said Vanya.

'What was he thinking of, I suppose. How he'd do it differently next time.'

Troy switched off the electric lights and sat down at the head of the table.

Strawberry's face, in the half-light of the candles, looked hollowed out, afraid.

'I'm really not sure about this, Troy.'

'It's just fun, Shortcake. Remember fun?'

We all laid our fingers on the top of an upended wineglass

that he had placed in the middle. Pattern's finger fat like a chipolata, Strawberry's fine as the handle of a bone-china teacup. Troy's long and powerful, Vanya's nicotine-stained, nail cracked. Mine, trembling slightly. I did not believe. But then, I wasn't sure I believed in my disbelief.

A hush descended. The undertow of levity was receding. Each person, I imagined, was thinking about someone dead. The glass remained still.

'Is anyone there?' said Troy in a slightly overwrought parody of a medium.

Vanya giggled, but it sounded forced. Strawberry and Troy *shhh*ed her.

Troy raised his voice slightly and raised his eyes towards the ceiling. This time his voice was serious.

'Is anyone there?'

Nothing happened. We all sat with our hands on the glass in silence for maybe a minute. Vanya coughed. Pattern sighed.

Then the glass gave a slight tremble and shifted a millimetre to the left. It paused, then shunted a few millimetres to the right. Then it started to move slowly, but with apparent randomness, around the table. It didn't move towards any of the letters, but made circular trajectories around the central point where it had started.

'Shit, Troy,' hissed Strawberry.

'This is bullshit,' muttered Pattern. But his shoulders were stiff with tension and he kept his finger on the glass.

'Shut up!' said Vanya, now apparently in deadly earnest.

Troy spoke. 'Who is it? Who is it speaking to us?'

Now the glass begin to slide across the table towards the perimeter of letters. I wasn't aware of exerting any pressure on it at all. If someone was, it wasn't detectable.

'Troy! Are you cheating?' hissed Vanya.

The glass stopped.

'No. No, I promise! Shut up! It won't work if we don't show it respect.'

After a few more seconds of silence, the glass started to move again, this time apparently indicating letters; but it spelled out only nonsense – A, F, P, W, L.

'The dude is obviously stoned,' said Pattern.

Strawberry, Troy and Vanya together issued an urgent 'Shhhh!' I remained silent and anxious. I wanted to leave, but didn't want to show my fear.

The glass kept moving, speeding up. Then it started to go crazy. It darted madly across the board. There was an E. Then it stopped for a few seconds. Then V. I wanted it to stop. I exerted pressure on the glass to stop it moving. But some-how, Troy sensed it.

'Adam's pressing down on the glass!'

'Adam,' hissed Strawberry.

'I'm not,' I said, releasing the pressure.

The glass started to move, again apparently randomly in the centre of the board. Then it travelled to the perimeter again – this time stopping at E.

The silence thickened. Even Pattern seemed drawn into the ceremony. There was no longer any sign of mockery on his face.

'What does E-V-E stand for?' said Troy, raising his face to the ceiling.

'Anyone know an Eve?' said Vanya.

The glass did not move. My finger was now trembling dis-cernibly on the glass.

'Bad connection,' said Pattern, very quietly.

'Are you OK, Adam?' said Strawberry.

I said nothing, but sensed bile heaving in my stomach.

The glass remained at the E. For a minute we just sat there. I began to assume the 'visitation' — if that's what it was — was over.

Then Troy raised his head again.

'Do you have a message for someone?'

The glass immediately began to move towards YES, where it stopped.

'Who is the message for?'

The glass stayed where it was.

'Do you wish to say something to someone here?'

The glass moved away from YES then back to it again.

'To whom do you wish to speak?'

Again it spelled out EVE. Than an R.

'Ever?'

'R. Is that short for "are"?'

'Ask it what it wants to say, Troy,' whispered Pattern. Clearly he had started to take things more seriously.

The glass picked out Y.

'Why? They're asking why.'

'No, he's spelling out "every".'

'I thought it was a she. I thought it was Eve.'

'I don't know what that means.'

Then the glass began to move again, almost frenziedly this time, at a terrific speed.

U DID IT

And then GILTY

The glass stopped. Then it smashed. Fragments scattered over the table. Strawberry recoiled. Vanya screamed.

I stood up, took the edges of the table in my hands and upended it. The board flew and the glass fragments spread across the wooden floor. Strawberry, Pattern and Troy looked at me in astonishment.

'What kind of stupid game is this?' I heard myself say. My voice was high and tremulous. My head was swimming from the wine I had drunk.

'Calm down, Adam!' said Vanya. 'Someone was probably just playing a trick.'

I swayed slightly, and went to kick what was left of the glass across the room, in fear and fury. As I did, I lost my balance. My legs went from under me, and the world turned upside-down. I was just about aware of the sharp pain of the impact of my head on the edge of the marble fireplace.

It took me several minutes to come back to consciousness. Strawberry and Troy were leaning over me. My vision cleared, taking in the rest of the room. Pattern and Vanya appeared to have left. Strawberry had propped my head on a pillow. She was holding a glass to my lips.

'Are you OK, Adam?'

'Urgh.'

I felt sick. I took a draught of water all the same.

Troy leaned over me.

'Did you drink too much?'

'I don't know. I guess. Did I faint?'

'You slipped and banged your head. You'll be OK. But you're going to have a bump.'

'It was a stupid game. Troy, I tried to tell you. Something like this always happens.'

I raised myself up on one elbow.

'It was the drink.'

'This is your fault.' Strawberry looked at Troy accusingly.

'Come on, Straws,' said Troy quietly. 'It was Pattern who

thought it would be hilarious. There's always one who takes it too far.'

'Pattern?' I said, my head clearing now.

'It was Pattern who was pushing the glass,' said Troy. 'He admitted it. He thinks we're all guilty, see. Guilty of everything. The Vietnam War, poverty, inequality, you name it. He was sending us a message. To "everyone". The E-V-E was the first letters of "everyone", but then he lost control of the glass. Sometimes that happens. Not because of supernatural reasons, but because other people, deliberately or inadvertently, start to exert equal pressure. Then he spelled out an R and a Y but we couldn't understand it. Then he found the rhythm again. Spelled out the rest before someone else took control of the glass again. And then he pushed down on it and broke it. For dramatic effect. The gimp.'

'Is that what upset you?' said Strawberry. 'The glass?'

'No. I thought it was a message. A message for me,' I said.

'That you were guilty?' said Strawberry.

'What did you do?' said Troy.

'Nothing,' I said. 'I didn't do anything at all.'

The next day I woke early, still fragile from my experience with the ouija board. There was a bump on my head like a half-buried ping-pong ball. I couldn't get back to sleep and I didn't want to inconvenience Troy, after nearly breaking his table, by demanding a lift. More to the point, I didn't want to wait for hours until they woke up – Strawberry had told me before she went to bed that she liked 'very long lie-ins'. I decided to head back to Lexham on the bus. I could walk or hitch from there to the boat. I pulled on my clothes, which smelled of cigarette smoke and incense.

Henry had told me there was a bus on the hour. I could make it if I dressed quickly. But I was overcome by the need to evacuate my bowels. By the time I had finished, I was cutting it fine. I hurried to the bus stop, half walking, half running. My head seemed to be expanding and contracting with every step, and each growth and diminution was accompanied by a diffuse flash of pain, like sheet lightning.

As I arrived, I could see my bus receding. After half an hour waiting for the next one, I vomited into the gutter. With each convulsion, it felt like someone was taking a pile driver to my synapses. It wasn't until eleven o'clock that the next bus arrived. The driver was heavy on the pedal. I made it back to Lexham shortly before noon.

I was heading for the road home when I became aware of singing coming from the church, St Jude's. I stood outside it for a while, just listening. I could hear the strains of 'He Who Would Valiant Be'. The sun was already blistering the tarmac and my head was crammed with broken glass. I craved cool and shade. I made my way through the porch and into the transept. I sat uncertainly, but gratefully, on one of the pews that lined the nave. As far as I could make out, no one had noticed me.

The hymn stopped. Wesley Toshack was in the pulpit. His skin tone had calmed down – it was now the colour of Mateus Rosé, the only wine I ever saw my father drink. Toshack owned his space like a prize fighter scoping out the ring. He began to deliver his sermon – some story set in Galilee and Judea, the point of which was lost on me. His voice, like his skin, had come down in tone. Although it carried easily, unamplified, throughout the space, it was measured and musical rather than the hectoring, brittle barrages of the day before.

The interior of the church was simple, with wooden pews and a flagstone floor. The temperature was so much lower than the outside air, I found myself shivering as the sweat condensed on my skin. The congregation was larger than I expected – maybe fifty heads. From what I could tell from the florid, balding pates and spun-coconut-macaroon hats, most of them were middle-aged or elderly. A sprightly congregant was beginning the collection – a ragged purple cloth bag was being passed along the rows. In the third row I saw Ash, or at least the back of her head. I was close enough to notice a mole just between her left shoulder blade and her neck.

The smell of seasoned wood and damp stone was in the air. Behind the altar there was a large stained-glass window showing Jesus suspended on the cross, with angels flitting rhapsodically in the middle distance. Although in this depiction nails clearly penetrated the Messiah's hands and feet, he didn't look as uncomfortable as you would expect. His expression suggested he was entirely at ease with his situation.

It was peaceful, sitting there. As I watched the sunlight push through the glass panels of the Crucifixion, tattooing patches and puddles of light on to the floor, I felt some of the weight that had been on my shoulders begin to lift slightly. My hangover likewise seemed to lose some of its force.

Toshack finished his sermon. There was another hymn, 'Onward, Christian Soldiers', which seemed to stir the congregation into a bit of a lather, with voices waxing martial and keen. When it finished, he began offering communion. One by one the congregation rose to kneel and be fed wafers and wine. The acoustics were sharp – I could hear Toshack whispering, like a stuck record, 'The body of Christ . . . the body of Christ.'

Ash was queuing with the other congregants. I had an urge to take communion myself, to atone and be blessed, but it passed, to be replaced by an urgent need to get out of the building before either Ash or her father noticed me. I had a vision of some bodged and embarrassing attempt at my recruitment into the fold — by either Toshack or Ash herself. At the same time, I imagined that my otherness, even my surliness, was a factor in me seeming to have some purchase on Ash's affections. I felt sure she wouldn't let a member of the fold anywhere near that provocatively moulded, poured-liquid body, that beckoning red mouth; yet I sensed that there was a need in her to transgress. Sitting at the back of her father's church wasn't going to help my cause.

I slipped out of the door, and took off around the town for half an hour. My hangover had miraculously lifted, so the minutes passed tediously rather than painfully. I bought a copy of the *News of the World* and a packet of cigarettes and sat down by the riverbank to smoke and read. But I found it hard to concentrate. Somehow the church — or the idea of the church — kept tugging at me.

I cautiously made my way back towards St Jude's. Neither voice nor music could be heard within. I edged into the building, and poked my head around the corner. It appeared to be deserted. I walked inside and sat in a pew at random, staring at the patches of sunlight. The feeling of peace I had experienced earlier returned.

I sat there in complete silence for maybe ten minutes. At one point I closed my eyes and offered up a prayer — but not to God. I had a sense instead that some part of my mind might find a way of forgiving some other part.

I found myself wondering about the church, and churches everywhere, and what they represented — what they *really* represented – and how there were thousands upon thousands of them, and how such effort and money had gone into them over nearly two millennia, all in the cause of a dream or a fantasy. Or *was* it a dream? Could so many people, some of them with brilliant minds, be so misguided?

I was about to rise and leave when I heard a slight noise. I turned and Ash was there, a few yards behind me, standing perfectly still as if afraid of startling me. Seeing me turn, she smiled and came and sat down beside me.

'This is a surprise.'

'Don't misunderstand,' I said.

'Meaning?'

'I've hardly been into a church in my life. I'm not into this stuff. I just like the quiet. The quiet and the light.'

'The light is special in here, isn't it? Like being inside a kaleidoscope.'

'I don't like sermons.'

'I get that.'

She lapsed into silence. But the peace I had enjoyed previously had dissipated. Conversation of some kind felt obligatory.

'You're a believer?' I said.

'After a fashion. Can I ask you something? If you're not a believer, why are you here?'

'I already told you.'

'Is there any more specific reason?'

I shook my head. I sensed Ash's gaze brushing my face like a searchlight.

'I heard about your mother, Adam.'

I turned and stared at her. She looked sad.

'What do you know about my mother?'

'Henry told me. Before my father and he fell out. Or

159

rather, he told my father. So I knew someone was coming down to the boat. Someone who was troubled.'

'What makes you think I'm troubled?'

'Anyone who watches his own mother die is going to be affected. You must be very distressed.'

I got up from the pew.

'I just had a hangover and needed a bit of cool air. I have to go.'

Ash reached out and touched the back of my hand. I recoiled.

'Are you trying to recruit me?'

'I'm trying to help. Don't you feel there's a weight that needs lifting? Something beyond grief? Henry said that you might have . . . if you had known more . . . about what was wrong with her.'

I took a step towards the door.

'I'm sorry if I've offended you,' said Ash, looking away. 'Do you still want to meet on Tuesday?'

'Sure.'

'OK.'

She looked up at me again, this time holding my gaze. She seemed to be asking me something, but I wasn't sure what.

'Look, Ash. I don't mean to be mysterious. It's just that I don't know you. You're just someone I keep bumping into.'

'OK. I overstepped.'

I looked up at the image of the hanging Christ. A long moment passed before I spoke again.

'You want to know the truth?'

'Only as much as you feel comfortable telling me.'

I searched my mind for what the truth actually was.

'I feel scared.'

'Of what?'

'I'm not sure.'

'Are you afraid for your future?'

'No. Not exactly. More of everything just . . . stopping. Now I know that it happens. Really, really happens. Lives ending. In the middle of breakfast. On an ordinary day. It makes everything seem so fragile. The whole living world, it . . . it's *disposable*. Temporary.'

Ash started playing with a small silver crucifix that hung round her neck on a slender chain.

'My father says God—'

'I don't want to hear about God. And don't tell me that Christians never die. Because they do. They just die in a cowardly way. They die not looking at things the way they are. Same as everyone else, filling their heads with shopping and sports and shuffling paper every day in an office. I can't do that any more. I can't sleep for thinking about it. Nothing cures it. It won't go away. It won't ever go away. Not unless you can make death go away. And you can't, however much you pretend.'

With that I left Ash behind me in the church, and walked out on to the pavement. I set off in the direction of the *Ho Koji*. As I walked, I could hear my footsteps echo in the air. Fading into nothing, and disappearing, each one, for ever.

Fourteen

It was Monday – the morning I had arranged to meet with Strawberry. I asked Henry if he wanted to join me, but he seemed unusally absorbed in that morning's mail. He was making pencil marks on a letter he had just opened. I noticed the crest of the local council heading it. Without looking up, he vaguely replied that he might come and join us a bit later.

Strawberry's shack was no more than five minutes' walk from the boat. There was no track leading to it – Henry had given me directions, but I got lost several times. I eventually found it in a clearing where a number of trees had been chopped down and the undergrowth cleared.

Henry had been harsh describing it as a shed. Certainly, it was small, but much sturdier and larger than a shed – perhaps twenty feet square, constructed of raw-looking planks. It had a pitched green tar roof. There was a pole erected on the roof, and hanging from it, limp in the still air, was a flag decorated with the black and white symbol of yin and yang. A narrow metal chimney stood parallel to the flagpost at the opposite corner.

There was a makeshift barbecue made out of old bricks and a rusty grill, along with a white-painted folding chair – now weathered into yellow – standing on the scrub outside. The shack had plastic-framed windows, which looked incongruous in such a rustic construction. There was no sign of curtains inside. There was an outhouse that I assumed held a toilet and perhaps a shower. From where I was standing, I couldn't see the door, so I walked round to what I presumed was the front. The door, made of rough pine, was aerosol-painted with the inscription COME IN! and a red, blurry heart about the size of a real heart. There was no knocker or bell, so I rapped on the small window that was set in the door.

The door swung open. Strawberry stood there, wearing a shapeless, billowing cream-coloured smock. Her feet were bare. She smiled and reached up – she was four or five inches shorter than me – to give me a kiss on the cheek.

'I'm glad you came. Wondered where you'd gone when we got up yesterday.'

'Took the bus. Didn't want to hang around. Didn't want to be a hassle for anyone.'

'You wouldn't have been. Having said that, we didn't get up till the afternoon.'

She beckoned me inside. I stepped across the threshold. The cabin was full of light. There was a smell of resin, and something like sour milk. I noticed an open carton of yoghurt standing by the sink, and presumed that was where the odour came from.

The interior was rudimentary. A futon was on the floor,

pushed up against the far wall, with a square of violently coloured Indian fabric on top. In the corner of the room there was a tiny kitchen area, and in front of that a couple of generously sized pillows. There was a trestle table with a some candles on it, a bookshelf and two tatty folding metal chairs. There were posters on the wall secured by drawing-pins – one an Escher print that she had presumably got from Troy. A tiny line of single type at the bottom identified it as 'When Falls the Coliseum'.

There were two more posters – one showing the phases of the moon, the other a Maxfield Parrish print of a mod-estly posed but naked pre-Raphaelite woman sitting with her legs pulled up to her chest on a rock, with the blue of the sea beneath her and the paler blue of the sky above. Other than a pine wardrobe, a chest of drawers, a pile of firewood, a wood-burning stove and her guitar, that was the whole thing.

Strawberry sat down on one of the cushions and indicated for me to do the same.

'What do you think of my crib?'

'I like it.'

I did, despite its rudimentary character and the nasty plas-tic windows. The light that came through the windows was dappled green. The shack was basic, even spartan, but held the space within it somehow very peacefully.

'Not too fancy?'

'Not so much. But it has a good air about it.'

'I think so. It's a place where you can just . . . sink into the moment. You know?'

She started coughing, as usual. I could see her ribcage struggle under the fabric of her smock. After around ten sec-onds the fit passed.

'Impurities are still coming out,' she said. 'It's a tough diet regime I'm following. Here, take a look.'

She picked up a dog-eared book from the table and passed it across to me. The words *Zen and the Macrobiotic Way* were written in a Japanese-calligraphy-style font.

'My boyfriend in California, Jerzy, he turned me on to this. I say he was my boyfriend, but really we just hung around together for a while – he used to get the most terrible headaches. Plagued him for years. He found out about this diet. His healer told him about it. Three days on it – well, it was hard. It is hard. But the headaches went. They never came back. And he'd tried everything up until then. You know? So he stayed on the diet. Said he never felt better in his life.'

'So what is it you're trying to cure?'

Strawberry looked at me as if I had asked a ridiculous question.

'It's not really about cure as such. It's about balance. The yin and the yang, you know?'

'Like the flag on the roof.'

'Exactly. And purity. It takes quite a lot of willpower.'

'Isn't it possible that it's making you ill?'

'Oh no. That's what Pattern says. I mean, I know it can look that way. To the untrained eye. But any good alternative practitioner will tell you: you're going to feel worse before you feel better.'

I noticed another book on the table. This one appeared to be about palm-reading. She followed my gaze, then pushed her cushion a bit closer to mine.

'Would you like me to read yours?'

'Are you any good at it?'

'People say I'm very in tune with that sort of thing. Of

course, it's not a science. But science is bullshit anyway, right?'

She beckoned for my hand. 'Don't be afraid.'

'I'm not afraid. It just seems a bit silly.'

I presented my left palm to her.

'Not that one. The right hand.'

'Why not the left?'

'The left hand is what you're born with. The right one is what you accumulate through life. For men, anyway. For women, it's the other way around.'

I gave her my right hand, and she rested it on her palm. I looked up at her and examined her face as she angled my palm slightly as if to get a better look. She appeared to be concentrating fiercely. The light came from behind her and gave her a blurry outline. It made her seem even more insubstantial.

She studied the creases and wrinkles for thirty seconds or so. I savoured the intimacy of her running her fingers over my skin.

'This crease is the life line.'

'How long have I got?'

'You'll make old bones. Don't worry about that. The line is substantial. But there's a break right here. Early on. Not in childhood, but not long ago.'

She showed me a wrinkle among what seemed to be a number of other random wrinkles.

'I can't see.'

'Not that one. This one.'

There was a line running along the top of my palm horizontally and a thick crease in the rough shape of a circle intersecting it about a fifth of the way up.

'The circle means depression or unhappiness.'

'I had a loss recently.'

'Someone close?'

'Yeah.'

'Well, it's written there.'

'What else is written?'

Strawberry laughed.

'Shit, I don't know. What do you want me to do, tell you if you're going to be a train driver when you grow up?'

'I thought that was the point of the whole thing.'

She concentrated again.

'You fall in love easily. And you get your heart broken easily. I know that because your heart line touches your life line. And you have a very deep, long head line. That means you're smart.'

'How many lines are there?'

'Heart, head, life and fate. This here, this is fate.' She indicated a line running south-west to north-east on my palm.

'What does my fate line say?'

'It's very deep. It means fate will play an important part in your life.'

'Meaning?'

'There's not much you can do about anything. So relax. It's out of your control.'

Strawberry dropped my hand.

'I guess you think it's all phoney, right?'

'I don't know.'

She reached out and picked a string on her guitar.

'You were good at the Fayre. Really good. What was that French song about?'

'It was about someone begging their lover not to leave them.'

'That never works,' I said, although I had no experience

167

whatsoever in the arena of love. I hadn't even had a proper girlfriend.

'Would you like me to sing you a song?'

I didn't say anything. I imagined that it would be embarrassing; it felt too intimate. But it seemed impolite to say so. Taking my silence as affirmation, she picked up her guitar.

'What would you like to hear?'

I shrugged.

She strummed a few chords, then started to sing 'Puff the Magic Dragon'. She looked at me as she sang it, and smiled. I tried to hold my eyes elsewhere – the whole thing was so unbearably intimate – but I kept flicking them back to her face. Towards the end of the song she began to cry. She leaned the guitar against the wall, and began another fit of coughing.

'Why did you cry?'

'When it says: dragons live for ever, but not so little boys. Don't you think that's just one of the saddest lines ever written?'

'I've never really thought about it.'

'It's a terribly unhappy song. All about loss.'

'I thought it was a kind of pothead anthem.'

'That too.'

'My mother used to sing it to me when I was a little boy. She could never remember all the words, so she used to hum a lot of it. But it helped me go to sleep.'

'Is it your mother that you lost?'

'I don't really want to talk about it.'

'Why don't you want to talk about your mother? What happened?'

I shifted on the cushion. There was nothing to support my back and I found myself perpetually off balance.

'She choked on something.'

'Shit!'

'I was in the room when it happened.'

'What did you do?'

'It's hard to talk about.'

'It's not good to keep stuff bottled up. Don't you think?'

'That's not what my dad seems to think. It isn't what my mum thought either.'

'Did you like her? Your mum?'

Moving branches outside produced shifting patterns of light inside.

'What kind of question is that?'

'I never liked my mother. She was a bitch.'

I felt shocked. I'd never heard anyone talk about their mother like that.

'My mother was nice. Nothing special. Boring really. But very nice.'

'How was she nice?'

'The usual ways. Fussing over me. Making me cups of tea. Worrying about me. Washing my clothes. Nagging. She was like all the other mums I knew. Just an ordinary parent. All pressed from the same mould.'

'Do you know that poem about your parents fucking you up? Not meaning to, but doing it all the same.'

'No.'

'Henry taught me it. My mum fucked me up. She was out screwing men half the time. Or in screwing men. I could hear her making out in the next room. This was like, when I was six, seven? Can you imagine your mum doing that?'

'Not really.'

'It's pretty disturbing. I couldn't work out what the noises were. I used to think there were ghosts in the next room.

'Cause my mum, she always said she couldn't hear anything. You know, when I asked her the next morning.'

'What about your dad?'

'He wasn't around so much. Not that he would have minded, I don't expect. It was the spirit of the times. Yeah. That's what he would always say, "the spirit of the times". My dad's not such a bad guy, though. He just had a habit of choosing the wrong women.'

'Where is he?'

'Oh, still around. Somewhere or other. He keeps in touch. When he feels like it.'

She got up and opened one of the windows. A slight breeze had arisen and I could hear the branches rustling. She sat back down again.

'I'm glad your mum was nice. And . . .'

'And what?'

The words came out with an edge. I stared at the floor. I could see splinters in it. 'I was just going to say I'm sorry that she's dead.'

'Right.'

'Do you feel guilty about it?'

'Sometimes.'

'Guilt's like poison. You got to get rid of that stuff. I'm sure you did all you could.'

'You weren't there.'

My voice came out edgy, harsh. Strawberry flinched slightly. But I couldn't quite stem the trickle of bile.

'Everyone's always sticking their nose in. Trying to be "sympathetic". It's just about making themselves feel better.'

As if to pacify me, Strawberry reached out to a white cardboard box sitting on the floor at arm's length.

'Don't be angry. Here. I've got some of those Greek cakes

I told you about.' She took a dusty white lump about the size of a table-tennis ball out of the box. 'They're made of almonds and honey. Too much sugar for me, but I think you'll like them.'

She sounded close to tears.

'Look,' I said, more softly. 'I know you meant well.'

'Forget about it. I'll shut up.'

'You see, it makes me . . . Thinking about it. It makes me want to . . . to . . .'

'Cry?'

'Vomit.'

It felt I had retched the word itself. Or at least that my stomach had rejected it, and it had come out involuntarily, leaving my mouth tasting bitter. I bit into the cake. It was sticky and floury and felt like cotton wool dipped in syrup.

'I know what that feels like. To think of something, and for it to make you ill,' said Strawberry.

'So maybe it's better to keep these things to yourself. Maybe it's better not to talk about them. Not to think about them.'

'You think that's healthy?'

The door to the shack opened a crack and Henry poked his head through.

'What in heaven and earth would you know about what's healthy?' he asked.

Fifteen

'Can I come in?'

'You're already in,' said Strawberry.

Henry pushed open the door, to reveal himself outlined by the timber frame, looking serious and puffing on his pipe. He was carrying a large cream-coloured canvas holdall.

He took the pipe out of his mouth and prodded the stem in the direction of Strawberry.

'Look at you. You're fading into nothing.'

'You're a water sign, Henry. I'm an air sign. I don't expect you to understand.'

'You're going to float away sooner or later. A blossom in the wind.'

Strawberry pulled her legs up under herself.

'What are you doing here anyway? You're usually writing at this time of day,' she said. 'In fact, come to think of it, you're *always* writing at this time of day.'

'I rather felt in the mood for a walk. Maybe to the lake. We could swim.' He held up the holdall. 'Towels. Swimsuits. And more. Refreshments.'

'I'd like a walk,' I said.

'What's going on, Henry?' Strawberry looked at him sideways as if suspicious.

'What makes you think there's something going on?'

'Because, like most lazy people, you're usually very careful to stick to your schedule. In case you sleep your life away.'

Henry nodded. He put down the holdall, extinguished his pipe, tapped out the tobacco on to the ground outside, and placed it in the right-hand pocket of his thin cotton pull-ons. Then he pulled the letter I'd seen earlier out of the same pocket and brandished it.

'It's finally happened. Was bound to sooner or later. They're trying to throw me off the reach.'

He stared at the letter, as if not sure what to do with it, then put it back in his pocket. He took a fat roll-up out of his other pocket, lit it and inhaled deeply. The aroma was unmistakable, a pungent reek. Strawberry grimaced and gestured impatiently towards the smoking joint. 'Not in here.'

Henry sighed, licked his fingers, extinguished it and stuck it behind his ear. His eyes were already red at the rims.

Strawberry touched him on the arm.

'Let me see the letter.'

'It's all in lawyer. You're not going to make much sense of it. They've set a date for a hearing at the end of August.'

'Could they win? What are the grounds?'

'They say I've broken the terms of the land lease, because I "concealed my criminal record". It was fifteen years ago! But they think it will play to the clause that I, quote, "conduct myself at all times with due decorum and appropriate

173

responsibility". They're going to need a lot more than that, though, if they're going to have any chance of success.'

'I guess they don't think drug smugglers are really of benefit to the local community,' said Strawberry, waving her hand around again to disperse the residual smoke. 'Which of course isn't strictly true.'

'It was one lid of weed. What the hell has that got to do with anything? It's Wesley Toshack that's behind it, him and and his greed, all gussied up as piety and community concern. I can't imagine how he found out about it. He is clearly a very assiduous and determined and dangerous man.'

'You'll be fine, Henry. It sounds like bullshit. You know your way around the law.'

'It is. I do. It's not going to wash. Still, I could do without it.'

'Why don't you just torch the fucking thing, Henry?' said Strawberry. 'The *Ho Koji*. It's insured up to the fundament. Take the money and run. You don't need this hassle. Buy a nice bungalow somewhere. You ain't Peter Fonda any more. Get a rock garden with a few fucking gnomes.'

'I'm not really a bungalow kind of person.'

He nodded towards the holdall.

'I'm not going to let the casual spite of small-minded people put a dent in this beautiful day. I'm heading for the lake. Coming?'

Strawberry turned to me.

'Wanna get wet?'

We followed Henry into the woods, trying to keep up with the long panther-lope of his legs. We walked for ten minutes, largely in silence – an open silence that asked nothing of us. I could hear small creatures, perhaps birds, tussling invisibly in the undergrowth. Tree branches screened out most of the sky, but the heat still penetrated right down to the ground.

We walked first in parallel with the river, and then veered off into another thicker sector of woodland. There was something magical about the landscape here. Soft green light shadowed the lush, thick grass, which was bedded with all manner of summer flowers growing wild. This part of the woods had a sense of being deserted – for ever untouched. It felt like we three were the only people that could ever possibly be there. I could feel the warm air sweet in my lungs.

'Can you feel it?' said Henry, stopping for a moment. It was the first thing he'd said since we'd started walking.

Strawberry and I caught up with him, then we all headed into the heart of the wood. The foliage became denser, and the overhanging leaves thicker. Although no path was obvious, Henry clearly knew where he was going, taking sudden angles of trajectory to the left or right. After we had been walking for maybe twenty minutes, we came to a large clearing.

'We are now precisely in the middle of the wood,' said Henry.

There was a pond, or perhaps more accurately a small lake, about a hundred yards across. There were dozens of water lilies suspended on it. Occasionally a breeze that had somehow penetrated the trees corrugated the surface. There were dragonflies punctuating the air, and butterflies.

Henry chose a soft-looking patch of grass and sat down on it, then beckoned for us to do the same. He reached into the canvas holdall and took out a bottle of red wine and a corkscrew. He opened it and poured it into a metal cup which he had also retrieved from his bag. He handed it to me.

I took a deep draught. It was thick, almost sticky, and held the tang of liquorice in its aftertaste.

'Aren't you having any?' I said.

'I'll stick with this for today.'

Henry removed the joint from behind his ear and relit it. I inhaled the fragrant smoke.

'Can I have a toke?'

'I don't think your father would consider it very responsible of me to offer my nephew marijuana.'

'So when did personal responsibility become one of your guiding principles in life?' said Strawberry.

Henry looked at her steadily. 'People can change.'

'Can they?'

'Aren't you trying to change yourself?'

'No. I'm trying to *be* myself. That's different.'

'I'm not sure that's true.'

'Shut up, Henry. Give the boy a toke if that's what he wants. Just stop pretending you give a shit about what other people do or don't do.'

Henry passed me the joint. I took a deep hit on it. I had smoked dope before, several times. It wasn't a big deal as far as I was concerned. I fought back a cough, leaned against a tree and inhaled again, deeply, a few more times.

I stared at the smooth surface of the pond, waiting for the drug to take effect. I could see a collection of tiny insects on the surface, with four legs spread like an X, and two small ones at the front. In the centre was a body the colour and shape of a canoe. The insects were tiny. What fascinated me was that they were walking on water, tiny dimples made in the surface tension by their thin, spindly legs. Not an easy stride – it was more like twitching, sending out violent ripples, then holding still again, balanced perfectly on the surface. I pointed to them.

'What are they'?

Henry squinted. '*Aquarius remigis*. The water strider, or the Jesus bug. Quite a spectacle.'

I watched as they skittered across the water's surface.

'They communicate with each other by the ripples. At least during breeding season. Those ripples are like our words.'

'I wonder what they're saying.'

'Probably praying,' he said.

'What would they pray for?'

'For the water to hold them up, I dare say.'

I took another toke.

'What do they eat?'

'Dead dragonflies, among other things. Ugliness consumes beauty. A little-known rule of nature. That's probably enough, Adam. It's heavyweight shit. Industrial-strength. Lebanese black.'

Henry took the joint from me, sucked out a final puff and made as if to throw it into the wood.

'For Christ's sake,' said Strawberry, rising sharply and grabbing the stub out of his hand. She extinguished it in the lake. 'Haven't you been reading about the forest fires? This undergrowth is like kindling.'

Now I could feel the dope affecting me. A surge of energy pulsed up my spine. My head was buzzing.

We sat there, the three of us, staring at the pool. The light had shifted. It was a shade of crystalline grey now.

Henry was right about the dope. It was far more potent than anything I'd tried before. Waves of disorientation threatened to shift me from my mental pivot. I wasn't sure if it was enjoyable or not. I felt on the edge of something, or at a crossroads. As if I could go either way, towards a kind of bliss or a state of paranoia.

The landscape around us appeared to be changing. I felt the ground soft underneath me, and looked down to see grass scattered with daisies. Little yellow faces with white frills. As I stared at them, transfixed – were they smiling? – something peculiar began to happen. It was as if time had speeded up. It seemed that I could see the grass grow, then rot and fall into the earth. From the compost more grass grew and decayed and fell.

The trees around me were doing likewise – palpably growing. It seemed suddenly as if everything was in motion, all the time, dying and regenerating. I could see the air move, as if in waves, and, high above, the spinning of the sun was apparent. It seemed to be darkening in colour, reaching a deeper and deeper red. I felt it would soon turn to black. I was suddenly anxious.

'Don't be afraid,' said Henry pleasantly.

'But everything's changing,' I said, as the rustle and thrum of the endless life and death around us filled my ears.

'Let's swim,' he said. 'It will freshen you up.'

He rose and I joined him, unsteady on my feet.

'Where are we going?' I said.

'Where are *you* going?' said Henry. 'We each travel alone.'

'I've no idea,' I said, feeling afraid again.

'Me neither,' said Henry. 'I'm grateful for that.'

He handed me my swimming trunks and I tried awkwardly and unsuccessfully to pull off my trousers. I didn't have any inhibitions about Strawberry, presumably because of the joint, but she had disappeared behind a tree anyway to get changed.

'But surely we're going somewhere?' I said, trying to stand on one leg in order to disentangle the other trouser leg from my foot.

'Why?' said Henry.

'There'd be no point in getting up in the morning if there wasn't some purpose.'

'Is that so?' said Henry.

I finally removed my trousers and pulled on my swimming trunks.

'Yes, that's so,' I said.

Henry, who had, without me noticing, taken off all his clothes, indicated the bank of the lake.

'You can learn a lot from water.'

He reached into his bag. To my surprise, he took a small toy sailboat out of it. I started to laugh. It struck me suddenly as the funniest thing in the world.

'Mary Poppins!' I said. 'Look, Strawberry. Henry is Julie Andrews. Get the umbrella out, Henry. The one with the parrot.'

There was still no sign of Strawberry, however. Henry ignored me and placed the boat on the surface of the water. He took out a small box which had a lever on it and a switch and a small light. He flicked the switch and the light came on. Then he gave the boat a push. A motor was engaged. It headed off towards the centre of the lake.

'I find this extraordinarily restful for some reason,' said Henry. He moved the lever on the box, and the boat responded. Then he turned the boat entirely round and it headed in our direction. It left a churning wake of milky white water.

'Isn't it lovely?' said Henry.

I had to admit – once my laughter had exhausted itself –

that it was, somehow, a beautiful thing to see. I had always liked to fly a kite, and watching the boat gave me a similar feeling as when I sent up my box kite in the local rec.

'Do you want a turn?'

I took the box out of his hands and started steering the boat. It made a low puttering sound that was barely audible, but somehow pleasant. I took the boat around in circles.

'Round and round,' I said. 'Round and round.'

'Going nowhere,' said Henry.

He looked over at the trees where Strawberry was changing.

'Strawberry! Are you OK?'

'I'll just be a minute.'

'I've launched the boat.'

'I'm coming. Just wait.'

Henry turned back to me and watched me steer for a while. Then he took the box back. I watched silently. All traces of anxiety had evaporated now.

'Look at it. What is that pattern of water behind the boat?' he said.

'It's called a wake. Awake. I'm awake!'

'Is the wake pushing the boat?'

'It's just bubbles. Bubbles and foam. Foamy bubbles.'

'Where's it headed?'

I gazed at the path the little yacht was taking. It appeared to be aiming for a small section of bank next to a large plane tree, overhung with a carapace of leaves stained the deepest of greens. I pointed to the spot. As soon as I did, the boat changed direction, suddenly moving away to the west, towards an entirely different spot on an adjacent bank.

'The boat is determined by the course of the boat. Not by the wake. And not by what you happen to assume is the destination.'

Strawberry emerged from behind a tree. I had not seen her this exposed before. She was little more than bare bones. Her ribs stuck out from underneath the line of her lemon-coloured bikini top, and her hipbones were clearly visible above the waistband of her pants.

'Tell him what point you're trying to make, Henry.'

Henry looked round. I could see that he was as shocked as I was by her appearance. But the expression – was it horror? Fear? – that briefly flickered in his features quickly disappeared, and he became calm again.

'It is the now that creates the then, is all I'm saying. All that is now in the past was created in the present.'

Passages memorized from my history books drifted into my head. The buzzing in my head had stopped and now my mind felt extraordinarily clear.

'The First World War was caused by the assassination of the Archduke Franz Ferdinand in Sarajevo. The Second World War was caused by the failure of the Treaty of Versailles. The assassination of President Kennedy was caused by a lone nut.'

'Trying to explain the present by the past is refusing to explain it at all,' said Henry. 'It's like driving a car using only your rear-view mirror. People are always looking over your shoulder to see what you should do. You want the past to tell you what to do. Like children with their parents.

'The universe began with a now-moment. It began with a big bang. In the beginning was a now. And there have only been nows ever since. The Big Bang is still happening.'

'Stretches your head,' said Strawberry, tentatively climbing into the water.

'Now and now and now and now. Now! Leaving the past behind it. Like the wake the boat. The past doesn't matter.'

Strawberry was swimming out towards the boat, which

was moving in her direction. She picked up a leaf from the surface of the pond and threw it on to the ripples that the boat was throwing out. The ripples continued to appear to travel outwards. The leaf stayed in exactly the same place, simply moving up and down slightly with the swell.

'Now. Let's swim.'

Henry threw himself into the lake and surfaced spitting water and laughing. Strawberry beckoned me in. I jumped, bombing, making a huge splash. For some reason – it might have been the effect of the joint – I felt closer to Henry and Strawberry at that moment than I ever had to my parents.

I felt weightless. But it was more than the lift of the water. I didn't know if it was Henry's words, or the joint, or the magic of the wood. But I had the strangest feeling, a feeling I couldn't remember having had for a very long time.

I felt happy.

The three of us swam close together. Strawberry reached out her hand to me, and I took it, treading water. Henry took my other hand, and joined hands with Strawberry. We floated in a circle. Then Henry let go.

'The thing is not to be afraid of the depths.'

He dived. I saw his undulating figure, distorted by the moving water, his legs kicking, down, down. Then he disappeared from view entirely.

Strawberry let go of my hand. We didn't speak. At least a minute passed. Henry had not reappeared.

Strawberry began to look nervous. She started shouting Henry's name.

But there was no sign of him. Her anxiety transmitted itself to me. I began to wonder if the letter about the houseboat, combined with the effects of the narcotic, had unhinged him in some way. That he had decided, madly, to end it all.

'Henry! Henry!'

Nothing. Strawberry looked around wildly. She began to cry.

'*Henry!*'

At that moment Henry, who must have been gone nearly two minutes, burst out of the mirrored surface of the lake, only feet where from where we were floating. He seemed barely out of breath.

'The pearl divers of the Pacific taught me that. It's not as difficult as——'

But he was cut off by the Strawberry throwing herself at him, scratching, punching, screaming.

Henry did not react, absorbing the punches. Eventually she ran out of energy, and Henry held her. She wept silently. Embarrassed, I struck back for the shore.

I wrapped myself in a towel and waited for them to join me. Strawberry began to swim back first. When she hit the bank, she headed without a word back to her changing spot behind the tree.

Henry arrived a minute or so later. He pulled a towel over his shoulder, came and sat next to me.

'I'm sorry about that, Adam. It was just a silly prank. I thought Strawberry had more faith in me.'

'You were showing off.'

'Yes, I suppose so. I'm the most terrible egotist some-times.'

We sat there silently for a while.

'Shouldn't she see a doctor?' I said.

'There is no way that's going to happen. Short of physically dragging her to a hospital, she's going to go through this diet, whatever it takes. She believes it's going to make her not merely well, but enlightened. I've tried to convince her otherwise, but she takes no notice of me. Why should she? She thinks she's exercising her free will, but I think she's in the grip of something she doesn't understand.'

He looked at me, but he seemed far away.

'What shall I do, Adam?'

I looked blankly back at him. I had no idea what to do. The drug focused my mind to a single, clarifying insight.

I didn't know a single thing about people.

Henry was looking past me, as if he had drifted off again.

'I expect she'll be all right. I thought she was looking a little better today. Don't you? She's put on a bit of flesh?'

To me it seemed that she was frailer than ever. I knew Henry knew that too.

'She had a difficult childhood,' he said.

He reached over to his cotton trousers, and fished out the letter he had brandished in the cabin. He read through it again.

'Why do they really want you out, Henry?'

'People can't stand the idea of other people living life differently from them. They hate it, because their lives are miserable and they're envious. It was different ten years ago. There was a different music in the air. Now we're retreating back into ourselves. Everyone, everywhere. Into our fortresses. Into our prisons. The prisons we build for ourselves. It's the new zeitgeist.'

'What's a zeitgeist?'

'The spirit of the times, Adam. The spirit of the times.'

It was only at that moment that I understood why Henry and Strawberry worried about one another so much.

Sixteen

The next morning, I showered, sunbathed for an hour, then dressed and went downstairs. Henry, as usual, was hammering away at his typewriter. I looked in on him as I headed out to meet Ash in the village.

'Thanks for yesterday, Henry. It will stay with me a long time.'

Henry looked up and gave me his big, brown-toothed smile. His front incisors reminded me of minature Chiclets.

'I'm glad. I get the impression you haven't enjoyed yourself very much recently. Just don't tell Raymond I got you undone on Leb. I doubt he would approve.'

'Ray's an idiot.'

'You're an idiot. Raymond loves you.'

'You don't know him.'

'Apparently, neither do you.'

'I just wish he wasn't so pissed off all the time.'

'He's lost his wife. What's he got left? You're his world.'

'He couldn't wait to get rid of me.'

'He wasn't coping. Give him some leeway.'

'If you say so.'

'I do.'

'He's jealous of you, you know.'

'I'm jealous of him.'

'Of Ray? Why?'

'Because he has a son.'

I noticed some official-looking papers spread on his desk, alongside the letter he had shown us yesterday. He followed my gaze.

'Are you worried?' I said. 'Do you think they might win?'

'These people keep going. Grinders. Eye on one point in the future. Stuck in joyless channels of purposefulness. Holy wars of greed and acquisition. But they're not shifting me. Christ, this is all . . .' He looked around him, at the river, at the boat. 'This is all I've got. This and my book.'

'And Strawberry.' I checked my watch.

'I should be going. I have to meet someone.'

Henry's eyes took on a mildly cynical cast.

'Ash the Pash has got her hooks into you, has she not?'

'How do you know I'm meeting Ash?'

'Who else would you be meeting?'

'I don't think she's as bad as you seem to believe. She seems very nice to me. And she's very . . .'

'Pretty? All that glisters, et cetera. I'd give her a wide berth.'

I felt a sudden prickle of indignation.

'You seem content to let Strawberry make her own mistakes. Perhaps you could extend the same courtesy to me. "A fool who persists in his folly will become wise." That's what you said, isn't it?'

Henry looked chastened.

'You're quite correct. I am hoist on my own petard. Go forth and prosper. Maybe you're right. Maybe she's not what I think she is. And she's got that certain something, hasn't she? I can't deny that. That mouth. Or is it in her eyes? The mockery. The intimation of corruption.'

Apparently I was now dismissed, because Henry returned to his typing. I paused, then, unable to contain my excitement any longer, I ran across the gangplank and out to the bike, which I had carelessly left thrown on its side next to the barbecue.

I arrived in Lexham fifteen minutes late, red-faced and panting with effort. Ash was sitting on the bench by the clock, holding a half-drunk bottle of milk. She looked up from a patch on the ground that she had been examining.

'Sorry I'm late. Henry was giving me a lecture on how you were best avoided.'

'Don't you think ants are fascinating?'

Her gaze returned to the ground, and I followed it. Ants were marching in a line, carrying leaves, shreds of grass. Ash put her foot in front of the line, and the ants marched across her shoe. She stared at them for a few seconds, then shook off the ants. Unable to dislodge all of them, she stamped her foot on the ground, crushing six or seven of the marching insects. She turned and smiled innocently.

'Henry dislikes me purely because of my father. And because I don't take him as seriously as he takes himself.'

She finished the milk, in a long gulp. I watched the undulations of her throat. Her lips were stained with white.

I sat down next to her, about a foot away. I stared at the

ground where she had been staring, and kicked at the earth, careful not to destroy any more ants.

'Hot,' I said.

'So everyone says,' said Ash.

'I haven't worked out my small-talk yet.'

I kicked a little more dirt up, but didn't raise my head.

'Shall we go and get a drink from the shop?' said Ash. 'I'm still thirsty, and you must be parched.'

She touched the edge of my mouth lightly with her index finger.

'The skin is cracked.'

She left the finger there for a moment longer, then removed it and put it momentarily to her own mouth, disturbing the thin film of milk. Then she let her hand drop, stood up and, without waiting for me, began walking towards the shops. She tossed the empty milk bottle into a bin. I rose, caught up and fell in step. I could still feel the imprint of her fingertip. We were walking towards the sun. I blinked and shaded my eyes, despite the amber shade afforded by my Foster Grants. I could see the spire of the church behind the parade of shops. Words were jumbled inside me somewhere that I couldn't untangle enough to speak, or even form into thoughts.

'You never answered that question. When we met before, with Henry. What it was like having a vicar for a father?'

'I don't know. I've never known anything else. What does your dad do?'

'He works in a shoe shop.'

'What's he like?'

'He's all right.'

We reached the newsagent. We were the only customers. The same matronly-looking woman I had seen the last time I had come into town was behind the counter.

'Hello, Ashley.'

'Mrs Wintergreen.'

'How's your dad? Fighting the good fight?'

'Doing his job.'

Mrs Wintergreen turned to me.

'Who's this? I've seen him before, I'm sure of it.'

'This is Adam. Adam, this is Mrs Wintergreen.'

I nodded, and examined the tray of sweets on the counter. I picked out a bag of space dust and a handful of liquorice chews.

'You're not from around here, are you, young man?'

'No.'

'He's staying with the notorious Henry Templeton,' said Ashley.

'On that boat?'

'He's my uncle.'

Ash selected a bottle of fizzy orange and a bag of crisps.

'He's a bit peculiar, your uncle, if you want to know what people around here think,' said Mrs. Wintergreen.

Ash turned to me. 'Henry's controversial.'

'I'm gathering that.'

'I don't mind it personally, but there are those that think his boat's something of an eyesore. Some say it's not legal,' added Mrs Wintergreen.

Ash took a note out of her pocket and laid it on the counter. Mrs Wintergreen put it in the till and handed her some change.

'You get all sorts turning up there, I hear. Not that your uncle isn't very pleasant in person. I've always found him to be charming. He's very well spoken, isn't he? Hasn't he been to Oxford or something?'

Ash picked up the fizzy orange and I gathered my sweets.

I tried to give her some money but she waved it away. We turned towards the door. Mrs Wintergreen called after us.

'It's just that we're very normal kind of people around here. Some of them that go there . . . you know. You hear things about drugs and what-have-you.'

'Goodbye, Mrs Wintergreen.'

'Say hello to your dad from me, Ashley.'

Outside, Ash dropped a few coins into the plaster model of a blind girl with a slot cut in her head for donations. The sky was absolutely clear, not even the vapour trail of a jet. Ash unscrewed the top of the fizzy orange and offered it to me. I took it and drank. It was warm and very sweet. The bubbles went up my nose and I sneezed. She pulled open the crisps and began delicately guiding them to her mouth, where she somehow chewed on them without making any noise. I could see spots of white salt on her lower lip.

'Why do you keep looking at my mouth?'

'I was just thinking how strange mouths are. Teeth-lined holes in the face. I was trying to imagine what an alien might think the first time it saw a mouth.'

'Has Henry been getting you high?'

'No. Well, yes. He did, actually. But that wasn't what made me think of it.'

I passed the bottle back to her.

'Do people hate Henry?' I asked as Ash took another swig.

'It's more that they can't make sense of him. They think he's got money – you know, because of his accent – so they can't make out why he would want to live on a boat rather than in a nice house. He's middle-aged and behaves like a young person. He's not married, he has no children. People are bound to question.'

'What do you think of him'? I asked as we continued to wander aimlessly down the main street.

'I don't know,' said Ash. 'I don't really know him. I wonder about him. Like what he's doing with that beautiful, skinny girl that's always at the boat.'

'Strawberry.'

She laughed. 'Yes. Her. Have you got to know her at all?'

'A little.'

Her eyebrows lifted. 'Really?'

'Not like that. She's just sort of . . . weird. In a nice way.'

'What's she got to do with Henry?'

I hesitated. Ash caught the hesitation.

'Don't worry, I'm not fishing for incriminating evidence. I'm just curious.'

'I'm not quite sure. They know each other from America.'

'OK. Well. That tells me a lot.'

'That's all I know.'

Ash looked at me sceptically. But she had clearly decided to let it go.

'What do *you* make of your Uncle Henry?'

'He's interesting. Not many people I meet are interesting.'

We had reached the borders of the little town, where the houses gave way to fields and trees.

'I read somewhere that tree roots go out as far as the trees go up,' I said, touching the bark of an elm.

'My father has a theory about that,' said Ash.

'He has a theory about trees?'

'Everything that brings life is below the surface. He says. Shall we go for a walk?'

'Isn't that what we're doing?'

'Somewhere nice, though.'

There was a small footpath that led to the river. Ash guided me down some ancient stone steps, beaten into a dull shine by footfall. The river was torpid. Leaves were held by the surface tension, the water, it seemed, too lazy to move them.

A comfortable silence had grown between us. I chewed thoughtfully on the liquorice tang of a Black Jack; I had not outgrown my taste for penny sweets. Perhaps when I did I would be finally grown up. The sounds of the town had receded to the occasional, faint rev of a car engine in the distance. The areas on the border of the river grew more thickly wooded. Ash stopped at a gap in the bushes and trees, and turned into it. I followed her.

There were nettles and thorny bushes tearing at my calves. I winced. A wild-rose tendril grabbed at my T-shirt. Ash reached over to unpick it, bringing herself close.

A thought without words came into my head, pure, like a sheet of light. I kissed her. She returned my kiss. She tasted of orange Corona and salt from the crisps. She leaned closer so that our bodies were touching. She brought her arms round behind me and pressed her hands against the small of my back. They felt so faint, like they were made of light, or shadow. She moved them under my T-shirt, cool against my bare skin. We kissed for minutes on end. All thought stopped. We became only physical. The sun came in sharply defined points through the trees. I could feel the outline of her breasts against my torso. The blunt stubs of her nipples. I could hear, somewhere in the distance, the lapping of water.

Then, as if on a predetermined signal, we separated. I looked away, not quite knowing what to do. She took my hand and held it. It felt tiny but somehow frighteningly strong.

Seventeen

The next morning, Henry handed me a letter that the postman had delivered. The postmark was Yiewsley.

I had never known Ray to write a letter to anyone. The letter was folded neatly into a buff business envelope. The paper was thin and coarse. Ray had written in a ballpoint pen, and his handwriting was childish, hard to decipher. There were smudges and blots.

Dear Adam

It was nice to hear from you at the shop the other day. I am sorry I was so busy and couldn't have a nice chinwag.

It has been raining a bit here for a few days, on and off. Makes quite a change after all the sunshine. People's feet smell worse in the summer. Sometimes it's hard to bear. I believe some people don't change their socks for days on end.

I have been working hard in the shop. We have a new area

manager, he is difficult. But I keep my nose clean and my head down. I can't see that he would have much to complain of, since I have worked here now for 21 years and have never had a day off sick!

I hope you are having a nice time down there with your uncle. I sometimes wander if I did the right thing packing you off like that! It being a hard time for you and everything as it is for me too. Anyway, not long to go now before your back. You must work hard and pass your exams. Your mother always thought you could do well if you made an effort.

Here, I mostly come home from work, make myself some supper. Nothing fancy, the old favourites like cheese on toast or baked beans. Mrs Gibbons sometimes brings me some soup, she has been very kind. Then I watch the old goggle box. Rots you're brain I expect.

Are you looking after yourself? I am not very good at this sort of thing. But every day I go in your room and make sure it is tidy. Which of course it is! I even give it a dust sometimes!

Well, that's all from me. I will see you in September.
Dad

For the rest of that day, I could not shake the image of Ray attending my empty room, a feather duster in one hand, the pointless rearranging of this book or that pillow. In my mind his face shifted, one moment clenched like a fist and focused on the task in hand, the other entirely empty of expression. In this last vision, which scared me, light poured into his eyes but found nothing there to illuminate.

*

When I started my revision, instead of heavy-heartedly grinding through my History, I sailed through it. Names, dates, places – they just stuck. Poincaré. The great naval race. Lord Kitchener. The Kaiser. The Siegfried Line.

My mind felt as absorbent as the parched, baked earth. Even though memories of Ash teased and tugged at me – flashes of her face, the compressions of her lips, the taste of orange and salt – I could concentrate perfectly. Ash had to work today – she occasionally waitressed in the town café, or 'buttery' as it was called – but I had arranged to see her again tomorrow.

By the time noon arrived, it occurred to me that I had not seen or heard Henry. Nevertheless, I was aware of movement on the boat below me. The clatter of cutlery, or the slight shift of furniture. I climbed down the steps.

Strawberry was in the galley area. She appeared to be preparing some kind of drink, and barely looked round when I walked into the room, even though I had taken care to make sufficient noise to alert her to my presence.

I coughed, and muttered a hello. Her beauty still frightened me. She looked round. She smiled, but traces of sadness lingered on her face.

'Henry's not here. He's gone into Bristol. Do you want to try this? It's wheatgrass. You pulp it, sieve it and add a little rainwater.'

I took the glass she held out to me, full of browny-green foaming liquid, and sipped. It was foul.

'Better than I expected,' I said.

She took the glass back, carefully wiped the rim with a clean white cloth, then took a draught. She grimaced.

'Being diplomatic doesn't come naturally to you.'

'If you want me to be honest, it's disgusting.'

'It takes a while to get used to, is all.'

I sat down at the table. She sat down next to me. I looked at the skin on her hands. The veins showed through, the thickness of woollen threads.

'Discipline is more important than pleasure. I've done the pleasure thing. I've taken that to the limit. This is why macrobiotics has been so good for me. I've felt so much more alive. You know? It's like I'm getting close to the essence.'

'Is it like calorie-counting?'

'Oh no. Not at all. Do you know about the yin and the yang?'

'Not much.'

'Suzuki says that all the physical and spiritual diseases come from consuming too much yin. Basically potassium. Or too much yang. Sodium. Usually it's too much yin. He says grain is the basic food, because it has the same five-to-one balance that you find in blood. So what I'm doing is increasing my intake of yang, which is salt, and taking in as little yin as possible.

'Some steamed green vegetables. Seaweed is good. It isn't just about physical health. It takes you into a place in your head that you've never been before. You know? Not even drugs can take you there. You should stay away from that shit Henry gave you, by the way.'

'I don't think it did me any harm. It was sort of interesting.'

Strawberry didn't seem to hear me. Her eyes, although tired, were alive. Then suddenly the light in them guttered. She yawned. The sadness seemed to gain the upper hand again.

'The diet takes a lot out of you at first. It takes a while. You're getting the poisons out of your body. So until you can get the balance right, until you can get pure, then you're going to feel worse before you feel better.'

'Right.'

'Are you enjoying yourself here, Adam?'

It seemed I had shown sufficient interest in her regime to merit some of Strawberry's attention, which otherwise – it then struck me – rarely seemed to move away from herself.

'I don't know.'

'What do you think of your Uncle Henry? Still think he's a queen?'

'Obviously not.'

'I think he cares about you.'

'He seems a good person.'

'No.' Strawberry's tone became very insistent. 'He's not good. Henry is *enlightened*. That is very different.'

I said I didn't understand.

'He says – what is it? I can't remember. Oh yes: "Goody-goodies are the enemies of virtue." Or something like that. Confucius apparently. Or some Chinese guy or other. It's a Zen trip. He told me he lives a "perpetually uncalculated life in the present". He's spontaneous. He's innocent. The thing that all the rest of us lost long ago. In making our Devil's bargain. He helps so many people. But he's suffered so much. It's made him who he is – but there are scars. I don't know who he is. Henry would say . . . what *would* he say? Yeah. That no one knows who they are. That you are too close to yourself to see yourself. And that's completely fine.'

She paused.

'I love him. Not in the way you think. But I do love him.'

Strawberry touched the back of my hand. She took a swig of her drink. It left a greenish crust over her lip, like mould.

I noticed there was a pale soft moustache underneath. Then I saw that there was a kind of downy furze all over her face. You could only see it if it caught the light properly.

'Why do you drink that stuff?' I indicated the empty glass.

'I told you. It helps to purify.'

'Why would you want to be pure?'

She made no reply, as if it was too stupid a question to reply to.

'How did you meet Henry?'

'I was hitchhiking. He picked me off the side of the road. I didn't have anywhere to go. I was lost. He took me in.'

I waited for her to continue, but Strawberry's train of thought seemed to get derailed before it reached the expected destination. She was often vague and abstracted. She gazed out of the window and stretched her limbs.

'That's not true, though?'

Strawberry stopped gazing out of the window, and regarded me steadily.

'Isn't it?'

I held her gaze unblinkingly.

'You're his daughter.'

Her eyes gave away nothing.

'Who told you that?'

'No one told me. I worked it out.'

'Was it Henry?'

'No.'

'Are you sure?'

'I guessed.'

She looked sceptical. Without speaking again, she arranged herself on the floor in the lotus posture.

She closed her eyes. She did not open them again. She just sat there, not moving.

'Are you OK?'

She didn't answer.

Weary of whatever game it was she was playing, I returned to the sun deck and my revision.

When I emerged a few hours later, Strawberry had gone and Henry had returned. He was at his typewriter, attacking the keys with such ferocity that I thought he was bound to break the thing. He didn't look up as I entered, but he stopped typing.

'My fingers are hurting. I need a break. I think I'm going to have a swim. Want to join me?'

'Why didn't you tell me that Strawberry was your daughter?'

He swung himself round in his chair to face me. He looked grave, but not discomfited.

'How did you work it out?'

'That phrase you use, "the spirit of the times". Strawberry said her father always used it.'

'I told Strawberry you'd guess. But she insisted.'

'You mean it was her idea to keep it secret?'

'Absolutely. Did you talk to her about it?'

'I tried. She more or less ignored me.'

'Please don't think badly of her. She's trying to work through some difficult stuff.'

'Why doesn't she want me to know that you're her father?'

'She says I have to earn it. I told you she had a difficult childhood. It was difficult partly because of me. Largely because of me, perhaps. For a long time she wouldn't acknowledge me as her father. That's one of the reasons she changed her name –

though why she chose something so childish as an alternative, I cannot quite tell. However, over the last year or so we have become somewhat reconciled. But there are still — what would you say? Issues. She says that when I have shown her that I can be a proper father, she will allow me to call her my daughter. To go public, if you will. But until then, we have to keep up this fiction that we are unrelated.'

'What did you do with her when she was a child?'

'To be honest, Adam, I'm not really comfortable talking to you about that. I think that information needs to come from Strawberry. If I give you my side of things, she will think I am pre-empting her. I cannot afford to take that chance — not now that we are close to finding an even keel again. So forgive me. She may share that knowledge with you in good time. She may not. I don't know. She is in many ways a closed book to me.'

'You've been lying to me all this time.'

'I haven't been entirely truthful. That's not quite the same thing.'

'Why should I believe anything you say now?'

'You don't have to. But whether you do or not, it is the truth. I hope before you return to London, you will find that out. Whether it will make you any more pleased with me, I do not know. My behaviour was regrettable. But I had no choice.'

He reached into his pocket and brought out a packet of Luckies. He held it out to me.

'Cigarette?'

Half of me wanted to take the packet and throw it in his face. But the other half of me — the half that believed in Henry, even, perhaps, loved him — prevailed. I took the cigarette. He lit it for me and I inhaled.

'You won't say anything to Raymond about this, will you?'

'Why not?'

'Because then Strawberry will think I broke my promise. I can't do that. Strawberry will hold it against me. And she already has a lot to hold against me.'

'I can't keep it a secret for ever.'

'I know. I'll talk to her. She can't keep this up for ever, either. Asking me to prove myself. But then again, she is a very wilful girl.'

He paused, and looked out of the window. His stare was hard and focused, as if he was inspecting something very closely. But there was nothing there. Then his gaze softened, and he turned back to me.

'So. What about that swim?'

I changed into my trunks, but when I came back down to the lower deck I saw that Henry had already stripped off and thrown himself into the river. His skin was a little loose and pocked on the arms. He beckoned to me as I stood on the bank, nervous of the shock of cold water.

'What's the temperature like?'

'Not too bad.'

'I don't believe you.'

'I could tell you more. Or you could just get in.'

I jumped. The river moved sluggishly along, tar-like almost, but the shock was crisp and enlivening. I struck out to where Henry floated. When I reached him, his attention was on something under the surface of the water. He indicated with his hand. A spray of iridescent droplets fell from his arm, were caught by the sun, and made a curtain of rainbow colours in the air.

'Where does the rainbow go when the water disappears?' he said.

He pointed at a spot in the water. Just under the surface was a small group of fish darting in oblique angular patterns. Gunmetal grey, they weren't particularly beautiful. But the patterns they made as they moved together in synchronization were fascinating.

'How does each know what the other is doing? Or is about to do?' I said.

'I have absolutely no idea. Marvellous, though, isn't it?'

I reached out to grab one. They swam away. Henry laughed.

'Like trying to catch yourself.'

I flushed my face with a handful of water. My body was warming up.

'Shall we swim?' said Henry. But instead of striking out, he turned and floated on his back and started talking to the sky.

'I have this dream of water. I dream of a river like this, silver and gold at twilight, that I swim along for hours. For days. For ever. It runs through empty space. This dream I have – I always wake from it happy. Perhaps the only time I feel completely that way.'

'Are you unhappy?'

Henry dipped his head under the water and brought it out again, shaking it to dislodge the water. He wiped his eyes with his hand, scattering droplets on to the surface.

'Happiness, unhappiness. They go together. All of a piece. You can't have up without down, or heads without tails.'

'There's no escape then.'

'You can learn how to not make it worse. You can work out how not to rub salt into your own wounds.'

'Is that what Strawberry's doing?'

'It's what people do.'

I began to swim, using first crawl, then breaststroke. Henry turned over on his stomach and drew up alongside me. He was a powerful swimmer, but so was I. Both using breaststroke at a casual, easy rate, we swam along with the flow. Henry's naked behind was intermittently illuminated by the sun, then, submerged, distorted into a kaleidoscope of pinks and browns by the flowing water.

After a while we came to a bank where a young family – a mother, a father and a young girl about five or six years old – were picnicking. Henry turned and floated on his back, seemingly unaware of, or unconcerned by, the family on the shore. The young girl began to giggle. The parents turned towards us, their faces darkening as their eyes fell on Henry. Henry waved. Instead of responding, they led the girl urgently away from the bank.

We carried on swimming for maybe ten more minutes, wordlessly. The river helped us with the gentle nudge of its current. The sunshine that came through the trees in patches between the branches, patterning light and dark, exerted a calming, almost mesmeric effect. As we reached a bend, Henry suggested we should swim back.

He struck back towards the boat. Upstream this time, it was more of a struggle. The family we had passed on the way down had gone. It took us thirty minutes to swim back. By the time we were on dry land again, I felt exhausted.

I went on to the roof to sunbathe and dry off. After maybe an hour, I fell asleep.

The sound of an unfamiliar voice woke me up and I made my way down to the living room. Henry, dressed in only a thin cotton shawl, was addressing a tall, skinny policeman, young and pale. His eyes never seemed to stop moving, darting about anxiously as if preparing for attack, and his mouth was working all the time, perhaps on a piece of gum. He had taken his helmet off, and was carrying it under his arm. With his other hand, he was wiping his face with a handkerchief. I only caught the last part of what he was saying to Henry.

'. . . and this isn't the first time there have been complaints.'

'I haven't broken any laws.'

'Exposing yourself to children is against the law.'

'I was just swimming.'

'You were swimming nude.'

'On a remote stretch of river. Surely that's not illegal.'

'What worries us is that you have a criminal record.'

He put down his helmet on the table, pocketed his handkerchief and fished out a notebook, which he started to examine.

'Not for exposing myself. And not in this country.'

The policeman read from the notebook.

'"Henry Templeton, possession of a controlled substance, Superior Court of California, San Diego, 1966. Six-month sentence, suspended on unspecified compassionate grounds, two-hundred-dollar fine."'

'Well, that's—'

'"Henry Templeton, supplying a controlled substance to a minor, Fresno County Superior Court, 1967. Three months' sentence, two months served."'

He put the notebook away. Henry looked momentarily taken aback.

'How did you come by that information, if I may ask?'

'That's really not your concern, sir. You don't deny these offences, presumably?'

'Of course not. But they took place a long time ago. If you're trying to make me feel guilty, I have to warn you that you are failing miserably.'

'And I have to warn *you*, Mr Templeton, that frankly your reputation and past suggests somebody who—'

'Somebody who what?'

'There's no call to interrupt me. Your reputation and past record suggest that your presence on this reach might not be entirely in the interests of the local community.'

'That's not for you to decide.'

'If you continue to be rude, sir, I'm going to have to—'

'I'm not being rude. I'm merely—'

Henry, clearly exasperated, checked himself.

The policeman stopped chewing his real or imaginary gum and his eyes stilled themselves and focused on Henry. A note of pomposity sounded in his voice, inflating its high, almost childish treble into a balloon of attempted gravity.

'Now look. Everyone has a right to live as he pleases. But there have been complaints about noise, about crowds, about drug-taking down on this boat. What with this latest incident, it all adds up to . . . Well, it adds up to the sort of disruption we could do without around here.'

There was a long pause. Henry and the policeman stared at each other. Then the policeman's eyes began to dart again, and his mouth to work. He picked up his helmet and placed it firmly on his head.

'However, I'm going to let you off with a caution this time.'

He paused, apparently expecting a 'thank you' from Henry.

'You mean you couldn't talk the parents into pressing charges for such an absurdly trivial incident.'

'If I hear reports of you swimming in the river with no clothes on again, you're going to be in a lot of trouble. Do you understand?'

There was a smudge of bum fluff under the policeman's nose. Henry, it seemed, couldn't quite bring himself to answer.

'Do you understand, Mr Templeton?'

'It's *Doctor* Templeton.'

The policeman buckled his helmet under the chin.

'I don't care if you're Doctor bloody Who. Just don't let me catch you in the river again with your kit off.'

He looked up at me, just long enough for me to register that I was of no importance. Then he made his way back towards where his police car was parked. He turned before he reached the curtain of trees that led off the reach.

'I'll be watching out for you, Mr Templeton.'

'Doctor,' Henry said, this time quietly, as if to himself.

As the police car disappeared through the fringe of trees, Henry sat himself down at the dining table, shaking his head in disbelief.

I sat next to him. He seemed downcast.

'Do you think this is to do with the hearing?' I said.

'I doubt that even Wesley Toshack was able to anticipate that I was going to swim naked and therefore plant a family on the riverbank. I suppose it could have an impact on the case. The lease specifically insists I act with "due decorum". Whatever that means. It's something for them to cling to, ludicrous though it is. But they didn't have enough to bring a criminal charge. And if the family won't press charges, then they are unlikely to want to put in an appearance at the hearing.'

'What if you lose the hearing?'

'I doubt very much that it will come to that. As I say, their evidence is very thin. Though I am rather surprised they've managed to access those old court records.'

'But what if you do?'

'Then I lose the case. Or, to be more precise, I lose everything.'

He stared out of the window and set his face in an expression that verged on bitterness.

'They're determined to get rid of me.'

'Who is?'

'Everyone.'

'But what about your friends? They'll speak up on your behalf. That must count for something.'

'Friends?'

'I don't know. Troy? Vanya?'

He gave a dry, almost bitter laugh.

'They don't want to hear what I have to say any more. They want the simplicity of magic. Or money. Or the delights of moral outrage. All the usual things on the infernal menu.'

He took out a cigarette paper and tobacco and started to roll them with hands that shook slightly.

'How are you getting on with your History revision?' Suddenly he seemed perfectly cheerful.

'Pretty well,' I said. 'I've got all the causes memorized now.'

Henry smiled. Outside the window, a gaily painted boat was chugging along, with a party of young, denim-clad daytrippers. They were drinking wine and laughing.

207

Henry waved and the people on the boat waved back and hooted.

We watched until they receded into the distance. Henry gathered up his legal papers, put on his glasses and began to examine them. I assumed this was the signal that my presence wasn't required any more.

Eighteen

I tried to write a reply to Ray. I found myself a blank sheet of thin, unlined A4 typing paper on Henry's desk, borrowed one of his antique English fountain pens, sat down at my own desk and waited for the words to come.

Dad.

Dear Dad.

Ray.

Hi.

That was as far as I got. However long I sat there, my mind could produce little more than a few generic sentences – 'How are you?', 'Hope you are well', 'Thanks for your letter'. Beyond those basic pleasantries, rummage as I might, I could find nothing.

I had never had any reason in my life previously to articulate my relationship with Ray. He was just there, being Ray. To write a letter to my grieving father, and to make it in any way meaningful, would require resources that I was unable to muster. To describe the parade of events and characters at the *Ho Koji* seemed merely to rub his face in the sense of inadequacy I could see he suffered over Henry. I could not tell him that he had a niece either – not without Henry's or Strawberry's say-so.

So how could I write anything that was not insincere or provocative? I knew that Ray would be pleased to get a letter from me whatever I wrote, even if it contained a series of trivial news bites and meaningless clichés, as his had. But I could not bring myself to fill the emptiness of the paper with still more emptiness. After half an hour or so I put Henry's pen down and gave up the struggle, leaving nothing on the page but *Dad* and an inkblot that, as it spread through the porous paper, came to resemble a black sun, out of focus, expanding.

That same day – Friday – I had arranged to meet Ash at the usual place. Henry immediately picked up on my mood.

'Someone's cheerful.'

'It's not a crime.'

I didn't feel inclined to say any more. Henry's hostility to Ash made me even more taciturn than usual.

'Any particular reason?'

'Not really.'

Henry looked at me shrewdly, then turned back to his papers.

'Sorry. Naturally nosey.'

I said goodbye and headed to where the grocer's bike lay. I lifted it off its side and began cycling. After I had negotiated the field and was five minutes into the journey into Lexham, I noticed a woman up ahead walking by the hedgerow. Her hair was exactly the colour and style of my mother's.

Out of nowhere, a great choking sob jerked out of me, so powerful I could no longer cycle. I abruptly stopped the bike and straddled the frame. The woman turned and looked at me. She looked nothing like my mother. She was fifteen years younger, with a sharp, cunning face and moist, loose lips.

'Are you all right?' Her voice registered slight suspicion rather than sympathy.

I nodded, and wiped my face with the back of my wrist. There was no dampness there.

'Do you need help?'

'It's OK.'

The woman shrugged and resumed her walk.

I dismounted the bike and lay on the ground on my back for several minutes, examining the sky for something other than hollowness.

I didn't know if I could meet Ash any more.

All the same, after a few more minutes, I clambered back on the bike and set off unsteadily for the village centre. I stopped briefly at a stream, washed my face and plastered down my hair. I cycled as hard as I could, exhausting myself, making my lungs burn.

The moment I arrived at the clock tower, Ash seemed to know that something was wrong. She moved towards me, inspected my face carefully, then enfolded me in her arms. I felt myself go limp.

After a while, I pulled away. I didn't feel as ashamed as I had expected to.

'Thank you,' I said simply.

'I didn't do anything,' said Ash.

'You were there. You are here. How did you know?'

'I could see you were upset.'

'Was it so obvious?'

'Was it because of your mother?'

Evie was part of it. But encroaching on to the ragged perimeter that surrounded her loss was the image of my father, dusting, dusting.

The loneliness of people seemed insupportable.

Ash continued talking in a low, soothing voice.

'I lost my mother when I was eight. It wasn't until much later that I found out that she killed herself. My father couldn't even bury her in the churchyard.'

'I guess that trumps me.' I attempted a smile.

'I don't normally talk about it.'

'I'm sorry. Being flippant. I guess I'm not sure what to say.'

'You don't need to say anything. I'm just trying to explain that I know something of what you feel. If it wasn't for my father . . .'

'How did he cope with it?'

'He was very strong. His faith got him through.' She took my hand. 'I love him more than anything, you know, Adam.'

I wanted, wished, hoped I could speak the same words about Ray. But they would not come – either because they were not true, or because they were too true.

'Would you like to meet him?'

This took me aback. I barely knew Ash. I was possessed by some kind of received wisdom that you only met the parents of a girlfriend when you were well on the way to engagement.

'I'm not sure.'

'Don't worry, I know what Henry thinks about him. But I have a strange feeling you two might get along.'

I hesitated, fearful that by agreeing I was making some promise, some commitment that I was barely aware of. I was also worried about betraying Henry. I looked at Ash. She was staring at the ground as if preparing herself for a rejection.

'I guess I have a right to form my own opinion. About your father.'

She took my hand again, and we began to walk.

We moved through the thick, sticky air towards the church. One or two people we passed stared with naked curiosity.

'Everyone feeds on everyone else's business here,' said Ash. 'The town runs on gossip.'

I started talking about the retake of my A level. Ash had already been offered a place at Bristol University to study Biology. She listened carefully as I told her how the exams had no longer seemed to matter after Evie's death. That I wasn't sure they mattered even now.

'It depends what you mean by "matter", I suppose,' said Ash. We were only a few hundred yards now from the rectory where Ash lived with her father. 'If you think your exams don't matter, isn't that the same as saying your future doesn't matter?'

We arrived at the rectory gate. The house was cartoon-cosy. Vines covered old red bricks. There was a green tile roof. The gutters were decorated with verdigris. The door was a thing of beauty, some rough-hewn piece of oak that looked centuries old and was twice the size of a normal door. Ash let herself in using an old mortice key that looked like it would open a dungeon or raise a portcullis.

The door opened directly into a large, light room furnished with what, even to my untrained eye, were exquisite antiques. The window was framed with heavy, tied-back floral curtains. There were real paintings on the walls, landscapes and portraits of sleek horses and ruddy-cheeked children. They had the sheen of antiquity.

Taking up most of the space on an overstuffed, distressed red-leather sofa propped against the furthest wall was Ash's father. He looked up as we entered. His thick, immaculate brown hair was brilliantined and clipped short at the sides and back. His trousers were brown corduroy and he wore a white shirt, a beige tie and a wine-coloured V-neck sleeveless pullover.

'Hello, Ashley,' he said softly. Even in this innocent greeting, his voice held a faint intimation of power, of conviction. He had a barely discernible Welsh accent. His eyes fell on me. I felt immediately that they were categorizing me, putting a brand on my forehead.

'You must be Adam.'

'Are you all right, Dad?' said Ash, looking concerned.

She left my side and walked quickly over to the Reverend Toshack. He held up his hand and smiled.

'Mrs Sparrow left us. I was at her bedside. I watched her pass.'

He looked up at me. 'Mrs Sparrow was one of our oldest parishioners. I must have known her for twenty years. Please sit down, Adam. I'm sorry. I'm sure this isn't what you expected. It's really not fair on you. I'm being inhospitable.'

I felt tongue-tied, but there was a space into which I was required to insert a remark.

'Don't you get used to it?'

Toshack looked at Ash, who shrugged, then back at me.

'Get used to what, son?'

'You know. Being a vicar? People dying?'

I immediately regretted the question. Embarrassment often had the effect of making me blunt.

'I'm sorry. I didn't mean to . . .'

Toshack stood up. His head almost touched the low ceiling. He walked over to me and held out his hand. I shook it.

'The answer is no. You never really do get used to it. And I don't mind you asking. You can call me Wesley, by the way. I'm genuinely sorry to have greeted you with such a drama. Could I get you a cup of tea at all?'

'I'd prefer coffee.'

'Mrs Taylor!'

He raised his voice very slightly. Once again, I felt the power that he held in reserve. A diminutive, pinch-faced woman entered the room. She was about seventy, had crimped white hair and was wearing a knee-length yellow floral-print dress. 'Could you fix Adam here a cup of coffee? How do you take it, Adam?'

'White, no sugar. Thank you.'

Without speaking a word or offering a nod, Mrs Taylor disappeared back into the kitchen. Wesley gestured for me to sit down. I did so, and rubbed my knees with my hands in small circles, nervously. Ash came and sat on the chair adjacent to mine and Toshack returned to the sofa.

'I think, before I say anything else, I should say that your uncle and I aren't really on speaking terms. Or rather, he's not on speaking terms with me. Of course, I'm happy to see him or talk to him any time.'

'Dad is on the committee trying to get his boat removed from the reach,' said Ash.

'I happen to be part of the committee, yes. It's nothing personal. It's a matter of precedent. Over the last couple of years, we've had a number of other boats trying to moor on that stretch of river, and we've had long and expensive legal battles to remove them. As long as Henry's there, there's a constant temptation for travelling people of one kind or another to set up home. Now I personally am not that vexed by it – I think we should be open to those who choose different styles of life. But a lot of the local community are not of the same mind. And as a councillor, as well as a representative of the Church, I am duty-bound to represent their interests and concerns. However, I understand that your uncle may well take it personally.'

'I heard that the rift between you was about something else,' I said. 'Some kind of appearance at the church?'

'Henry made a speech in the church. It was a little . . .'

'It upset some of the parishioners,' said Ash.

'I know it seems strange to be talking about these matters when we only met a moment ago. But I feel I would be talking to you, inviting you into my house, under false pretences if I didn't come right out and say this. To clear the air, as it were. You might feel some issue of loyalty, I don't know. I just want to tell you right out that I bear your uncle personally no ill will. However, if the fact of a dispute between us makes you uncomfortable, I will understand completely if you wish to save . . . this meeting for another time. Or avoid it altogether.'

Mrs Taylor walked in with the coffee and biscuits, and set them on a table next to me. Ash stared at me expectantly, waiting for me to accept the offering. I picked up a biscuit and bit into it. Crumbs flaked on to the carpet. Embarrassed, I bent to try and retrieve them, but Wesley indicated for me to leave them alone. Mrs Taylor had now delivered a cup of tea to him.

'Is it true that he set fire to a bible in your church?'

'Henry was rude,' said Ash.

'I'm sure he didn't see it that way,' said Wesley. 'I think the points he was trying to make were a little too . . . subtle for our congregation.'

'Is that the real reason you're trying to drive him off the boat?'

'Absolutely not. The two issues are not connected. That's water under the bridge. It's simply that if your uncle is allowed to continue staying there, in law a precedent will be set. You see, since a houseboat is not a permanent structure, it occupies the same category as a caravan or, for that matter, a tent. An encampment of some kind could be established, and if we tolerate the boat it will undermine our power to do anything about it. We have a gypsy problem around here, apart from anything else. I personally like Henry very much. But we can't have one law for him and another law for the rest of us. Naturally, Henry doesn't see it that way.'

'So – if you don't mind me asking, Mr – Reverend – Toshack, on what basis are you trying to get him out?'

'I'll be honest with you, Adam. Any method we can. As far as I'm concerned, it's for the good of the community. As you may know, there are stipulations in the lease about the behaviour of residents. Sometimes Henry sails close to the wind there. His "gatherings". Rumours of drug use. I've heard he has some girl down there who's little more than a skeleton. What's going on there?'

'I suppose you're talking about Strawberry.'

'Is that her name? She doesn't look like there's much juice in her.' He gave a thin laugh.

'She's someone Henry is helping. She doesn't live on the boat. There's a cabin a little way off where she stays. There's nothing between them, if that's what you're suggesting.'

'I'm not suggesting anything,' said Toshack. 'Your uncle knows he's always very welcome at the rectory. He also

217

knows that I like him greatly. I hope you will send him my best wishes.'

He looked at Ash and Ash nodded.

Now he smiled at me.

'So. How did you come to meet my beautiful daughter?'

Ash and I walked back through the town to where I'd parked my bike. I felt that the sun had barely moved since we had set off for the rectory. Time itself was slow that summer, as if snagging on some invisible impediment. Ash and I held hands. She seemed, at that moment, in the nature of a sun herself, rising rather than falling, a source of heat and light and nourishment.

We stopped as we passed a huge oak tree, one of several that decorated a patch of open green space in the middle of the town. I began kissing Ash. She kissed me back. She was so tender, so slight. It was like a breeze in my mouth.

People were beginning to stare, and we broke apart and continued walking back to my bike. I knew she had a shift at the buttery in thirty minutes. She held a plastic bag with her uniform in – a white pinafore dress and a pale green cotton blouse.

I didn't want her to go.

'Do you believe all that stuff?' I said.

'What stuff?'

'God. Jesus.'

'Some of it.'

'I've always wondered about the Holy Ghost. Is it really a ghost? Where does that fit in?'

'I'm not sure I'm very good on the fine points of theology. You should ask my father.'

'Would you call yourself a Christian?'

'Why do you keep asking me about that? Does it really matter so much?'

'The kids at school who were Christians were all freaks.'

Time seemed to be speeding up as we approached the bike. I felt for my padlock key in my pocket.

'I think my dad liked you.'

'When can we meet again, Ash?'

'I'm coming to Henry's "happening" tomorrow night.'

'Really? Why are you doing that? I thought you disliked him.'

'It's not that I dislike him, Adam. I just think he was rude to my father. And I'm coming because I want to see you. But I'm bringing that girl you saw me with first time we met. Wendy. We'd arranged to go out ages ago, and I can't really break it. I've talked her into coming down, in the hope there might be some available boys. She's desperate for some kind of romance.'

'Oh.'

'Do you mind if we play it cool? Wendy doesn't know about us. She's still got that "best friends" thing going on. She'll be jealous if she knows about you.'

'I don't mind.'

'Thanks for understanding.'

She gave me a final kiss. At the same time her hand brushed lightly – and, I was sure, deliberately – against my groin.

Nineteen

When I arrived back at the boat, there was a Citroën Dyane parked in the field. I recognized it as Troy's car. Troy was sitting across from Henry on the strip of land next to the boat, *Easy Rider* shades perched loosely on his nose and a pair of Bermuda shorts slung low enough to reveal the first inch of the furrow that separated the cheeks of his rear. His shirt was off and his back was arched to bask in the sun. Henry was examining some papers on his lap. Strawberry was lying down on a beach towel next to them. Her tan seemed to be fading, overtaken by a porridge-like wanness.

Troy looked up. He raised a hand.

'Hi, kid.'

His smile was lazy and seemed to have the stretch potential of an accordion. I nodded. Henry barely glanced at me. His attention was concentrated on the sheets of paper in front of him, which I now saw were covered with numbers serried in neat columns.

Strawberry had her eyes closed. I could see her eyeballs moving under the skin. I wondered if she was dreaming, and if so, what she dreamed about.

Troy followed my gaze.

'Amazing woman,' he said, lowering his voice, either to indicate intimacy between him and myself or to prevent Strawberry hearing him. The voice had an attractive growl to it. 'Incredible will-power. Anyone else would have given up weeks ago. Not Straws. She takes it to the limit. Every time, she takes it to the limit.'

I sat down. Troy offered me a cigarette, which I took.

'Where have you been?' Henry looked up. I noted a rare hint of sharpness in his voice.

'In Lexham. Seeing Ash.' I paused. 'And her father. He seemed nice.'

Henry stared at me.

'You met Wesley?'

'I went to the rectory, yes.'

'I see.'

He paused, as if he was shuffling through a number of potential responses. In the end he just said:

'Watch yourself, Adam. They're not all that they seem.'

'I know you fell out with Wesley, but he doesn't seem to bear you any grudge.'

Troy began to laugh.

'Fell out? That's putting it mildly. Toshack would have ripped his fucking head off if he'd had the chance. And then fed it to the congregation with a side of brimstone.'

At that point the sound of Strawberry retching interrupted the flow of the conversation. Troy handed her a tissue and she wiped her mouth, where there was a thin trace of liquid. She was smiling with delight.

'That must be nearly the last of the poisons. Look, there's hardly anything of it.'

'You're brave, Strawberry. Deranged, but brave.'

I looked at Henry. He said nothing.

'She doesn't look well,' I said.

'She knows what she's doing,' said Troy.

'Don't talk about me as if I'm not here! Suzuki says—'

'I *know* Kenzaburo Suzuki,' said Henry. 'I'm going to write to him. I think, Strawberry, you have misunderstood the diet.'

'How can I have misunderstood it? It's there in black and white.' She pointed to the book, *Macrobiotics and the Zen Way*, which was lying on the grass beside her.

'Take it easy, Henry,' said Troy. 'You know she's recovering. You know this is better than what there was before. And you know the way she was before and who that was down to. So just leave her alone.'

'You've always said I've got to find my own way. Make my own mistakes.'

Henry went back to staring at the figures. Troy looked at me and winked.

'What are you doing, Henry?' I said, trying to make out the contents of the page.

'He's trying to make some of that do-re-mi for once in his life.'

Henry ignored us both and turned over another page. Troy came and sat next to me. His right leg bobbed up and down as if he found it difficult to keep still.

'The world is changing. When the world changes, there's fortunes to be made. All you need is two things. Imagination. And some cap-ee-tal. I got the imagination. Henry got the capital.'

'*Access* to capital,' said Henry, without looking up. 'I have a banker acquaintance who would make a loan to the business on my say-so. If I'm convinced there's something in it.'

'Together, Henry, we'll be an unbeatable team. The only problem is—'

'The only problem is that your "crystal healing powers" are horseshit,' said Henry quietly.

'Maybe they are, maybe they're not. Who cares? People *believe* that they help them. Maybe they do help them. Where's the harm in that? And it's just the beginning. There's medicine – natural medicines. Homeopathic. Organic. Flower remedies. This stuff is flying off the market stalls.'

'You know the medicine shows in America at the turn of the century?' said Henry. 'They used to sell sugar and water and tell everyone it was a potion that would solve all their ills. People made millions. People aren't that gullible any more, Troy. This is just a blip. When people see through it, they'll put it behind them. It's a passing fad.'

He put the papers neatly into a pile and got up.

'What's your point, Henry?'

'What I'm saying is, I'm not going to ask my friend to put money into conning people with sugar-water and rocks. And even if I was, it would never make a long-term profit. People simply aren't that dumb.'

Troy shook his head in disbelief.

'You've said a few things that have shocked me in our long and fruitful relationship, Henry. But that is the most shocking. People aren't stupid? Are you kidding me?'

'No, they're not stupid. They're just ignorant. People like you make sure they stay that way.'

'So let me get this straight. You're not coming in on this?'

'No. No, I'm not, Troy. I'm sorry. I'd really like to help. But that's how I feel.'

Troy snorted, and snatched the papers back from Henry.

'And you think the people who buy *my* stuff have got their heads up their asses. That's a good one, Henry. Yeah. From the chief head-ass guy.'

Henry looked at me and smiled fondly. It was as if he was seeing me for the first time that day.

'Hi, stupid.'

'Hi, stupid.'

'How about a swim?'

'Sure. Why not?

When we came out of the water, both Strawberry and Troy had left. Henry and I towelled ourselves down.

'Are they angry with you?'

'Most of Strawberry's anger is reserved for herself. As for Troy, he's never angry for long. Underneath his untram-melled materialism and irreducible rascality, he has rather a sweet nature. I find him frustratingly likeable.'

I threw my towel down and put on a robe.

'Uncle Henry?'

Henry sat down naked. I made an effort to avoid looking at his genitals.

'I don't get all this. I don't get the set-up. In fact, I don't get you.'

'What do you mean?'

'My dad said you'd done all these things. I found some of the things he said hard to swallow.'

'"Things"?'

'Is it true that you knew The Beatles?'

'John and George better than the other two. But yes, I know them.'

I duly noted the present tense. Henry got up and put on his robe and gestured that I should follow him back to the boat. Once we had boarded, he reached into one of the cupboards that was built into seats in the main room. He found an old biscuit tin, speckled with rust spots, and rummaged around. After a few seconds he brought out a black and white photo. Sure enough, there was Henry with John Lennon and George Harrison in a bar somewhere, holding bottles of beer and wearing flower garlands around their necks. They were all toasting the camera. John had his arm around Henry.

'That was in Rishikesh. I was getting drugs for them,' Henry said matter-of-factly.

'You were a drug dealer?'

'A very good one. Honest. Dependable. Personally abstemious. It's a rare quality in that trade. Of course, that's all way behind me now.'

He put the photo away and closed the cupboard.

'I'll show you the rest of my gallery before you go back to London. Right now, I'm famished.'

He began clattering around in the galley area. Outside, darkness was gathering.

'You want something to eat?' He inspected a few cupboards and the fridge. 'I could make *pasta all'amatriciana*. Or I have some very good lamb cutlets.'

'I'm not hungry, thanks. Tell me about what happened in the church. With the bible? Telling people to wash their mouths out when they said the word "Jesus".'

'Such a fuss over nothing. It's no different from saying, "When you meet the Buddha on the road, kill him." The point is not to mistake the map for the territory. The symbol

225

for what is being symbolized. That's all I was saying. It was a kind of joke. Not everyone has the same sense of humour as me, it appears.'

'How did you even get to know Wesley Toshack in the first place? You don't seem like natural soulmates.'

Henry popped the cork from a bottle of red wine. He poured a glass for me, but took only water for himself.

'I only became friends with Wesley last year. We bumped into one another in a pub in Lexham. I have a doctorate in Divinity, and him being a man of God, we got talking. He learned that I had once been an episcopal priest in America.'

'You were a priest?'

It occurred to me, not for the first time, that Henry was a fantasist, despite the photographic evidence of his friendship with The Beatles. His life seemed too improbable to be fully credible.

'I had my own chapel in Chicago. It was very popular with the public. Congregations were busting down the doors to get in, whereas before my arrival church attendances were ailing. We tried out all sorts of new things. Theology was a very exciting field at the time.'

Henry told me how he had run the church using religious influences from a variety of different traditions. There had been chants and dancing, rituals borrowed from Hinduism and Buddhism, prayers and hymns, candles and incense. The Catholic Mass had been appropriated for its air of mystery. It had been, according to Henry, 'a radical experiment in pluralistic spirituality'. It turned into — again, according to Henry — the most popular church that the diocese had ever known. From half-empty pews, there were people queuing outside. The parties Henry held after the services became legendary.

But Henry's excessive liberality proved to be his downfall. Drugs and drink began to make appearances among the congregation, the former in a semi-sanctioned attempt to enrich spiritual life. Sexual contact between the congregants was given the stamp of approval.

It didn't take long for a newspaper exposé to get under way. The bishop who ran the diocese grew tired of the controversy surrounding Henry's activities and made it clear that if he didn't resign, he would be defrocked.

It was shortly afterwards, Henry told me, that he went to India. He spent years there, travelling, dealing, living on the road. Then he returned, lived in a squat in Chelsea for a while, spending much of his time looking after a friend who was seriously ill. It was the friend who owned the houseboat. Henry supported him with what was left of the money from his drug-dealing days, then the friend died. He left the boat to Henry in his will.

Henry refurbished the *Ho Koji* – which had been entirely decrepit – and came to live in it, but it turned out he had also inherited legal complications. The lease, Henry admitted, was riddled with difficult and problematic terms which strictly controlled the behaviour of the residents on the boat – since the freehold on the land belonged to the Church.

I steered Henry back to the story of the burning bible.

'It's not easy to explain. I think there was a breakdown in communication about what I was going to be talking about at the service. Wesley knew I was once an ordained priest. He also knew that I styled myself as a radical theologian. I just don't think he thought through what that meant. But I genuinely didn't mean any offence.'

'You didn't mean any offence by burning a bible?'

'I was trying to demonstrate the difference between faith and belief.'

'What is the difference?'

'Belief is about crawling into a hole and pulling the hole in after you. Faith is crawling out of a hole and pulling the space out after you.'

'I don't think I'm out of my gourd enough to know what that means.'

'I think I am expressing myself perfectly clearly. I merely suggested that there should be a very respectful burning of bibles once a year, to remind us all that for all the beauties and profundities of Christianity, we shouldn't get hung up on it as the final version of reality. It is simply a clue.'

'That's when people walked out?'

Henry paused.

'That's right. Wesley was unhappy – as you might expect. Ashley, on the other hand, was incandescent.'

'Ash honestly didn't seem all that bothered when I talked to her about it. Although she did think you were rather rude to her father.'

'What Ash is and what she says are very different things, I suspect. I don't mean any disrespect to her. I know you've become fond of her. But that is my experience.'

'He's forgiven you, you know. Wesley.'

'Is that so?'

'He sends his best wishes. Says you're welcome at the rectory any time.'

Henry shook his head.

'I genuinely believe that Wesley would utterly destroy me if he had the chance. A chance that he's looking out for all the time. Furthermore, his daughter would do a jig on my corpse while whistling an accompanying tune.'

'But why would he pretend to forgive you?'

'Because pretending is what people do,' said Henry. 'I'm going to attend to the chops. Sure I can't tempt you?'

'I'm fine.'

It seemed that the subject was closed. Henry resumed clattering in the galley. I returned to my room. A picture of the Archduke Franz Ferdinand stared up at me from my open textbook on the desk. Lacking anything better to do, and aware that I had been tardy about my revision that day, I began reading about Gavrilo Princip's assassination plan.

Only it seemed he didn't have much of a plan. On the day itself, another of his associates from the Black Hand — or the Young Bosnians — had thrown a bomb at the carriage carrying the archduke through the streets of Sarajevo. The archduke then, against all common sense, instructed his driver to take him to hospital to visit an Austrian officer injured by the earlier bomb, rather than abandon the procession immediately. The driver took the intended original route in error. Realizing he had gone the wrong way, he pulled up to reverse — and stopped right in front of Princip.

Princip, seizing the opportunity, turned his head away so that he couldn't even see his target, and, with a gun that he was ill-trained to use, killed both the archduke and his wife Sophie, with two shots — something the most brilliant and highly trained assassin might have struggled to do.

Circumstance and luck. The whole history of the twentieth century resting on a series of accidents. I wondered if my own life was simply fluke. And what a relief it would be if it was.

Twenty

By late afternoon the next day, Henry was more or less fully prepared for his 'Vibrations and Polarities' lecture that evening. There were smells of garlic and curry powder spicing the air. Oil burners heated three metal trays containing vegetarian curry, lamb stew and chilli con carne. There was an earthenware pot of dhal, a paper plate of brown rice and a huge potato salad, dressed with sour cream and chives, in a Tupperware box.

Arranged beside the main dishes on a trestle table were ceramic cereal bowls filled with crisps and peanuts, along with piles of paper plates, disposable beakers and plastic cutlery. The wine was Spanish, and of rather poorer quality than anything Henry had ever offered me. There was a jug of beer that he proudly claimed to have brewed himself. The rank, raw odour turned my stomach slightly.

I had helped, laying out the plates and cutlery, setting up the table. I put out condiments – mainly Indian chutneys –

along with bottles of wine and soft drinks. I threw scatter cushions in front of the blackboard Henry would refer to during his talk. I had also set up the sound system outside, trailing an extension lead from the generator. Henry had supplied a microphone ready to be plugged into the amplifier. He was worried that not everybody was going to be able to hear him.

'How many people are you expecting?' I asked as I rearranged the scatter cushions, trying to get them into some kind of order that was neither too symmetrical nor too chaotic.

'I don't know. Maybe thirty. At least twenty. I've got a modest reputation around here.'

'You have a following?'

'Perhaps that's too concrete a description. A reputation, perhaps.'

'A reputation as what?'

'A spiritual entertainer, you might say. Others would say a genuine fake.'

He laughed, and added another pinch of something to a simmering copper pot.

'I'd be inclined to agree with them.'

Henry whistled tunelessly to himself and attended to final details – straightening the paper tablecloth on the trestle table, laying out some napkins, testing the PA. He spread a few blankets in the spaces between the scatter cushions.

The event was scheduled to begin at 7 p.m. At six, Henry lit a pile of logs and kindling for a fire, which blazed cheerfully a few yards to the right of the blackboard. At six-thirty the first visitor arrived. He was a middle-aged man who looked a thoroughly improbable candidate for the lecture. He was clean-shaven with oiled hair, and was wearing heavy leather shoes beneath rather shiny grey trousers.

'Mr Templeton?'

He was stretched and tense, as if he carried struts and wires within that had been adjusted for maximum torque.

'Yes, I'm Henry Templeton,' said Henry, stretching out his hand. The man took it and shook it briskly.

'I'm from Lexham District Council.'

'How delightful.'

'Fire and Safety,' said the man. 'As you know, there have been a lot of forest fires recently. We just wanted to make sure that regulations were being followed.'

'You're not here for the talk?' said Henry.

'Not exactly. No, I'm here to make sure it's all in order. May I ask to see your licence?'

'Licence?'

'For public gatherings of more than twenty people, you need a licence from the council.'

'Oh, I understand,' said Henry. 'You're Wesley Toshack's man. His stooge.'

'I'm an officer of the council. Not of the Reverend Toshack.'

'You know of him, then?'

The man looked shifty.

'I know of Wesley Toshack, yes.'

'Fancy!'

'I'm just here to make sure everything goes without a hitch. My name is Pritchard. Now. Do you have a licence?' He took a notepad and pencil out of his pocket.

'No, I do not. And I do not need one.'

Pritchard made a note on his pad.

Henry opened his arms in a welcoming gesture.

'Well, since you're here, you can help yourself to some food. There's plenty.' He waved towards the table.

'As for the licence – that only applies if there's an entrance fee for the event. Otherwise it is, legally speaking, a private party.'

'There is an entrance fee, Mr Templeton. One pound, I believe.'

'That's not an entrance fee, it's a voluntary contribution. It is my pleasure to feed these people. I would not be much of a host if I did not offer them something to drink. This is simple hospitality. The voluntary contribution is not for profit. It's simply a matter of covering my costs.'

'Do you have a licence to sell alcohol?' said Pritchard.

'I'm not selling alcohol,' responded Henry, now glancing around him as if losing interest. I saw that he was looking towards the gap in the willow trees, where more people were arriving. 'There's a few glasses of wine on the house. The donation is to cover soft drinks and food. Hey, Strawberry!'

Strawberry had emerged from the curtain of willow branches. She was followed by Pattern, Vanya and Troy, walking arm in arm.

Henry turned back to Pritchard.

'I can recommend the dhal. The Maharishi Ji gave me the recipe. Excuse me. I've got to circulate.'

Pritchard was left looking uncertain of what to do next. Henry's knowledge of the law, whether real or feigned, along with his air of intimidating self-confidence, seemed to have stymied him.

Troy was marching towards us, his accustomed concertina grin firmly in place.

'I told you Troy would get over our disagreement,' said Henry.

He moved to greet Troy and the others, hugging them

each in turn. As usual, he was looking faintly angry. He held up a hand in greeting when he saw me, and I returned the wave. Vanya wandered over and kissed me on the cheek.

'How's the self-abuse, boy?'

'Good.'

'Make sure you think good thoughts.'

'I try to think about women who are scantily clad now. Instead of naked.'

'That's what's known in the women's movement as consciousness-raising.'

I noticed that Henry greeted Strawberry rather formally, merely touching her shoulder rather than kissing her on the cheek. It was as if she was now too delicate to even embrace.

Now Pattern greeted me with a pat on the arm.

'Hi, Adam.'

'All right?' I said surlily, and moved away so his hand was no longer touching me.

'You're angry with me, right?'

His voice softened. 'Look, Adam. It was a stupid thing to do, what I did at the seance. I thought the whole thing was so dumb, no one would ever take it seriously. It was just a joke. A laugh. I was a moron. Let me off the hook, will you? I don't want you to think I'm an even bigger dick than I actually am.'

He looked genuinely sheepish.

'Forget about it. I was three sheets to the wind.'

He smacked me on the back.

'Thanks, Adam. Thanks, man. You're a dude.'

Henry kept checking his watch. It was five-past seven. Then ten-past. Then quarter-past. No one else came. It was just the five of us and Pritchard.

Henry looked at Pritchard and said, as if unconcerned,

'Well, it seems you won't have to worry about it being a gathering of more than twenty people anyway.'

Despite his insouciance, Henry's shoulders had dropped, and he paced listlessly up and down. He looked over the laden table of food, which had hardly been touched. The fire, which had caught and was roaring, sent grey clouds of smoke across the blackboard where the lecture was meant to take place. Henry stopped pacing and took his place next to the PA, ten feet to the side of the fire, in front of the cushions. The smoke was blowing in his face, and he coughed. It seemed he wasn't quite ready to start — if he intended to go ahead at all. Clearly he had a fading hope that a few more people might turn up. He gazed anxiously at the trees at the edge of the reach. As if on cue, the curtain of willow trembled and two more people walked through.

It was Ash and Wendy. They were both dressed as I had first seen them, in their contrasting overalls. Wendy was smoking. Ash carried a light canvas bag over her shoulder. Henry looked relieved to see them.

'Is eight a quorum, Adam? Including Mr Pritchard?'

'I don't know. It's up to you.'

Ash shot me a glance, tipped me a wink. They made their way towards Henry.

'Hello, Wendy,' said Henry. 'This is a bit out of your comfort zone, isn't it?'

'What do you know about my comfort zones?'

'Still smoking those vile peppermint cigarettes?'

Wendy threw her cigarette on the ground. Pritchard looked at her, alert. She stomped it out under her sandal.

Henry turned to Ash. 'Surprised to see you here.'

'Nothing much else to do,' said Ash. She offered £1.

'Forget about it. This isn't really a public event any more. And if it becomes one, apparently I would be breaking the law. You should mention to your worried friends in the town what kind of influence I have in this area. Won't you get paid by the old man for the undercover work, anyway? I should introduce you to Pritchard, your associate from the council.'

He indicated Pritchard, who, satisfied that Wendy's cigarette was fully extinguished, was spooning chilli con carne into his mouth.

'You're a cynic, Henry.'

'I'm as far away from a cynic as it is possible to be. Which is why, I think, people like your father take such exception to me.'

'Where's the loo?' said Wendy. 'I'm busting.'

'I'll show you.'

Henry led Wendy towards the boat. Ash and I were left alone. She touched me lightly on the arm.

'Don't be upset that I'm here with Wendy.'

'I'm not.'

'She's an unhappy girl. She's lonely. I'm looking out for her.'

I tried to reach over and kiss her, but she pulled back.

'Can we just cool it while we're here? I told you, Wendy doesn't know about us.'

I called across to Henry, who had given directions to Wendy and was heading towards the blackboard.

'Are you starting, Henry?'

'No,' said Henry. 'Not right now.'

I turned back to Ash. 'Would you like me to show you around?'

She looked over at the boat.

'Wendy will take about twenty minutes tarting herself up, knowing her. Go on then, give us a quick tour.'

I showed her around the boat – my room, Henry's, the main area. She clucked her approval, offering an occasional 'nice' or 'characterful' or a less complimentary 'tatty'. Seeing that Wendy was still apparently in the loo, and with no sign of Henry starting, Ash insisted I give her a quick tour of the grounds as well. After checking with Henry that we had time, we took a brisk walk down the path that led to Strawberry's shack. In a few minutes we reached the clearing where it was sited.

'What's this? The garden shed?'

'It's where Strawberry lives.'

Ash frowned. 'It's tiny.'

'It's rather nice actually. I'm sure Strawberry wouldn't mind if we took a look inside.'

I stepped across and opened the door. Ash stuck her head in, looked around carefully, sniffed and withdrew. I closed the door again.

'See? It's nice.'

'It smells of cabbage.'

'Wheatgrass.'

'It's a hovel.'

'"Judge not, lest ye be judged." Henry's always quoting that at me.'

Suddenly Ash pulled me towards her and kissed me, her bag dropping to the ground. I nearly overbalanced. After a minute, we broke apart. I could see my saliva on her lips. She stood with her legs apart. She was breathing heavily. We said nothing.

Then I heard a call, distant but distinct.

'Adam!'

It was Troy's voice.

'We'd better get back.' I grabbed her hand and pulled her after me.

When we arrived back at the boat, Wendy was there, still doing her make-up in a pocket mirror. She glared at Ash.

'I've got to stay with Wendy now,' said Ash. 'See you later.'

I hurried off to where Henry seemed to be arguing with Troy. The approach of night made the fire brighter. Ginsberg had appeared. He foraged for crisp crumbs, then slid back into the river. The sky was turning deep scarlet, and the air was thickened with the perfume of the pines and the incense.

'Adam! Where have you been? Henry's trying to call the whole thing off. I was hoping you could convince him.'

Henry looked at me sadly.

'I suppose it's up to Henry really,' I said feebly.

Troy looked disappointed.

'Come on, Henry! I've paid my money and I want my lecture.'

'Troy, I will be very happy to return your money of course, but . . .'

'We want to hear you, Henry,' said Strawberry, who had come to join them.

'That's right!' chimed in Vanya. 'You're the man, Henry.'

Henry looked doubtful.

Pattern was the last to add his voice.

'Come on, Henry. We all want to hear what you have to say. Even if it is bollocks.' He started a chant. 'Come-on Hen-ry! Come-on Hen-ry!'

Everyone joined in apart from Pritchard, who stood a little way away, chewing on some pitta bread and looking bemused.

Henry held up a hand.

'I'm afraid it would simply be too absurd. But anyone who wants to talk to me about anything – well, come right over and chat. And there is lots of food and drink. Let's do what the rest of the world does. Let's stop thinking, and have a party!'

He punched the button on a cassette player. The music that boomed out – he had run a wire from the boat and erected the Wharfedale speakers – was 'Monkey Man' by Toots & The Maytals.

Henry began to dance – a Jamaican skank, such an absurd yet graceful performance that there were outbreaks of laughter, not mocking, but delighted. He gestured for us to start dancing too. Strawberry rose and began moving in her own way, a spidery, rather gothic shimmer. Ash and Wendy followed suit, Ash bumping and grinding, Wendy awkwardly swaying. Even I, self-conscious as I was, could hardly help but shuffle my feet and sway my hips a bit.

Vanya came over to me, sipping at a plastic cup of white wine. I had watched her knock back several of them already, and she had acquired a slightly glazed look.

She gestured over to Strawberry, who was dancing, not quite with, but in the same general vicinity as, Pattern. They were talking animatedly at the same time. Pattern was jabbing his finger at Strawberry as if accusing her of something. She raised her eyebrows and shook her head.

'Pattern seems even more indignant than usual,' I said.

'He's knocked Moo up again. Can you believe it? After all that drama. Trying to get her to terminate a second time. I told her to hold out for herself. But she's weak. Can't imagine life without a man. Why do women love men like that?'

'What's your husband like?'

'He's all right. Bit of a standard model. Doesn't listen. Misses the point. Likes cars and football. But decent enough.'

'Not a rapist then?'

'I doubt he'd be up to it. Troy says I cut his balls off years ago.'

Strawberry looked over and waved.

'That girl is a proper mess,' said Vanya.

'So everyone says. But maybe she's right. Maybe she really is purifying herself.'

'Needs more than a few grains and vitamins to unfuck her head. After what she's been through.'

'What has she been through?'

'Let me explain something to you.'

She held my leg for balance as she lowered herself on to a scatter cushion.

I sat down next to her and she put an arm around me. She smelled of oranges and tobacco. Also, inevitably, patchouli oil, although it could have been coming from any of the women around me. All of them seemed to reek of the stuff.

'What the hell is that patchouli stuff made of? Some kind of flower? Or do they mix it up in a lab somewhere?'

She ignored me. 'So I was telling you about Strawberry.'

'Yeah.'

'What do you know about her and Henry? About their relationship? To . . . one another. I'm not giving away any secrets, right?'

I hesitated.

'You mean that they're . . . sort of . . . related?'

'You're not as dumb as you pretend to be. What else do you know?'

'Not much.'

She leaned in to me conspiratorially.

'What I heard is this. Henry took off when she was about five to travel America. That whole Kerouac *On the Road* shit. He drank with bums, slept on park benches. In the end he became a bum himself. A drunk, a street rat. Then he cleaned up. Not before he nearly died of whatever. But he didn't go back to look after Strawberry. Too busy discovering himself. Went to India and joined an ashram, which is where he started on all this spiritual shit. He was gone ten years. Ten fucking years, leaving her with her crazy mother, who was a whore, to put it mildly.'

'I thought he became a priest.'

'Never heard that one. Henry told you that?'

'Yes.'

'Did he tell you that her mother had Strawberry out turning tricks at the age of thirteen? Did he tell you that during that time he never once got in touch with her?'

I was aware of my blink rate increasing.

'Did he tell you that a bunch of guys practically raped her while her mother stood by and did nothing?'

'Bullshit.'

'It's true. Unless Strawberry's making it up. And why should she make it up? She told us at *Shrew* in a consciousness-raising group. Did she tell you that she was strung out on DMT for half the time?'

'Something like that, yes. Why are you spilling all this?'

'Because,' said Vanya, 'I want you to understand something about people that you don't yet understand. That you don't *want* to understand.'

'What's that?'

'That people are terrible, Adam.'

She took my face in her hands and gazed directly into my eyes.

241

'Under the surface, they're terrible.'

She let go of me, then took a deep swig of wine.

'Myself included,' she added. 'Very much.'

'Not everybody's terrible,' I said.

Vanya shrugged. 'If you say so. I mean, I guess everyone has different experiences.'

'So how did Strawberry end up here?'

'Henry rolled back into town – Sacramento – when Strawberry was fifteen. By then her mother was in a crazy-house, and Strawberry was sleeping on the floors of "friends". So-called. Henry had come by some money, somehow. I heard he stole it from the Maharishi Ji himself.'

'It was drug-dealing.'

'Whatever it was, he brought her back to England. He's been looking after her ever since. Or what he calls "looking after", which seems to involve him leaving her alone in order to slowly murder herself. Big of him, I guess. Big old Henry.'

'You're bitter.'

'I'm not bitter. Life is bitter. I'm just pointing it out. You'll understand when you're older.'

Henry loomed up.

'What are you two talking about?'

'Vanya thinks people are all rotten.'

'Vanya's wrong. People aren't bad. But they are, very often, of rather poor quality.'

'You should know, Henry.'

She got up and staggered off in the direction of Pattern, who was scowling at no one in particular and picking violently at dry, brown tufts of grass.

I looked around for Ash, but she was nowhere in sight.

Twenty-one

'Why do you think no one turned up?' I said to Henry over the blare of the music, which was still reggae, something I didn't recognize, very bass-driven and heavy in the air.

'Clearly I should have given away free crystals as an inducement.'

'Seriously.'

He turned back, a puzzled look on his face.

'It's hard to say. I think what I am saying is perfectly simple and uncontroversial. But everyone seems to either take exception to it, or find it of no interest. It baffles me.'

He stopped, searching for words. It was something Henry rarely did. He always spoke so fluently that it seemed as if someone was speaking through him.

'I don't know. It's as if people are not satisfied or willing to understand the world. Or other people. They want magic – not cheap magic like mine, but real magic. Crystals and angels. Or they want power. Or they are angry and they want retribution. Or justice. Or confirmation of their victimhood. Or some way of thinking that will make them better than everyone else. And I don't have anything like that to give.'

Strawberry shouted over the music: 'Come on, Henry, give us *something*. Please. Not the whole lecture. Just something.'

There was a round of 'Yeah's and 'Go for it, Henry's.

Henry looked around at the faces, which seemed genuinely expectant, and held up a hand.

'Listen to the music for a moment. Consider it. *Feel* it.'

The thudding bass dominated everything, almost shaking the ground. Everyone stopped dancing and just listened. I tried to feel the bass line with my body.

'Strawberry, could you turn it off, please?'

Strawberry reached over and hit the stop button. I looked around for Ash, but she seemed to have disappeared somewhere. Henry fixed us, one by one, with his eyes. We all fell silent. When he spoke again, his voice had changed – it was more intimate, it drew you in.

'Let me tell you a story. I was friends with a woman once who had been blind since birth. A wonderful woman, a poet and a seer. She loved gardening. And yet she could never see the colourful plants and flowers that she brought to fruition with her fingers and her skill.'

He paused, took his pipe out of his pocket, lit it and pulled on it. He briefly closed his eyes, as if lost in thought, then opened them again.

'This woman, she didn't know what colour was – obviously. But more interestingly, she didn't know what *darkness* was either. She didn't know what *blackness* was. Why? Because she had nothing to compare it with.

'This demonstrates a very important principle. That we only know what we know *by contrasts*. And that is why we have vibrations. That is why we have rhythms. That is why we have life counterpointed by death.'

He paused.

'You're looking blank.'

There was laughter.

'Let me explain further.'

From somewhere, he produced two tuning forks. First he struck one on the edge of the blackboard. It sounded high and pure. Then the other – low and rough.

He paused for effect.

'Why is the low sound so grainy?'

Nobody answered.

'It is grainy because sound is a vibration – a series of peaks and troughs, a sequence of consecutive interruptions of sound and silence. In the high-pitched sound, they come so quickly one after the other that we do not notice them. In the low sound the gaps between the sound and the silence are much greater, so there is a roughness. It is sound, then silence. Sound, then silence. An alternation.'

He paused again.

'*Everything* is a vibration. A coming then a going. Light is vibration – waves and troughs. So-called solid matter is a vibration – of electromagnetic impulses. The beating of your heart is a vibration; the coming and going of your breath is a vibration. The cycles of a woman are a vibration.'

Vanya's body language shifted. She crossed her arms and her facial expression, instead of being simply drunken, became defensive and alert.

'So what?' said Pattern.

'This *means* something. It is why babies love to play peek-a-boo. It is why the sun rises and falls — yet another vibration. We are governed by these comings and these goings, these presences and absences. Do you see? They are the secret pattern behind everything. We fight against evil, we fight against the dark, we fight against death, against nothingness. But they are all necessary, so that their opposites can manifest.'

There was a general air of puzzlement, but Henry was unfazed. He puffed at his pipe with a contented air. He was clearly in his element.

'These vibrations, these rhythms, are so ingrained in our everyday consciousness that they have become invisible to us. We do not see that we ourselves are vibrations — vibrations of the very earth, which breathes out its newborn and breathes in its dead. Rhythm is at the heart of everything. That is why we dance to it.'

'For example: men and women. Male and female are not poles *apart*. They are poles of the *same thing*. There is common ground between poles. The circuit runs from positive to negative.'

Vanya stood up unsteadily. She had helped herself to a half-full bottle of wine from the trestle table, and had repeatedly topped up her cup.

'So which is the negative pole?' she demanded.

'I don't mean it in *that* sense, not the popular, pejorative sense of the word "negative". More in the scientific sense. As with the poles of an electrical current.'

'The negative pole.'

'Between women's legs is the space that gives birth to everything and from which everything comes. Out of nothing comes everything.'

246

'You're saying women are nothing?'

'I am all in favour of nothing.' He walked a few steps across to where Vanya was sitting. 'Do you think nothing comes from nothing?'

'Of course.'

'Then how to explain this?'

And at that he reached behind her head and a pigeon flew out of his hand as if from nowhere.

There was laughter, and the argument was defused. Vanya, helpless now, sat down again, joining in the chorus of approval.

The wine, which I had been knocking back with almost as much alacrity as Vanya, was beginning to make me drowsy and inattentive.

'But what do you *believe* in, Henry?' said Pattern edgily.

'Uncertainty. Transience. The urgency of the present. The intractability of death. The secret self that guides us.'

Henry had put away his pipe and was now smoking a cigarette. He blew a perfect smoke ring, then another one that floated through the first one.

'This is what we are. Dissolving smoke.'

Everyone applauded. Henry smiled.

'Now, we need to finish up. I don't want Mr Pritchard from the council accusing me of infringing some by-law or other.'

He looked around for Pritchard, but he was nowhere to be seen.

'Thank you for listening.'

It was clear his talk was over. There was a smattering of slightly puzzled applause. Strawberry, however, was nodding vigorously, cheering and clapping.

Ash got up from where she was sitting and came and crouched next to me. She smelled of hairspray.

'Your uncle's a nutter,' she said.

'Where did you go?'

'When?'

'Just before the talk started.'

' I forgot my bag. I thought I might have left it back in the woods. Yeah. It was there.' She swung her small cloth bag lightly on her arm and patted it.

Henry now appeared to be debating a point with Pattern. I became fiercely aware of the closeness of Ash's body. There was a fire in it as radiant and as real as the one that now lay smouldering by the side of the blackboard.

'They will get rid of him, you know.'

I took another swig of my wine and went to fill up my plate with vegetable curry. I had grown used to spicy food, even begun to enjoy it. The pot on the table was empty, but I was sure I had seen some more left on the stovetop. When I got into the galley, Pritchard was there. He looked up amiably when I entered.

'Mr Templeton is quite a character,' he said, scribbling on his pad. I noticed he had a tape measure. He started measuring the boat's dimensions from floor to roof.

'Do you have permission to do that?'

'What?' said Pritchard, idly checking the tape at floor level. I repeated the question more assertively.

'Do I need it?'

'Let's find out.'

I headed out to Henry, who was drinking a glass of water and talking to Vanya. I beckoned urgently to him. He nodded, apologized to Vanya and walked directly across to the boat and Pritchard, who was still happily measuring and scribbling.

'What are you doing?' Henry demanded.

'I'm measuring your boat to see if it conforms with—'

'I invite you on to my boat in a spirit of hospitality. You offer no fee or donation. Your intentions are far from congenial. Yet still I welcome you. You turned up with no warning, and now you've started . . . measuring things. What is it with you people and your measurements? Are you afraid you're going to run out of inches?'

'I'm sure you'd want to be seen to be obeying the law, Mr Templeton, if that means—'

Before he could do any more, Henry snatched the tape out of his hands and hurled it through the open window into the river.

'That tape measure belongs to the council,' said Pritchard. He appeared genuinely shocked.

'This land, and this boat, belongs to me. And I'd thank you to get off it. Right now.'

Pritchard looked nervous. Henry didn't often lose his temper, but when he did, he managed to generate an intimidating amount of heat. Holding Henry's gaze for less than a second, Pritchard turned and made for the exit.

'We'll be in touch, Mr Templeton.'

'Dr Templeton. I'll look forward to it immensely.'

Henry returned to his place next to the blackboard. Everyone was now standing in a clump by the guttering fire as Pritchard marched out, muttering, still apparently outraged by the loss of his tape measure.

'I think we're finished for tonight. We need to clean up and close down. If you could put the cushions and blankets into a pile, that would be most helpful. Thank you all for coming.'

He threw a glass of water on the fire. It hissed, gave a gasp, and died.

Twenty-two

After I had spent almost a month at the houseboat, I phoned my father again. However, once again I found that I had little to say to him, or vice versa. I told him that I was doing well with my studies and enjoying my stay. I was careful not to go into too much detail about the closeness I was experiencing with Henry – I had at least that much residual sensitivity. I just informed Ray that Henry was keeping me safe, looking after me tolerably and not forcing me to inject myself with heroin or ingest peyote. This seemed to satisfy Ray, at least enough to prevent him from driving down to check on me. There was a part of me that wanted to see him, but a larger part wanted to keep my new, bewitched, fire-and-water world private and inviolate. I hoped, in the meantime, that he had stopped dusting my bedroom.

The date of the hearing was closing in. Henry remained convinced that the terms of his lease had not been breached.

Even with Toshack's spies at the boat lecture, nothing unseemly had taken place. There had been no drugs or drunkenness. There might be suspicions, but there was nothing they could bring into county court in the way of hard evidence. As for the family to whom Henry had allegedly exposed himself, nothing more had been heard from them.

The weather remained uncompromisingly hot and dry, with only the occasional welcome thunderstorm to relieve the turbid, heavy stillness of the air. The days had taken on a rhythm. In the morning I sunbathed and revised while Henry worked on his book and his court case. In the afternoons, I would often meet up with Ash. Sometimes we would go to her room at the rectory, to clandestinely kiss and explore one another's bodies with the thin skin of our fingertips while Wesley worked at his desk, no more than yards away, on the far side of a floor and a wall. Most of the time I struggled with the prophylactic of an outer layer of clothing, but several times Ash allowed me to trace the outline of her nipples under her still-buttoned blouse.

On one occasion, I took courage and ventured to put my moist, trembling hand down the front of her pants. I was astonished when I momentarily met no resistance. Then she gently prised my hand away, and planted a kiss on my mouth. The kiss was angry and apologetic and yet at the same time held a note of encouragement, even abandonment.

Outside of that enchanted room, that temple where our bodies prayed to one another for release, we would walk, or picnic, or cycle. The days seemed very long, and yet we did not feel the weight of them. There was a sense that any movement was half imagined, illusory, as if lightly sketched

in a flick-book. Only the awareness that I would be returning to London in a few weeks pressed down on me.

Even the oppression I had felt since my mother died
began, at times, to lift. But although that grief was fading –
the grief that had long been concealed under the drab,
smothering garments of sterility and numbness – I could find
no solution to the guilt that chafed and cut at me.

My self-recrimination was so unrelenting it was boring,
even to me. It had carved out a channel in my head which I
paced endlessly. I found the walls too slippery or indistinct
to climb. Or – as Henry had suggested to me on one occasion – perhaps I didn't want to climb out. Henry said that so
long as I felt the experience of guilt I could hang on to the
illusion that the world was controllable. So long as I believed
I might have acted otherwise, I could imagine myself to be
powerful. I understood what he was saying. But it didn't
make any difference to the unreachable itch that inflicted
itself relentlessly on my conscience. The distance between
the language of the mind and that of the heart seemed to span
oceans.

Despite the fact that we were roughly the same age – she was
born in the same year, only two months previously – Ash
appeared more mature than I felt. She listened carefully to all
I had to say – I had started to gabble a lot when silence fell and
I became ill-at-ease – and seemed able to understand the
meanings between the words as well as the words themselves.

She was a serious person, in her way. I saw myself, on the
other hand, more as a shallow person being lent the patina of
gravitas by my colourless, soul-tiring depression. Nevertheless,
despite our differences, we had established a certain closeness

that went beyond simply passing the time, flirtation and the accumulations of casual familiarity. I knew that I would miss her, sharply, when the summer was over. However, I wasn't convinced that she would be more than slightly dislocated by my absence. It was her father who was the chief subject of her love. Wesley Toshack, who – I came to learn – she saw as all-knowing, all good, indestructible.

Ash kept herself at one remove, physically and emotionally. Although we would kiss and touch, and on a few occasions she fumbled with my zip and rubbed clumsily at my crotch – enough, sometimes, to bring me off into a hastily convened pink tissue – it was for the most part innocent stuff. We were little more than children – the 1970s maintained a semblance of innocence, at least in regard to sex, at least in Somerset.

I assumed that Ash had ventured as far as she was going to go, confounding what I now could only think of as a childish, Mills-and-Boon fantasy that she was holding an unruly passion in strict check. But then, one day when we met at the town clock, she informed me in a matter-of-fact tone that her father had gone away for a few days and we would have the whole house to ourselves. The implication – the invitation – was plain enough.

When we arrived at the rectory, Ash took me by the hand and led me into her bedroom. It was the same as ever – plain and pleasant and like any teenager's bedroom. There was a poster of Marc Bolan on the wall. On the bed, three teddy bears. There were two small tables, each with a single drawer, on either side of a single bed with a pink eiderdown. There was a glass of water on one of the tables. A wardrobe, a larger chest of drawers, a mirror and a dressing-table with flounces.

Ash and I faced one another. I imagined she was waiting for me to do something – perhaps she wanted me to overwhelm her? But Vanya, during one of her drunken lectures at the party at Troy's, had given me strict lessons about consent between the sexes. I shouldn't push myself forward too hard.

I just stood there. I could go over and kiss her, but it felt a bit feeble. I sensed that she wanted something more from me. I swallowed.

'You look nice,' I said, and immediately regretted it.

'I'm not nice,' she answered.

Then, keeping her eyes on my face all the time, she began to slowly undress. I had not expected this – it was so . . . brazen. First her T-shirt, revealing a black lacy bra. Then her shoes, then her jeans. Matching tiny black knickers. Her white socks stayed in place.

My body began to tremble, despite the fierce heat of the room, which faced south and had little in the way of ventilation. For some reason – to ensure privacy from the ears of neighbours? – Ash had insisted on keeping the window closed.

She reached behind herself and unhooked her bra, and it fell to the ground. Her breasts were heavier than I had imagined them to be, on the many occasions when I had imagined them. The skin there was marked by the pale outline of a bikini top. The nipples were raised up in dark islands of pigmented skin, areolas the size of daisies.

She rolled down her knickers. The furze underneath was pale, a sparse crop. Ash's clothes were in a pile at her feet. One of her legs was held straight, the other had its knee slightly bent. I could see a line of pinkness between her legs. She faced me full on, flagrantly, fragrantly.

The silver crucifix she always wore remained around her neck. But she was working at the catch. She undid it and placed it on the bedside table. It seemed to me that she was separating herself from her vows, whatever those vows were. I allowed myself to imagine, anyway, this was the rune she intended me to read.

Still she said nothing. The wispy triangle of hair seemed to advertise the gap between her legs. Still keeping her eyes on my face, not smiling, her pupils large and black, she threw the soft toys from the bed then arranged herself, reclining on the counterpane. She propped a pillow behind her head, clenched her hands behind her neck and just lay there, looking at me, her face gathering seriousness. She was as silent as a midnight cathedral. She just looked at me, lips slightly apart, legs separated by two or three carefully calibrated inches. And waited.

Then I noticed her tongue moving slowly between her lips and my paralysis came abruptly to an end. I tore off my clothes as quickly as I could, almost tripping over my jeans as I struggled to remove them. I didn't care what the etiquette was any more. I didn't care what I was supposed to do. I didn't care about Vanya and her prescriptions. Ash laughed – a deeper, hoarser laugh than I had heard from her before.

I threw myself on top of her and pushed my tongue into her mouth. She responded, fiercely. I could feel her small hand, the arc of her nails lightly touching the tip of my cock. She tasted intensely of sugar. She moaned slightly – it was like the most beautiful, dark chord that had ever been conjured.

Still on top of her, balanced on one arm, I drifted my hand over her skin – neck, collarbone, the top of the arms, the rise of her breasts, the eruptions of the nipples. I felt I was navigating an uncharted landscape that I nevertheless knew since I had traversed it compulsively in my dreams. A thrill of bliss ran through me, blotting out all the negative feeling that I dragged after me like a leg iron. Henry had once said that the real god was hidden in the present moment, and I suddenly knew what it was to be at one with Henry's god. Future and past were entirely obliterated.

I hesitated before moving my hand further down. But Ash grabbed it and pushed it towards her groin. She took a single finger – the index – and guided it to the space between her legs. I started to search, gently, not sure what I was aiming for.

'Harder,' she said, quite sharply.

I felt— No, I had stopped feeling. I was only being. I was reduced, or rather expanded, to the sum total of my nerve endings, and my instinct, and my imagination. I continued prying and probing, this time more violently, trying to find half-imagined passageways and turnings. I detected an area of swelling that as I touched and rubbed it seemed to produce a reaction in Ash, a vibration, a sigh. Her face was flushed, her lips distended. She was a furnace, a lava pit. Outside, more heat fought to enter the room. It was ninety degrees in the street.

I pulled my hand away and rested myself on both elbows above her now. My cock was at around her stomach level. I knew I was in position but I wasn't sure what to do.

Ash's eyes were fierce. It was written in them that this was going to go further than I had ever imagined. The furthest.

Then pragmatism, that passion killer, struck me.

'Do you have any . . .?' I said.

Ash looked impatient.

'There's no need. Trust me.'

I wasn't interested in debating the point. But I still wasn't quite sure what to do next.

She had my cock in her left hand now and was lightly running her fingers up and down the shaft. I thought I was going to disgrace myself at any moment, but I held on.

'Wait a minute,' she said.

Suddenly she pushed me off her. I crouched by the side of the bed. She fumbled underneath the left-hand bedside table. I heard the sound of some kind of adhesive tape being removed. She produced a small tube, about the size of a toothpaste tube, with the clinical inscription KY JELLY.

'What's that for?'

'It's a lubricant.'

'Oh.'

This took me aback. From the exploring I had done so far she seemed pretty adequately lubricated. It was like a warm, scented, drenched sponge. But then I had no experience of these things.

'Stay there.'

She squeezed some out and reached down between her legs. Then she dropped the tub, grabbed me by the cock and pulled me on top of her. I balanced on my elbows again. She raised her legs, high, higher. Now her ankles were resting on my shoulders. She guided me with her hand, down, down. Down. And forward.

Almost immediately, before I knew what was happening, there was a pressure, then a parting, then I was inside her. First just the tip. She winced. Then further. She cried out. Further. I thrust. It was tighter there than I had expected. More hollow. Waves of excitement broke over me and felt I myself fighting the largest wave that I could sense in the distance, already approaching, approaching.

I held on. She arched her back and opened her mouth. I could see her teeth. The colour of her eyes had disappeared behind her eyelids. There was only a slit there, and it showed white, like a suffering saint, like a martyr.

I pushed in again, but it was too tight for me to go all the way. She seemed to groan from the depths of herself, from the cellars and sounding-rooms. I pushed harder, and thrust faster. Deeper. She screamed – a quiet scream, perhaps modulated for the neighbours, but a scream. Unable to resist what I thought of as the seventh wave – though it might have been the third or the twentieth – I felt myself go under, nearly black out. Her head fell back, limp, her eyes staring wildly at the ceiling as if she could see nothing at all.

The energy drained out of everything, leaving only a low corona of electric afterglow. It could only have been five minutes since we'd lain down together. But I felt that I had evacuated every part of my being. Lost my soul, gratefully. There were final contractions – mine, hers. Then I pushed myself off her, lay flat on the pillow, loins jerking, legs trembling. Gasping. Fighting for breath.

I felt immediately, as thought returned, that I had fallen short. It was over so quickly. The present now disappeared, pushed away by the past and future moments that always crowded life, strangled it.

'I'm sorry,' I said.

'What about?' said Ash.

She jostled up to me, briefly rested her head on my chest. Then she reached for a box of tissues that was on the other bedside table, and wiped me carefully. She threw the tissue in the bin.

'Remind me to flush that down the lav. Dad checks my room sometimes.'

Then, as if she had been jolted into remembering something, she picked up the tube of KY Jelly and replaced the lid. She found a roll of Sellotape, reached under the bedside table and secured it in the hollow there. From the outside it was entirely invisible.

'He would never look there, though. Hasn't got the imagination.'

She returned to me on the bed. We lay in silence. Outside I could hear the faint passing of motor cars and the music of voices. They all seemed very far away.

Eventually I found the honesty I needed to turn and look her in the eyes. She simply smiled at me. It was as if her soul, having been transported, had returned to her body and now was shining out at me.

'You're beautiful,' I said.

'I'm dirty.'

'That too. But mainly beautiful.'

'Thank you.'

She still had her white socks on. One was at the calf, the other was pushed down to her ankle. She sat up and began to secure her crucifix back on her neck again. I helped her to fasten the back.

'You're not such a good Christian after all,' I said – purely in a spirit of teasing.

She glanced at me. Her eyes now seemed to hold a mystery.

'Aren't I?'

'I thought you were meant to save that up until you got married.'

'Save what up?'

'Your virginity, obviously. Although, of course, I'm assuming that you're a virgin. Were a virgin.'

'I was a virgin, yes.'

'Me too.'

'I sort of guessed that.' She stopped smiling. 'I still am. Didn't you get that?' she murmured, reaching for her knickers and pulling them slowly on.

I had no idea what she meant.

'But. I felt. It was . . .'

'I'm still a virgin.'

'You can't be.'

'So are you.'

'What are you *talking* about?'

Now she deftly clipped her bra on.

'I'm a Christian, Adam. Pre-marital sex is proscribed by the Church. I shan't have intercourse with a man until I fall in love and I'm married.'

I felt a deep, deep puzzlement – and not only because I had started to imagine that she had fallen in love with me. Why else would she give herself to me?

'Are you playing a game with me?'

'No. But if I am, it was a good game, wasn't it?'

I thought about the tube of KY Jelly under the bedside table. I was reaching for a solution to the deep puzzle that my mind was shying away from.

'You're saying?'

'I'm saying that I stayed true to my faith. Work the rest out yourself. It's not that uncommon in Catholic countries, apparently.'

I remained still on the bed as the truth began to soak in.

'Actually, I can't believe the real thing would be any improvement. Or any more real, for that matter.'

'But surely . . . The Bible. Your beliefs.'

'If something slipped through God's net while he was

telling the faithful how to live, that's hardly my fault.'

Now, just as I had penetrated her, by gradations, the knowledge finally penetrated me.

I had no idea how to feel. Puzzlement flashed through my head. Then a shiver of revulsion, then finally, and definitely, excitement – the excitement of the dark, the forbidden.

'You're debauched,' I said, with genuine astonishment.

She laughed now. 'My soul is still spotless.'

I laughed too. I understood, and it was OK, and I had gone beyond the imagined possible without even knowing it.

'You're a catamite, Ashley.'

'A what?'

'It's a word Henry taught me.'

My mind wandered across far spaces, making improbable connections.

'Now I get it!'

'You get what?' she asked.

'Troy.'

'Who's Troy?'

'He's a friend of Strawberry's. And mine. You saw him at the boat. With the big hair. I could never understand how he could do that kind of thing.'

Her face did something strange. It was not so much a hardening of the eyes as a withdrawal of the entity behind them.

'What are you talking about?'

'Troy. The one with the big hair. Surely you must have noticed.'

'What – that big strapping American?'

'He's from the Midlands, actually.'

'Even so. What? He's a queer?'

There was something distinctly nasty in the way she pronounced the word, as if she was chewing on a bitter root.

'He's gay, yes.'

She reared up from the bed and started briskly pulling on the rest of her clothes. She turned back to me, stretching her T-shirt over her torso.

'A man with a man. How can they do that?'

'Are you joking? After what you just had me do?'

'There's nothing in the Bible against that. *Nothing.*'

'What is wrong with you?'

'How can you be friends with such a person? He probably molests children.'

'Rubbish! He's not doing anyone any harm.'

'It's not a matter of whether he's doing harm. It's a matter of whether what he's doing is right.'

She opened the window. It was as if she wished to fumigate the room. It provoked me.

'I kissed him, you know.'

She looked round at me furiously.

'It was at a party. For a dare.'

'That's revolting. What were you thinking of? I can't believe you.'

'It's true though.'

'Did you *like* it?'

I decided not to mention that I'd bitten Troy's tongue.

Twenty-three

I received the results of my other A levels, forwarded by my father with a desultory *Well done!* scrawled on an accompanying note. I had achieved a B in English and a C in Physics, both which were fine with me. Bs, Cs, As — it was all the same crazy, made-up rat race.

Nevertheless I remained grimly committed to finishing my revision for my retake. I rehearsed all the necessary facts and arguments, and now, at least, I cared enough to make an effort to pass. But the dilemmas of history still pressed on me, which was odd, since I was not a particularly academic child. Why did the First World War happen? Why did anything happen? That was all of it, but who was ever capable of untangling those things? Henry said that history was just 'accidents that no one could understand'. The idea appealed to me. Perhaps it rather conveniently got me off the hook over my mother's death. But then, as Henry pointed out, who wants to spend their life dangling from a hook?

My main worry, as the summer drew on, was Strawberry. Her health had continued to be poor, if anything getting worse. She was still functional, but she seemed perpetually tired, rarely leaving the cabin now, except when Troy occasionally came to pick her up and drive her into Bristol to do some shopping for raw food and dietary products.

One morning I decided to pay her a visit. Strawberry and I had become close, but in a different way from my feelings for Ash. Although she was older than me — she told me she was twenty-three — there was a part of her that seemed for ever a child. She seemed to have no sex life whatsoever.

She would giggle like a child, she craved sweets ('That's the worst thing about this diet, and this country — no M&Ms'), she made daisy chains and read *The Little Prince* over and over again as if it was the Oracle. It was as if the very act of starving herself was an attempt to keep herself a child. Yet there was something so old and tired about her at the same time, as if she had contracted some reverse version of progeria. Her body was young, as were parts of her mind, but the soul that peered out from her eyes sometimes seemed weary and shrivelled.

I supposed it was simply damage. She was crippled inside, badly — that was obvious even to me. Sometimes I would hear her crying when I walked near the cabin. She would wring her hands as if trying to rub them clean, like Lady Macbeth. She was developing a tic on the side of her mouth, and her hair had started to look dry and distressed. There were cracks and chaps on her lips.

Henry was not insouciant about her condition — in fact he was profoundly concerned — but he was also, to my mind, wilfully blind. 'A fool who persists in his folly will become wise' remained his mantra, his point of principle. He insisted that he had no power to force her to abandon her diet. He had tried to do so on a number of occasions, without success. I felt sure I could detect a tinge of paternal pride at her wilfulness, even as it seemingly wrecked her from within.

I set off for the cabin in my cut-off jeans, but no pants, socks or T-shirt. My skin was tanned now, my hair sun-streaked, my body lean and defined. Physically, I had never felt better. I didn't even bother with my sandals as I made my way along the riverbank and then turned towards the clearing where the cabin was.

As I made the clearing, I heard a scream. It was the most awful sound, worse than anything I had heard in a horror movie. Like the fox I had heard in the night that first week, only darker, more desperate, louder.

I wanted to turn and run. Crazily, I decided that Strawberry was being murdered. I forced myself to stand firm.

The scream stopped very suddenly. I waited, rooted to the spot, outside the cabin. I heard a weird thudding noise, a shuffling and a faint moaning. I wondered for a moment if she might be having sex, but then dismissed the idea. Without thinking any more, I pushed the door open.

Strawberry was alone, spread out on the floor, face up, eyes wide open. Flecks of foam speckled her lips. Her arms and legs were twitching compulsively, and her head was banging against the floor, as if she was frustrated and having a tantrum. Her back was arched. The heel of one foot struck repeatedly against the wall in a dull tattoo. There was a broken glass of what looked like carrot juice to one side of her head. She was within an inch or two of the shards of glass.

Immediately, I found myself back in my kitchen with my mother – terrified, impotent. But there were no telephones here, no neighbours. Then, to my own surprise, the feeling passed and I became very calm and focused. I called her name to see if she could hear me – but, as I expected, there was no reply.

I swiftly cleared up the scraps of glass with my fingertips. I had worked out that she was fitting, so I carefully found a pillow and pushed it under her head. Her blank eyes stared at me, nothing behind them. Her mouth worked and worked, grinding. I saw a flannel by the sink, grabbed it, rolled it up and forced it between her teeth, to stop her swallowing her tongue.

I sat still, hoping that the fit would pass, by no means certain that it would. After maybe thirty more seconds, a light returned to her eyes – she seemed to work at focusing. A few more seconds and she looked up at me and tried to smile, but the cloth in her mouth made it impossible. I wasn't sure she recognized me. Her limbs had become still. She relaxed her back. She looked exhausted, but beautiful. I reached over and took the flannel gently from her mouth. It was coated with sputum and a little blood.

She pulled herself up slowly on to one elbow, and shook her head from side to side, as if this might enable thought to return. She seemed unconcerned, dazed. She noticed the spilled orange liquid on the floor. A trail of the same liquid was trickling down the side of her mouth. She wiped it with her sleeve.

'Did you do that?' she said, pointing to the remnants of glass, now on the draining board.

'No.'

'Who did?'

'I imagine you did.'

'No,' she said. 'No.'

She staggered to her feet and nearly fell over. I caught her. She was so light. I felt her hand around my wrist. She looked at me again, as if seeing me for the first time.

'I'm so tired.'

I said nothing. She looked suddenly puzzled and angry.

'What are you doing here? How long have you been here?'

'A few minutes. You were having some kind of fit.'

Strawberry corrugated her brow. The anger fled her face.

'You were lying on the floor. Twitching. Eyes open. I propped your head up. That's why you had a flannel in your mouth.'

'I had a flannel in my mouth?'

She looked incredulous.

'To stop you swallowing your tongue.'

Her face cleared. Her features drooped. She sat heavily down.

'Oh. *Grand mal*. Shit.'

I sat down on the cushion opposite her. 'What?'

'*Grand mal*. I thought the purification process would get rid of it. Haven't had an attack for more than nine months. Gave up on the medication, and the diet kept it at bay. But it's come back. Fuck.'

She looked disgusted.

'"*Grand mal*"?'

She reached for some kitchen towel and started clearing up the carrot juice. Without looking at me, she spoke again.

'I've had it since I was a kid. Epilepsy. Only lasts maybe a minute. I can't remember anything about it.'

She looked at me now. Momentarily, there was a pleading in her face, but it gave way to a vague sadness.

'You helped me. Thank you. But I'd have been OK. I just black out.'

I was feeling very shaken.

'You screamed. A really . . . I've never heard anything like it. Like you were being possessed.'

'Did I? Yes, I've heard that that happens. I can't remember.'

'It sounded like you were very scared.'

'Perhaps I was. I don't know. But I'm OK now.'

She stepped uncertainly over to me and gave me a kiss on the cheek.

'Thank you for looking after me, Adam. It was sweet of you. Would you like some oatmeal biscuits? No sugar in them, I'm afraid. But I made them myself.'

'No thank you.'

Her eyelids flickered.

'I'm so tired. I'm always so tired.'

'But are you OK?'

'Oh yes,' she said sleepily. 'I'm fine. Just need to rest.'

'Don't you think . . .?'

I hesitated. I didn't want to upset her. But she looked like she was already drifting off.

'Don't you think your diet might have sparked off the attack?'

She shook her head woozily and lay down on the futon.

'Helping. Used to get them every six months. Now nine months since . . . Suzuki wrote to me. He told me to carry on. Just side-effects.'

Her head lolled to one side. She was asleep.

I headed back to the *Ho Koji* to tell Henry what had happened. I found him in his office, typing. When I told him the news, he banged his forehead with the heel of his palm.

'Jesus! Susan. What the hell is wrong with her? What is she putting herself through?'

'She says it was nothing to do with her diet.'

'You believe that?'

'How would I know?'

'Is she OK now?'

'She's fallen asleep.'

He began slowly rolling a cigarette. His hands trembled slightly. He dropped the paper, and had to pick up the scraps of tobacco and reroll.

'It's true that she had occasional bouts of epilepsy before she embarked on this fad. But it can be brought on by stress, both mental and physical. The diet is likely to be a factor.'

'Have you asked her when the diet's going to finish?'

'I don't think it *is* going to finish. She sees it as a permanent choice. Although, hopefully, it will be moderated at some point. Perhaps when she has disappeared altogether.'

I hesitated.

'How much danger is she putting herself in?'

Henry finished rolling the cigarette, successfully this time. He lit it and inhaled. The smoke emerged in bitty, nervous exhalations, manifesting as intermittent blue clouds.

'She's been through fads before. Plenty of them. She always comes to her senses in the end. She will again.'

'What if she doesn't come to her senses?'

He spat out some tobacco.

'Well – what do you want me to do about it? I can't tell her what to do. She's very, very stubborn.'

'She needs to see a doctor.'

'Try telling her that and see how far it gets you.'

'She's tired all the time. She looks like she's about to get heart failure or something.'

'Come on, Adam. Don't exaggerate.'

'I couldn't bear for it to happen again.'

Henry looked up sharply.

'It's not going to happen "again", Adam. She'll be OK. She's not entirely crazy. I've written to Suzuki, explaining the situation. He's the only person she'll listen to. I'm sure if he understands that her health is in jeopardy, he will write a note telling her to ease up. I've met him on more than one occasion. He's misguided, but he's not a monster.'

'He's already written to her. He says she's doing fine.'

Henry pulled on the rollie, but it had gone out. He threw it at the bin, with more force than was necessary, and missed. He sucked on his teeth.

'She didn't tell me.'

'Why should she tell you? You're only going to try and talk her out of it.'

'Well, I guess that's my point entirely.'

'So you're washing your hands of this.'

'I'm not doing anything of the sort. But I'm not God.'

'How much longer do you think she can survive in that state?'

'You're not a doctor. Neither am I.'

'That's what she needs to see. A doctor. Soon.'

'That's not for us to decide.'

I looked at Henry — now searching for stub that had missed the bin — and he suddenly angered me. Despite his obvious concern for Strawberry, there was within him a quiet certainty, a deep acceptance of the inevitability of wrongness, that was at the same time elevated and vaguely inhuman.

I shrugged. 'Well – I guess that's up to you.'

'It's up to Susan.'

He found the stub, deposited it in the bin and then started to type again, signalling that the topic of Strawberry had been exhausted. I felt at a loss as to how to get through to him – how to get through to either of them.

'How's the book going?' I muttered.

'Good. Very good. I've nearly completed a second draft. Then it will be ready for submission. Five years' work. I'm very pleased with it. Yes. I'm delighted.'

He didn't look up from the Remington.

'Are you not going to go and see Strawberry?'

He hit a few more keys, then stopped.

'Hmmm? Oh yes. Of course. But you said she was OK, right?'

'For the short term.'

'No, you're right. I should go and see her.'

He stood up.

I made my way out of the boat and stared blankly in the direction of Strawberry's cabin. Henry followed, then started taking leisurely, casual paces towards the clearing.

It was then, as I watched the infuriating slowness of his stride, that I decided what I had to do next.

It took me fifteen minutes to pedal into town. When I reached the rectory, I banged on the door furiously with my fist. I realized I was in a panic, and started to take deep breaths to try and calm myself down.

Wesley Toshack opened the door. He almost entirely filled the doorway. I still hadn't quite got used to how huge he was. His black hair was thick and crinkly and oiled back. His jaw was as angular as a chair-back. I was still breathless from the bike ride, despite my attempts at deep breathing.

'Adam.'

'Reverend.'

'Call me Wesley. Please. I assume you're here to see Ash.'

I wasn't sure why I was there, or what it was I had to do. I just knew I had to come here.

'Is she here?'

'She'll be back in fifteen minutes or so. She's popped down to the shops.'

He looked at me shrewdly for a long moment. 'Are you all right, Adam?'

I made no reply. He gestured for me to come in. I hesitated, then stepped across the threshold. The room, with its old, dark wood, rugs and religious icons, had the air of a confessional booth.

Toshack made me a cup of coffee and brought it to me with a sugared biscuit. We sat and made small-talk – how my revision was going, how things were on the boat, what my life was like when I was in London. He was clearly practised in listening, and asking questions that might open you up. It made me faintly uneasy, but I was also aware that at some level I welcomed it.

After twenty-five minutes, Ash had still not returned. Wesley tapped his finger three times on the wooden arm of the chair he was sitting in, regarding me curiously.

'There's something wrong, Adam, isn't there?'

I felt a stab of loyalty towards Henry, who, I knew, would be mortified to know that I was talking to Toshack like this. But then I thought of Strawberry. Her blank, staring eyes. Her tiny body shaking as if caught in a cruel wind.

'Perhaps we should wait until Ash comes back.'

'You can never tell with Ash. When she says fifteen minutes, she can mean anything up to an hour. But you probably
know that already. So what's the matter, Adam?'

I sensed that some invisible clerical vestment was being
slipped on. His body language opened, inviting me to open
up in return. He leaned forward slightly.

'It's hard to talk about.'

'Your uncle told me about the death of your mother.
Tragic, tragic. Is it that which is troubling you?'

I shook my head.

'No. Well. Yes. That's always there. Always with me. But
no.'

Still I held back. But Toshack held me steadily in his gaze,
which was like a tractor beam. It seemed to leave me no
place to hide. He said nothing, but eventually the silence
became unbearable.

'It's Strawberry.'

'Strawberry?'

'Yes. The girl you talked about. Skinny.'

'Yes,' said Toshack. 'I remember her. She didn't look well.
Skin and bone. Has she some kind of disease?'

'Not exactly. She's just very determined.'

I paused. Then the words tumbled out, the words that I
knew marked the early gradient of a hazardous slope.

'I went to her cabin today. She was having some sort of fit.
She's recovered, but I think she's in a serious condition.'

Ash walked into the room, carrying two shopping bags.

'Hello, Dad. Adam! What are you doing here?'

She kept moving, depositing the shopping bags in the
kitchen.

'There's a bit of trouble down at the boat,' said Toshack.

'Nothing to worry about. Nothing we can't sort out. What kind of fit, Adam?'

'What's happened?' said Ash, sitting down beside me on the sofa.

'She said it was *grand mal*. Some form of epilepsy.' I told them about the scene that had confronted me.

Ash put her hand on mine. It was comforting.

'You must have been terrified.'

'I think she may be very ill. Dangerously so. And she won't go to a doctor.'

'What does Henry have to say about this?'

'He doesn't know how to help.'

Ash and Toshack exchanged glances.

'We have to do something. Don't we, Dad? We have to?'

'As Henry says – what can we do?' I said.

'I'll think of something,' said Toshack. 'But I need to pray first.' He stood up. 'Is there anything else you can tell us about this girl, Adam?'

'Nothing that matters.'

'Are you sure?'

I felt Ash pressing my hand. At the same time, words fizzed on my tongue, demanding utterance. Before I allowed myself to think any more, I blurted them out.

'She's Henry's daughter.'

Rationalizations crowded my mind, trying to obliterate the sense of betrayal I immediately felt, like heartburn. Vanya had known, and therefore probably all her group knew – Pattern, Troy, probably Moo. What difference did it make anyway?

'Henry's *daughter*,' repeated Ash slowly, as if tasting the information, feeling it on her lips for flavours.

'Does it matter?'

Toshack's face was dark, but there was another look there, beneath the darkness. I couldn't put my finger on it, but it worried me. Wesley was again exchanging glances with Ash. It was as if they had suddenly excavated a deep common purpose.

'Come and see us tomorrow, will you, Adam? Once I've had a chance to sleep on it. We'll work something out. Come at around noon.'

I agreed. Wesley shook my hand, and Ash walked me back to my bike.

I wanted to tell Henry of the meeting, but my shame choked me. When I returned to the houseboat, I went to my room and stayed there, without speaking a word, until the light died in the sky.

Twenty-four

The next day, as I had promised, I made my way back to the rectory. The benefit of a night's sleep had reassured me somewhat. Yes, Strawberry was Henry's daughter. But she was twenty-three years old. She was not Henry's responsibility.

The heat shimmer that hovered over the tarmac as I cycled towards Lexham gave the ride an eerie, premonitory quality. It was eighty-seven degrees. We had seen no rain for a fortnight. Forest fires had caught on the Somerset Levels, even coming close to Bath on occasion. I thought of the Long Hot Summer of 1914, before everything incandesced. How forces built up and then, when some mysterious tipping point was reached, released themselves uncontrollably.

I arrived at midday. Wesley and Ash were outside waiting for me. To my consternation, there was also a policeman, standing by an Austin Allegro squad car. It was the same tall, skinny policeman with bum fluff under his nose who had cautioned Henry for 'exposing' himself on the river. The passenger door was open.

Wesley was wearing his clerical garb. Ash was in an innocent cotton dress, white punctuated with tiny blue flowers. Wesley held a large black bible in his right hand. He spoke in a low, even tone that somehow implied absolute determination.

'I'm sorry, Adam. You had something of a wasted journey. We're going to head down to the boat. We had no way of letting you know.'

'We couldn't turn up without you. It didn't seem right,' said Ash.

I stared at them both, uncomprehending. I gestured towards the policeman.

'What's he doing here?'

'Constable Urquhart is concerned there may be issues of abuse and neglect,' said Toshack. 'And it may be that, if we cannot talk sense into the girl – let me speak plainly – we will have to compel her to seek treatment.'

'Abuse and neglect by who? She's a twenty-three-year-old woman.'

Ash and Toshack exchanged glances.

'We have information that she is only seventeen years old, and therefore technically a minor. As such, she is in her father's care.'

I laughed.

'That's ridiculous. She told me herself that she was twenty-three.'

'And you find her testimony entirely reliable, do you, sir?' said the policeman. The way he pronounced the word 'sir' made it clear that he was entirely without respect for my viewpoint. He was Toshack's man all right.

'But how would you know different?'

A flicker crossed Ash's face. She would not meet my eye.

'We have access to . . . certain documents, which make the facts . . . unassailable,' said Toshak.

'What documents?'

I looked at Ash again. Still she was looking at the ground.

'Have you been through Strawberry's things?' I said, grabbing her by the shoulder. She shrugged me off and glared at me defiantly.

'It doesn't really matter where the documents come from. They show that her eighteenth birthday is still a matter of months away,' said Toshack.

Something clicked.

'Ash,' I persisted, 'where did you go when you disappeared at the lecture on the boat?'

Her gaze didn't falter.

'You must see that this is for Strawberry's own good.'

Puzzle pieces were falling into imaginary spaces.

'Did you go to Strawberry's cabin?'

'Listen, Adam,' said Wesley. 'Let me speak plainly. Anything Ashley did, she did under instruction from me. And it's as well she did.'

'I found her passport,' said Ash, very quietly, still looking at the ground. 'Her name really *is* Strawberry Shortcake.'

The policeman laughed.

'But her date of birth shows she still three months shy of being a legal adult,' said Toshack.

I could feel the sting of acid in my throat.

'You can't just turn up at the boat without Henry's

permission and drag Strawberry out of there forcibly. She still has a right to her own choices.'

Ash looked at me sadly, but with a tinge now of defiance, of disdain even.

'Is this something Henry has told you?'

'He does say that, yes. But I agree with him.'

'Even if she is still technically a child?'

I felt my confidence evaporating under the weight of the sunlight.

The policeman looked at his watch.

'Shall we get to it?'

'What are you going to do? Handcuff her and drag her screaming out of the cabin?'

'It may not come to that,' said Toshack.

'"May not"? You mean it could come to that.'

Now another disturbing thought occurred to me.

'Will this have any effect on the outcome of Henry's court hearing?'

'I don't suppose it will help his case.'

'Shit. Oh, shit.'

'You're being melodramatic, Adam. We're just going to talk to her. Having a policeman with us – well, it's for show as much as anything else. I think probably Strawberry hasn't had to deal with too much authority in her life. Perhaps Constable Urquhart will provide her with the shock she needs to start to see sense.'

'And if she doesn't "see sense", what then?'

Instead of answering, Toshack began to intone: '"Beware of false prophets, who come to you in sheep's clothing but inwardly are ravenous wolves."'

He exchanged glances with Ash.

'The harvest must be gathered in,' said Ash.

They were both looking at me. There was nothing in their eyes but will and judgement and determination and triumph.

There was no compassion at all.

'You're a spy. A Judas,' I said bitterly to Ash.

'I'm simply someone who knows the difference between right and wrong,' she replied.

My fury overwhelmed me. She had been playing me. All that had passed between us had been artifice, the unfolding of a larger scheme. Now she was being pious, unbearable.

'But not, apparently, someone who knows the difference between her arse and her fanny,' I spat back.

'Don't use that filthy language here,' barked Toshack, rising to his full height. 'Don't you dare speak about Ashley in that manner.'

'Why not?'

'Using such vulgar metaphors is revolting.'

Ash shot me a pleading look.

'They're not fucking metaphors.'

'Whatever they are, shut up about it.'

'They are literal descriptions of your daughter's behaviour.'

I could hear the echo of Henry in my own voice – only it came out pompous and green rather than easily authoritative.

'I don't know what you're talking about.'

'Do you *want* to know? Because I understand you're very keen on the truth.'

A shadow passed across Toshack's eyes, a faint glimmer of dawning understanding.

'You had better not say another word. You are treading on thin ice, Sonny Jim.'

'Then let me speak plainly. As you are so fond of doing. Your daughter is a catamite. An enthusiastic one.'

'Don't be absurd. You're hysterical.'

'What's a catamite?' said Urquhart.

'A catamite is the passive partner in anal intercourse,' I answered.

'Adam . . .' Ash was looking at me desperately now.

'It's a lie,' said Toshack. 'A filthy, revolting lie.'

But the confidence had left his voice. He sat down on the edge of the police car's passenger seat, knitting and furrowing his brow.

'Anal . . .?' said Urquhart. 'Cata-what?'

I felt myself in the final act of some weird cross between a Joe Orton farce and a 1960s horror film. Toshack was sitting absolutely still. His eyes swivelled slowly towards Ashley.

'Catamite,' I said, looking at Urquhart's plain, stupid face. 'There's probably a dictionary inside the rectory. I suggest you go and look it up. Permitted as part of God's perfect plan, apparently. So long as it's a daughter that's being taken up the aisle and not a member of the same sex.'

'Shut your filthy mouth!'

'If you don't believe me, go and look under her bedside table.'

Toshack stood up. He raised his hand to strike me. I didn't move. His hand drew back at the last moment, a half-inch from my face. I carried on looking at him steadily.

Urquhart did nothing to reprimand him. He walked round to the driver's side of the car.

'Ashley,' said Toshack, still looking at me. 'If I go and look under your bedside table, what will I find?'

Ashley hesitated for a fatal split second.

'Nothing. Nothing at all.'

Toshack grabbed Ashley by the shoulders.

'Look at me. And tell me the truth.'

She said nothing.

'Well?' said Toshack again, waiting for a confirmation of her denial.

Still she said nothing. Now he looked at her desperately. She stared back, her face a pool of tenderness and regret.

'I love you, Dad.'

'Ashley, if you tell me there's nothing for me to find, then I will believe you. Just promise, in the Lord's name, and the name of your mother, that you're telling me the truth.'

Her mouth worked as if chewing on unsayable words, but she could not spit any out.

Toshack's shoulders fell. There was a heavy silence.

'We need to go,' said Urquhart.

He climbed into the driving seat of the car. Toshack took one long, final look at me, then climbed into the passenger seat and slammed the door shut. Ash opened the door at the back.

'No,' said Toshack through the open window, with a deadly restraint.

She looked wildly around.

'But Dad, I—'

'You will stay here, Ashley. You will not leave the house. You will not speak to anyone. You will not try and contact anyone. We will talk when I return. You will have had plenty of time to clear up any evidence of your transgressions by then. But you will not be able to hide them from God.'

'Dad! I have lived as . . . I have tried to live as . . . you taught me . . . and—'

Toshack cut her off. 'Shame on you. For your mother's sake, shame on you.'

The expression on Ash's face was no longer a crucible, but a mirror turned inwards that showed, simply, fear. With a final, unreadable glance at me, she turned and walked heavily back towards the rectory.

I ran for my bike. The policeman called after me, but I ignored him and began pedalling furiously. I pedalled faster than I had ever pedalled before.

There was a short-cut across the fields, if you could negotiate the dry ruts and ditches without coming out of the saddle. I bumped and rocked, panting. I had no idea what I was going to do when I got there, or if I had any chance of getting there before Toshack and Urquhart. There were roadworks on the single-lane route from the town to the track that led to the forest and the boat, so it was possible that they would be delayed. But I had to warn Henry, even if it was too late to do anything about it.

I was there in twenty minutes. I had taken my shirt off but I wore an undercoat of sweat. My hair was ragged and drenched. As I pulled up beside the boat, I could see, maybe five hundred yards away, the police car approaching down the dirt track. I had, at least, got there first.

I started calling desperately for Henry. There was no answer. I had no time to check inside the boat. I began to run towards the cabin. I imagined I had been spotted, because suddenly the siren sounded. I ran harder, still exhausted from the bike journey. I could hear a theatrical squeal of tyres as the police car pulled up next to the field gate.

As I ran towards the cabin, I called Strawberry's name. I didn't know if I wanted her to run or to stay. I just knew I didn't want to be guilty again.

Toshack and Urquhart could only be seconds behind me now. I increased my pace. The cabin came into view. As I came closer, the front door opened.

It was not Strawberry that walked out, but Henry. Henry, holding Strawberry's delicate frame cradled in his arms. His skin was floury, despite his tan. He looked up at me but didn't seem to see me.

'Henry! What's wrong with her?'

He shook his head.

'I can't wake her up.'

He carried on walking towards me, not increasing his pace.

Then Urquhart and Toshack appeared, striding purposefully through the edge of the wood and into the clearing. Toshack was still holding his bible. Seeing Henry, both broke into a run.

'Lay her down,' commanded Toshack.

Henry looked up and shot Toshack a look of wild warning such as I had never seen. It blazed through the screen of pain behind his eyes.

'Get away from me,' he said simply.

Toshak took a step backwards and fell silent.

Urquhart looked out of his depth. But then, very softly, he said: 'Please put her down, sir. Perhaps I can help her. Please, sir. Please.' He indicated a soft spot with thick grass and fallen leaves. 'There.'

Henry threw one more burning gaze at Toshack, then he sighed and the muscles in his face, contorted in agony, seemed to relax.

Gently Henry laid her among the leaves of the undergrowth. Her face had a certain look, a particular, terrible stillness. I recognized it. I had seen it on my own mother's face.

Unclouded.

Pure.

Urquhart leaned over and gave her artificial respiration. Doing it expertly, nothing like the muddled attempt I had made on my mother.

He cleared her mouth of any possible blockages and moved the lower jaw forward and upward. Then he placed his mouth on hers and pressed, creating a leak-proof seal, and clamped her nostrils closed with his hand.

'No,' said Henry simply.

Urquhart was red-faced, perspiring.

After a minute there was no response from Strawberry.

Another minute, nothing.

Urquhart breathed into her, pulled away when her chest expanded, maybe twelve times per minute. Every time he reared back, he put his ear to her mouth to see if he could hear her exhaling. At the same time he gave her regular chest compressions, fast, maybe one every second.

'We need to get her to hospital. Now,' he said.

Henry picked her up, still a dead weight, and we began to hurry back to the car. When we arrived, Henry laid Strawberry in the back and joined her there, her head on his lap. Toshack went to get in the front.

Then I saw Strawberry's eyelids flicker and her chest begin to rise and fall. But still her eyes did not open.

Toshack hesitated, then meekly stepped to one side and let me in instead.

The car started. Just before it pulled way, Toshack leaned down to the open window where Strawberry was cradled in Henry's arms.

'You did this,' he said. 'It was you, Templeton.'

Henry didn't look up from Strawberry's face.

'I'm sorry I robbed you of the chance to be a saviour, Wesley.'

The engine roared and we drove away. I looked back and saw Toshack straighten up and begin to walk to back in the direction of the town, alone.

Twenty-five

Strawberry remained in a coma for two days at Bristol Royal Infirmary. Her eyes flickered open in the early afternoon of the third day. Henry and I were waiting by her bedside.

Her first words were woozy, but distinct.

'What the fuck?'

'Susan,' said Henry. 'Susan. You're with us.'

She closed her eyes again, and fell asleep.

Then the nurse moved us out of the room and called a doctor to conduct an examination. We waited for fifteen minutes until the doctor, a tired and tiresome-looking man in late middle age with a lofty Roman nose, a spotless white coat and an air of casual superiority, finally entered the waiting room.

'You're the father? Is that correct?'

'I am,' said Henry.

'And you are?' He gazed at me from the summit of his formidable nose.

'I'm her . . .' It hadn't occurred to me to think of Strawberry in these terms before.

'I'm her cousin.'

He looked back at Henry, an expression of faint disapproval passing across his face like indigestion.

'This girl has been sorely neglected. I think you know that I have had to pass the information on to the relevant authorities.'

Henry stood up. He towered some several inches above the doctor.

'The "authorities" know all about it. The "authorities" have it in hand. Doubtless I will be hung, drawn and quartered for allowing her to make her own decisions. So be it. I am a wicked man. Let's all agree on that, shall we? Now. Can you tell me — without the pious lectures — is she going to be all right?'

'I don't think there's any need for that kind of tone, Mr Templeton.'

'*Doctor* Templeton. And I don't give a tuppeny damn whether you think there's any need for that kind of tone or not. I want to know about the state of my daughter's health. That is your job. So please, could we waste no more of our time? Thank you.'

The doctor's face took on a fresh layer of pomposity, but it was clear he was not used to such dressings-down. He took refuge in inspecting his notes. Without looking up he started speaking.

'Your daughter should make a full recovery. If she is looked after properly, and if she abandons this ridiculous so-called "health" regime that she is clearly addicted to . . .' He paused to let the weight of these words sink in. '*If* she is looked after properly, there is no reason she shouldn't return to full health.'

'Thank you, doctor.'

'I have to tell you that I believe that the neglect this girl suffered—'

'Thank you, doctor. That will be all.'

The doctor paused, as if deciding whether to press home the point. Then he said, 'What kind of doctor are you anyway?'

'I'm a doctor of Divinity. Is that relevant?'

The medic gave Henry a hard stare.

'Apparently not. I imagine that you can come and collect your daughter in a couple of days, after we've completed the appropriate tests. If you phone the hospital they will let you know the details. But she's a very lucky girl. Very lucky that there were some people, other than her father, prepared to take an interest in her health. I bid you good day, *Doctor* Templeton.'

Henry was silent on the drive back to the boat. In fact, he had been more or less silent since the day Strawberry had been taken from the cabin to the hospital. He had not issued recriminations against me, or railed against the Toshacks. In fact, he had shown very little emotion at all, continuing to work on his book and keeping to his normal routine.

When we were close to the mooring, without looking at me, he said: 'It's all over.'

I said nothing, merely kept staring straight ahead at the road in front of us.

Henry nodded, as if in confirmation of his own thoughts.

'They're bound to award the court order against me. I can muster all the legal defences I want, but what underlies the whole action is the question of whether I am a responsible citizen. They object to my unconventional lifestyle. That's what's at the root of it.'

'Are you a responsible citizen?' I said quietly. 'Or a responsible father?'

'I understand that you wish to judge me,' said Henry. 'I understand that you blame me. But you don't understand how hard I have tried to help Susan in the past. I wasn't prepared, as Toshack was, to simply bully her into a hospital. Perhaps I was wrong, I don't know. But I passionately believed I was doing the right thing. And if you don't stand on your beliefs, what are you? A straw in the wind.

'I have nothing now, you know. I will lose my home. They will take Susan away from me. It's over. And do you know something? I'm not sure that I really care. There are mansions in the mind, Adam. I can find comfort there.'

'You need money to live.'

Henry looked vague.

'I have a great affection for Mr Micawber. Something will turn up, I dare say.'

We arrived at the boat and Henry, having embarked, immediately returned to his book. I spoke to him only once more that day, to ask him how it was going.

'It's almost finished. A few more days. I'm pleased with it. Yes.'

It suddenly occurred to me that I still knew almost nothing about the book.

'What's it called?'

'At the moment it's called *Book*.'

'You can't just call a book *Book*.'

'Why not?'

'I still don't understand what it's about.'

'And you won't until you've read it. Which I very much

hope, one day, you will. But if you want a simple answer, it's a book about why the world doesn't make any sense. And before you ask, "Why doesn't it make any sense?" – well, that's what I spend the book trying to explore.'

I was none the wiser. I left Henry to it, wondering, not for the first time, if he was deranged, or someone living out his life on a higher plane than the rest of us. During all the time Strawberry had been in hospital, although unusually quiet he had betrayed no other signs of anxiety. It struck me as inhuman. Or, possibly, more than human.

The day of the county court hearing reminded me of the atmosphere at Evie's funeral. Henry packed up all his paperwork for his defence. There were reams of the stuff. Most of it he could fit into his briefcase, but the remainder had to be stuffed into a plastic shopping bag.

There was time to visit Strawberry before the hearing. She had been given the all-clear, and was sitting up in bed. She informed Henry that she had given up the diet completely, and was happily scarfing any of the vile hospital food that was put in front of her. She had not accepted that she was misguided in following her regime – she was, on the contrary, somewhat proud of herself that she had taken it so far. But she finally recognized that there was a time to stop. The poisons, she declared, had left her body. The coma was their last gasp.

She nevertheless seemed to have grasped, at some level, how close she had come to death, and this had had a moderating effect on her formidable will-power. She now talked of acceptance, of 'going with the flow', of bending with the wind and living a balanced life rather than an ascetic one.

Before we left for the court, she handed Henry a letter.

'Look at it in good time before the hearing,' she said. 'And then read it to the court. Please.'

We drove the last few miles in silence. Henry, dressed in not even his best suit, turned to me and smiled once or twice, but it was clear he had already resigned himself to the outcome.

The court itself was within an ugly 1960s concrete building, already showing signs of staining from the weather. The interior was no more attractive. The small room where the hearing was taking place had little of the majesty of justice. There was pine cladding behind the judges' bench, and below the level of the bench, where the litigants and the public sat, there were long narrow tables with single sofa-seats, all clad in some nasty veneer and black plastic. There were plastic beakers of water on the tables and a coat of arms above where the judge sat.

The judge wore an ordinary grey suit, and seemed brisk and cheerful, smiling without discrimination at the small congregation below, although the smile was unconvincing, like that carved into a Hallowe'en pumpkin. On one side of the room, myself and Henry. I scrabbled around on the desk, trying to help him to find documents and notes. On the other side, lawyers from both the church commissioners and the local council. There was a stenographer, a few court officers and a reporter from the local paper. Also there, to Henry's great consternation, were Pritchard, Constable Urquhart and one of the parents of the girl who had seen Henry swimming naked.

In the public gallery sat Pattern and Moo, Vanya and Troy. There were a few faces I didn't recognize. And there was Toshack, in full church regalia, gazing down like Zeus, eyes shooting sparks.

The proceedings didn't take too long – I suspected Henry's heart wasn't in it any more. He defended himself against the charge that he had concealed his criminal record when he had taken over the lease, arguing convincingly that not only had the offences taken place years previously in another country, but that no such information had been required of him when he signed the lease. The allegations by Pritchard that there had been an illegal gathering at the boat were also dealt with efficiently by Henry, who had done his homework and demonstrated convincingly that no by-laws had been transgressed.

The judge beamed down as if delighted by the whole spectacle of the proceedings. When the allegation of indecent exposure was made, he smiled even more widely. Henry pointed out that no action had been taken at the time, and that he had a right to swim unclothed in a remote stretch of river.

Even the complainant, a nervous sprig of a man in a grey suit who looked leaned-upon and shifty, seemed uncertain of his ground. The judge continued to beam, and scribble occasionally on the notepad in front of him.

The atmosphere in the courtroom changed for the final complaint, however.

Testimony by Urquhart – unopposed by Henry – that Strawberry Shortcake, née his seventeen-year-old daughter Susan Templeton, had been slowly starving to death under his care drained all levity out of the room. Photographs were produced of her after hospitalization – she looked, from the angle they had been taken, like a concentration-camp survivor. Urquhart's description of the scene when he and Toshack had arrived at the cabin was surprisingly poetic. He talked of his 'profound disquiet' and 'intense sympathy' for the girl. He and Toshack swapped glances. It was fairly obvious that the police constable had been schooled.

Lastly came Toshack. He pulled out all the stops, presenting himself as an Elmer Gantry, although I thought of him as Robert Mitchum in *The Night of the Hunter*. He was holy, he was upright, he was a proud man of God, he was forgiving, but he was stern: this must not stand. And so on.

Finally it was Henry's turn. He faced the judge. I waited for his defence. I was sure he wouldn't go down without a fight. When he spoke he called on all his reserves of gravitas, which were considerable. A certain electricity entered the staleness of the proceedings. People in the court, including the clerk and the stenographer, sat up sharply and attended to the rumble and boom of his voice.

'Your Honour. I have today been standing here fighting for my home, my honour and my reputation against a number of unfair and unfairly presented slanders on my character. They are not motivated, as they present themselves, by human charity and decency, but by greed and cynicism. The council wish to remove me from the reach because they consider my boat an eyesore and, worse than that, *unusual*. A different way of living. This threatens them in some irrational and obscure way that makes them seek my destruction.

'As for the church commissioners, they have been got up to this by a certain person in this court who stands to benefit and profit from my removal from Lexham Reach. I will not name him as I am aware that the law of slander still pertains in civil law. But he knows who I am talking about. He knows.'

'A damn lie,' muttered Toshack audibly.

The judge glared at Toshack. Henry continued, ignoring the interruption.

'I have defended myself, I believe, successfully regarding three of the four charges that have been laid in front of you today, alleging contravention of the terms of the lease. It is very clear to me that the evidence brought against me in these cases is weak, and well short of the balance of probabilities that is required for a verdict against me.

'However, in the fourth case, that of my daughter Susan Templeton, who chooses to call herself Strawberry, I have little in the way of a legal defence. She is my daughter. She is technically a child. She did come to harm under my care.'

There was a silence, as I waited for Henry to parry his own thrust.

'Before I continue, I would like to read out this letter from my daughter, if the court will permit me. She was not fit to leave hospital today, but she was passionate about wishing to make her side of events heard.'

There were objections from the other bench, but the judge overruled them.

'The letter reads as follows:

Dear Judge and members of the court

My name is Susan Templeton, and I am the daughter of Dr Henry Templeton.

I would like to enter my plea that my father be allowed to stay on the Ho Koji. He has looked after me well since I came to England from America last year, and shown me all the love and consideration that a father owes a daughter. Part of that love and consideration was, I believe, to allow me to make my own decisions about my body, and how I should treat it.

This may not be what the law requires of him. I do not know. But I for one will always remain grateful. If harm was inflicted, then it was inflicted by myself, on myself. My father allowed me to follow my own destiny — to take charge of my own biology. He is a good man trying to his best to be true to his own values. Even if the judgement goes against him, as Henry informs me it probably will, I want you to judge him purely in law and not as a man. He is my father. I would once have wished for a better one. But not any longer. He had the rare courage to let me be who I chose to be.

Love and peace,

Susan Templeton

He handed the letter around for inspection. In the meantime, the lawyers for the Church Commission and the council were on their feet, complaining of duress, second-hand testimony, etc.

The judge, after little more than a few seconds' consideration, instructed that the testimony be struck from the record, agreeing with the objecting lawyers that it had no legal relevance. Henry nodded, as if it was exactly what he had expected.

'Do you have anything else to say, Dr Templeton?' asked the judge.

'I have nothing else to say on the matter, Your Honour, other than that I believe I am guilty of nothing more than infringing a technicality of the common law because of my moral beliefs. I do not shrink before my own conscience or the judgement of others. And I would ask you finally to consider, if your concern for my daughter is so profound, how precisely it will benefit her to make her father, and therefore her, effectively homeless. Thank you.'

It was a desperate last throw. Henry sat heavily down. The judge sighed and cleared the court.

The verdict took fifteen minutes.

Henry had thirty days to get off the boat.

We met with Pattern, Vanya and Troy afterwards in the lobby. Troy gave Henry a hug. Vanya kissed him on the cheek.

'It was all set up before it started,' said Pattern, shaking Henry's hand with the air of an old fellow-combatant. 'The fuckers.'

'For once, Pattern,' said Henry, 'and perhaps for the only time, I do believe you're right.'

Twenty-six

The day after the hearing, Henry had to go to the hospital to pick Strawberry up and return her to the place that would be her home for only a matter of weeks. Ray had arranged to collect me that coming Sunday, only two days later.

Troy turned out to be a surprisingly good friend to Henry. Understanding that there was no money for him to invest in the crystals business, he offered Henry a partnership all the same. 'You have the mystique, man. I'm just a dumb hippy but you can talk the talk.' Henry calmly responded that he would give the proposal serious consideration, but I knew his pride wouldn't allow him to do it.

After Henry left for the hospital – he was meeting Troy there and they were returning together – I found some of the home-made beer he had served at his lecture and decided to get stuck into it. To celebrate Strawberry's return, I told myself. It didn't taste as bad as it smelled. It was strong. After two pints my head swam pleasantly.

I was lying on a sun lounger, staring at the sky, nursing a half-empty glass, when the solution to everything occurred to me.

The idea enveloped me like a blessing. I took another swig of beer, gargled it and swallowed, smelling rather than tasting the acrid smack of the hops.

Henry had always told me to trust my instincts – not to overthink. Not to weigh the pros and cons like my father did, but to dive into things using intuition and the guidance of the unconscious, which, he said, was 'ancient and wiser than reason'. 'Go left or go right, but do not wobble' was the Zen saying he was most fond of.

I turned the idea over in my mind, examined it, held it up to the light. I could find no flaw in it.

After lying there for several more minutes, I rose somewhat shakily but determinedly to my feet. My vision, blurring slightly now, located the rusty barbecue. I staggered over to it and wheeled it into the field, halfway between the boat and the forest, a distance of some thirty feet either side. The wheels squeaked and protested as if trying to dissuade me from my still-crystallizing purpose.

I went and looked in the fridge. There were chops, sausages, a steak, some red peppers and halloumi cheese.

I set up a barbecue to welcome Strawberry home. That's what I would say.

There was a brisk breeze coming off the river. I gathered brushwood, then laid a path of thin twigs between the barbecue and the forest, and another between the barbecue and the boat.

I found some coals and poured them into the base of the

barbecue, then replaced the grill and laid the meat, cheese and vegetables – 'for Strawberry' – tenderly on top.

There was a can of kerosene in a lean-to outside the boat. I fetched it, then emptied a quarter of the contents into the briquettes.

I used the rest of the liquid to douse the brushwood kindling.

I checked my watch. I expected Henry, Troy and Strawberry to arrive in about forty-five minutes. By that time, the work should be done. I pulled a box of matches from my pocket. I took another swig of beer.

Go left, go right, but do not wobble.

I was fighting with the thought that what I was doing was insane. But with so much other insanity going on around me, could I be blamed? I was still, legally, a child. They wouldn't lock me up, even if they read my crime in the story of the embers. The thing was to act spontaneously, sincerely and without regret.

Henry couldn't find fault. After all, he would lose the mooring in thirty days anyway, and he had nowhere else to put the boat. Without me, all was lost for him.

The insurance on the *Ho Koji* would set him up to start again.

I slowly moved the match towards the charcoal. I was contemplating finally calling the whole thing off when the vapours caught and the thing went up with a giant *whoosh* – far more violently than I had expected, almost catching me in the face. The wind swung the tower of flames around in all directions. Sparks and, almost immediately, dollops of hot fat began to take to the air.

I staggered back, astonished at the force I had released. I gazed, mesmerized, then, intoxicated not only by the beer but by the sheer beauty of destruction, I took another match and threw it on the brushwood that led to the forest. It too caught immediately, running at the trees as if possessed by a spirit of fire. The brush leading to the boat went up with similar violence.

I felt a purifying sense of liberation. The primal erasing of things. Henry had talked to me of Kali the destroyer and Prometheus the fire-god. I felt as though they were working through me, compelling me. The flames were already at the willow curtain and swallowing the scrub under the trees. I sat down on the grass, lit a cigarette and watched the conflagration.

The *Ho Koji* began to catch with the same urgent readiness. Black smoke poured out of the roof and flames licked through the windows. I stood and peered through the open sash. I could see the Wharfedale stereo system light up, as if some unheard music had manifested itself physically in the vapour pouring out of the cones and membranes.

Heat radiated towards me from two sides, the forest and the boat. The violence of the sun above completed a triangle. Out of the corner of my eye, I saw a bird with its feathers blazing, screeching, running wildly in circles. I just had time to see that it had a yellow ring round its leg before it was consumed. I looked around for water to pour on him, but there was none. Ginsberg's screeching soon died away.

I watched, transfixed, stunned, as the blue and orange flames advanced into the study. I wondered if Henry's typewriter would melt.

Henry's typewriter. It was only then, through the cloud of alcohol, that I remembered his book.

The book about everything.

Five years' work.

I staggered to my feet. There were flames on either side of me now, ten feet away, raging. The forest beyond the first fringe of trees had taken. It would be clearly visible from some of the habitations a mile or two beyond the fields, and they would have telephones. The fire service would be called, but it would be too late.

The single sheet of flame that had first ignited *Ho Koji* was swelling into three dimensions. I started towards the boat, holding my hand up as if it could protect me against the flames. I staggered closer. I could almost feel the lick of the flames. I could see Henry's study through the porthole, full of smoke, but no flames. I tried to force open the window, but it wouldn't budge.

I looked around for something heavy, and found a statuette of a Buddha on the edge of the deck. I raised my arm and smashed it into the window. It gave way immediately, leaving a star-shaped hole full of jagged edges. I struck again, but it was still framed with sharp-angled glass. I dropped the Buddha in the river and climbed through. I felt the glass against my skin, and had a sense of the blood running down my arm, but it didn't hurt. The smoke invaded my lungs. Licks of black and orange flame were pushing through under the study door and caressing the legs of the desk. I was coughing desperately. I lay down on the floor to breathe more easily; the smoke was thinner there. I crawled on all fours, trying to locate the manuscript.

The wooden desk had caught now. I spotted the manuscript in a three-tier tray at the bottom, a clump of paper maybe six inches thick. It had already ignited, was blackening at the edges. I drew myself up and made a grab at it. The fire burned me, the fire of the paper, the fire of Henry's words. But I held on.

The pain was intense. The smoke was overwhelming. I felt my consciousness slipping. The manuscript was turning black before my eyes, then grey and red, a pulsing heart of blue.

I felt strong arms around my chest and then a sharp tug. Someone was dragging me away from the desk.

'The book.' My voice was barely audible, even to myself. I held on to the last intact desk leg.

'Let go. For God's sake, let go!'

I recognized Troy's voice. The desk leg slipped from my hands. Then Troy was somehow dragging me out of the small broken window. I felt the jags of the glass tearing at my legs.

He hauled me across the small gangplank and on to the singed grass, which was cloaked in black smoke. He found a spot that was clear and laid me down. I coughed violently. My head began to clear. I looked at the palm of the hand with which I had been scrabbling at the manuscript. It was black, with patches of vivid red. It started to hurt.

Trance-like, I turned my attention back to the boat. It was nearly gone now. I turned back to the field, where I had started the fire. I saw Henry standing there, and Strawberry, clearly stunned but looking healthier than I had ever seen her before.

Troy remained standing over me, hands on hips, half breathing, half choking. He grabbed a bucket, ran to the river and started hopelessly to try and douse the flames.

Neither Henry, Strawberry nor I moved.

'What is this?' said Henry quietly.

'I've saved you,' I said simply, slurring my words only slightly. 'I've made it right.'

Henry didn't even glance at the boat.

'Where's the book?'

I stared at him. I said nothing, but it was clear that he understood.

He ran his hand through his hair. He took two deep breaths. Then he started taking off his clothes.

Strawberry screamed at him.

'What are you doing? Have you gone fucking crazy?'

The flames climbed either side of us. Troy had realized the futility of his task and was making his way back to us, tears streaming down his face from the smoke.

Henry continued undressing until he was completely naked. Strawberry turned away.

Henry's body shook. He was bent over, shaking.

I thought he was crying. But then I saw that he was laughing.

Laughing joyfully, uproariously.

He began to dance, his head thrown back. The flames threw shadows on to his body as they grew ever closer. It seemed like the river itself was on fire.

I heard the faint sound of sirens in the distance.

'Do you hear that?' said Henry. I thought at first he was talking about the sirens, but he was looking in the other direction.

'The water,' was the last thing I heard Henry say. 'The river. It's singing.'

Before any of us could do anything to stop him, he slipped into the water and began slowly to swim downstream.

Strawberry sat down on the grass, the flames licking closer to her all the time.

Troy didn't take any notice. The tears on his face, I now saw, were not from the smoke.

I watched Henry quietly as the flames licked the river

orange. He was swimming away towards the bend. He didn't look back. His stroke was strong yet relaxed. His face turned every few seconds to take in air, then returned into the water.

Cinders fell on to the river, surrounding him like rain, some falling on his hair and back. Nothing interrupted his stroke.

I turned back to Strawberry and Troy. The flames were now only a few feet from us. We were practically surrounded by a circle of fire. The smell of kerosene was everywhere. I looked back at the river. Henry had gone. There were only ripples, the illusion of movement, spreading outwards.

'We have to go,' I said, grabbing Strawberry by the arm. Troy was covered in ash and his face was blackened. He held up his hands. Like mine, they were blistered and burned.

There was still a gap in the forest that for some reason was untouched by the fire. In a line of three, we walked through it, into the clear air, the safe space on the other side.

Sirens approached, and I registered two fire engines come racing down the track towards the reach. As soon as the first one got to us, a fireman leapt from the cabin.

'Is anyone hurt?' he shouted as other firemen disgorged themselves from the engines and began to work the hose free.

'Yes,' I said in a voice flat and dead and even.

Ignoring the firemen, we walked across the field, none of us sure where we were going, the fire at our backs, the sun punishing our faces.

*

The next day was a Saturday. My hand had been dressed and bandages put on my cuts, which, fortunately, were shallow. The pain in my hand, though, had become almost unbearable and I swallowed as many paracetemol as I dared.

I had spent the night after the fire at Troy's, where Strawberry was also staying. The first thing I did after I woke up and dressed was to go and find a telephone box.

I rang my father's shop, cradling the receiver gingerly in my bandaged hand. Ray's voice, as ever, was harassed, impatient to get back to the shop floor and deal with whatever customers were demanding of him.

'Dad,' I said. My voice came out stiff and cracked, as if it had been burned itself.

'Adam. What's the matter?'

'Dad,' I repeated.

'Are you calling about tomorrow? I'll be there. As promised. Why are you calling?'

'Because . . .'

I picked at a piece of chewing gum that was stuck to one of the window panels, as if it could help me unpick my own confusions. When I spoke again, I felt myself blurting, without thought.

'Can you come and get me, Dad? Can you come and get me now? Today?'

'Adam. It's Saturday. It's our busiest time. We're understaffed. I'm coming tomorrow.'

For the first time since my mother died, I began to cry.

'I know, Dad, but – I've hurt myself. I've hurt myself, Dad.'

I vomited up sobs, I retched out wails. The pain in my bandaged hand was becoming too much to bear.

There was silence at the other end of the line. A woman standing outside the booth stared at me impatiently, her eyes hard and accusing.

After maybe thirty seconds had passed I spoke again, this time in resignation at what I assumed would be my father's answer.

'Dad. I should go now. Someone's waiting to use the phone.'

In twenty-five years working in the shop, my father had never taken an unscheduled day off for any reason. To take a Saturday off was unthinkable.

The silence continued.

Then, quietly, distinctly, I heard Ray say: 'I'm leaving right now.'

No one ever saw Henry again. He was presumed dead but no body was found. I feel deep in my core that he's alive somewhere, following his own path, navigating his own river. Perhaps in Mexico, perhaps in India, with some woman, or alone, working again on his book, the book that will explain all the secrets of the world.

I passed my exams in History. I got a B. Henry had told me, 'Play your life as if it were a game.' And although the questions and the answers I gave to them were both meaningless, I played the game, and I was given my prize, my magical piece of paper.

Living with Ray was different afterwards. He ruffled my hair sometimes, and I didn't demur. Occasionally we would watch some comedy on TV and laugh together. Ray was boring and unadventurous, but he was my dad. I admired Henry; he captivated me. But I loved Ray. There was all the difference in the world.

All the same, living on the boat had changed me, and I could no longer be held by the magnetic torpor of Buthelezi House. Shortly after my A-level result arrived, I went to live with Troy for a while. Strawberry had moved in with him while she waited for the legal processes that would allow her to inherit the substantial insurance payment on the *Ho Koji*, which she came into shortly after her eighteenth birthday. The story that was told to the loss adjuster about the barbecue that went wrong was accepted by the insurance company without demur – apparently it was a common enough event that summer.

Troy looked after her with great compassion and care. She fattened herself up, and they went into the crystals business, using the capital from the boat. Her radiant health and good looks helped sell the product – she would ascribe it all to the right exposure to rose quartz, or aquamarine, or chalcopyrite. They made good money.

Eventually, she married a farmer and they had a child. She called him Henry. So far as I am aware, they are living quite prosperously in a small village in the Somerset Levels. We don't see each other much. It was another time.

I never saw Ash again, or Wesley Toshack, although I did bump into Pattern and Vanya from time to time while I was living in Bristol. Moo had a child, then another. Pattern signed up for the nine-to-five – he ended up a manager in an IT firm. By all accounts he was a good father and a good manager.

Vanya divorced her plumber husband after he beat her senseless one day in a drunken rage after his football team had lost and she had chosen the wrong moment to ask him to vacuum the stairs. She opened a small shop selling antiques and bric-à-brac. She never married again. She told me she was very happy on her own. She had realized that it wasn't just men that were the problem. It was people.

The burn on my hand never healed. Even now it looks as if it is part liquid. Still, sometimes, it hurts. I use it to remind me what Henry told me — that everything, even matter, flows. And within the flowing there is pain.

Things happened to me or I made things happen. Perhaps those are just two different ways of looking at the same thing. I don't look for causes any more. Life flows through me, containing in every instant the possibility of freedom; but only the possibility.

Sometimes my life seems more like history — accidents that no one can explain leading to consequences that no one can foresee.

There are moments I am shot through with piercings of joy. At other times, I feel the scouring beauty of grief. Each, I know now, depends on the other. Neither of them lasts. In between are stretches of nothingness, of neutrality, flat and unbound.

I have a house by the water now, where I have wanted to live ever since that distant season. Sometimes I walk down to the river, and in the summer I see the water striders, standing perfect and graceful and so fragile. They do nothing, they are still. The water holds them aloft on the elastic bed of surface tension. Even though they are cruel, and even though they cannot help but feed on the living beauty around them with their pitiful jaws, they seem to me inspiring creatures, those Jesus bugs, living lives of grace and beauty and economy and sustenance.

Then a hungry fish will come from underneath, and they are consumed by the water they trusted. Again and again they are consumed. But the others that remain on the surface, they do not see, or they forget, or they are brave. So they keep on praying, and trusting the hazardous, predatory depths beneath them.

They keep on trusting all the same.

Acknowledgements

Thanks to Christina Ostrem at the Portixol Hotel, Mallorca, and Penny and Kit Noble at Nonsuch House, Dartmouth, for their kindness and hospitality. Also Mike Jones, Suzanne Baboneau and Clare Alexander. And Rachael Newberry, who does things that matter while I make stuff up. A final shout out to Ruby, Cissy, Lydia and Esme, my remarkable daughters.